T0267707

UNDER THE SAND

A LESLIE ELLIOTT MYSTERY

(Book Four)

Susan Hanafee

Under the Sand is a work of fiction created by Susan Hanafee. All names, characters, their actions in this novel and the outcome of those actions are products of the author's imagination.

Cover photograph by Rick Montgomery. Graphics by Jim Hartman.

Copyright © 2024 by the author. All rights reserved.

No part of this book may be reproduced, stored in a retrieval system, or transmitted by any means without the written permission of the author.

Print ISBN: 978-1-7324894-7-9
eBook ISBN: 978-1-7324894-8-6

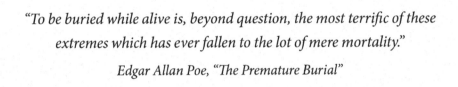

"To be buried while alive is, beyond question, the most terrific of these extremes which has ever fallen to the lot of mere mortality."

Edgar Allan Poe, "The Premature Burial"

CHAPTER 1

Victor Clerk was outraged. He guessed he was outnumbered but couldn't see because of the covering over his head. While he wanted to toss expletives and more at whoever had forced him from his home, he kept his mouth shut as the powerboat he was riding in skimmed over the water toward what was, for him, an unknown destination.

He remembered most of what had happened. Had it been an hour ago? He had lost track of time. He was talking to the sheriff's deputy on the phone when two armed men entered his home after blowing up the patio door and some floor-to-ceiling windows on the lower level. The deputy urged Victor to go to the safe room, but Billie—stupid bitch that she was—had locked the secret door to a closet in the main bathroom and kept screaming that she couldn't figure out how to open it.

Frustrated, he left the bathroom. He didn't want the intruders anywhere near his safe, which was in the same room where Billie was hiding. He resigned himself to lying in wait for them in the bedroom. He had a knobkerrie—a Zulu fighting stick he bought during a trip to Africa. If he could land a blow to the head of one of the men, he could disarm him and shoot the other. That was the best plan he could devise to protect himself until help arrived.

Where the fuck are the police? he repeated over and over in his head until the armed men burst through the bedroom door and Victor came to the distressing realization that his rescuers were not going to make it in time.

CHAPTER 2

Monday, July 12, 2021, 2:50 p.m.: Day One

Mark Foxx hadn't slept well. He never did, but this night was worse. Maybe it was the call from his father who needed $350 for a new medication, and could Mark help? He had told his dad he'd mail a check that morning, along with the money for August. He had dropped it in the mailbox on his way to work.

Likely, it was the other thing nagging at him. He thought he'd taken care of every detail, but in these situations, you could never be sure. Disaster was a misstep away, especially with this crew of unknowns. They could speak English but rarely talked except to one another. Even then, it was in Russian or Polish. Foxx couldn't tell the difference.

He parked his 2015 silver Kia hatchback alongside the two-story bridge administration building, started to get out of the car, and realized he'd left his lunch at home. Would someone notice he didn't have his brown bag with him? Something small like that could throw things off. He reached into the glove box for the energy bars he kept for emergencies. The Florida heat had fused them into a sticky lump. He pried two loose and stuffed them into his jeans pocket. He wasn't going to have much time to eat, but you never knew when you might need something.

When he started across the walkway to the bridge tender's house, he saw Cap Collier coming his way, his limp more pronounced than usual. Foxx glanced first to one side, then the other of the swing bridge. No boats were waiting, so it was obvious Cap had taken a chance and departed the house a few minutes early. Cap would think it was no big deal; his replacement was on the way. But to Foxx, it was the kind of sloppy thinking that had gotten guys he had known killed in Afghanistan.

"You watch the game last night?" Cap asked when both men reached the midpoint and exchanged hellos. It was well known among the swing-bridge tenders and tollbooth workers that Cap was obsessed with baseball in general and the Cincinnati Reds in particular.

On Foxx's first day on the job as a bridge tender six months ago, Cap had told him about meeting his hero, Pete Rose, at the Mirage in Las Vegas in 2006. "Paid seventy-five dollars for an autographed photo. Pete joked with me like we were old friends," he said with a grin, his brown eyes animated with the memory. "We went to the same high school, you know. After all these years, the guy belongs in the Hall of Fame, but I can't see it happening. I guess a lotta the sportswriters that vote you in still think the gambling he did was a sin."

Over time, Foxx had heard various versions of Cap's encounter with the disgraced Charlie Hustle and always tried to act interested. Cap didn't appear to have much going on in his life except work and his preoccupation with America's favorite pastime. What was a few minutes of Foxx's time and attention if it made Cap feel important?

"Didn't see it," Foxx said. "The Reds win?"

"Yeah. I think they're a contender," Cap said, pulling a handkerchief out of his back pocket and wiping the sweat off his fleshy neck and face. "I got a good feeling about it."

Despite the endless retelling of stories, the clichéd observations, and the occasional work slipup, Foxx liked Cap and admired him for his service in Vietnam five decades earlier. They shared the bond of two men who had been in foreign countries, dodging bullets and watching boys their age die for causes that never made sense. Cap received a Purple Heart and a bum knee. Foxx was left with nightmares of burning flesh, the sting of barbed wire around his neck, and the sensation of water filling his mouth and throat. He would awake gasping for air, afraid to close his eyes and face those unholy terrors again.

As he left his friend, Foxx wondered if what was about to happen would supplant the Pete Rose story in Cap's repertoire of memories.

In the distance, he could see the sailboat with its thirty-foot mast headed in his direction on the Intracoastal Waterway, cutting through the water with the aid of an engine. Behind it were two forty-foot Sea Rays, plodding along so as not to create turbulence or draw attention to themselves in the no-wake zone. He could feel his heartbeat quicken. Everything was on schedule.

Inside the bridge tender's house, he flipped through papers on the desk—not really seeing what was in them—and checked the small mirror someone had attached to the window casing. Since he had stopped using Just for Men color gel, the black beard he touched up every couple of weeks now had a light-brown undercoat but still hid the white marks on his chin and neck. Unless he shaved, they remained undetectable, like the scars he bore inside.

A voice on the VHF filled the small space, bringing Foxx back to the moment. "Boat approaching from the west, requesting next bridge opening." It was followed by a prolonged horn blast, a three-second delay, and a final, short blast.

"Bridge opening at 3:00 p.m.," Foxx responded, then pushed a series of keys on the computer.

Five minutes later, the metal crossbars on either end of the bridge started down, dislodging an osprey roosting on top and halting the vehicles intending to cross the causeway from both directions. Red lights flashed, followed by warning signals. When the crossbars snapped into place, the swing bridge started to move, giving the illusion of a giant metal bird unfolding its wings.

Once it was fully open, Foxx reached into his pocket, pulled out a flash drive, and stuck it into the computer. His fingers traveled across the keyboard again. When he pushed *Enter*, a series of hieroglyphics flickered on the screen. It went dead, leaving the bridge locked open.

"That should do it," he said as he removed the flash drive and stuck it in his pocket.

He stepped outside the bridge tender's house and leaned against the aluminum railing, waving to the people in the sailboat and then to the driver of the first Sea Ray as they passed below him. The other speedboat was idling, hanging back.

Foxx gazed at the water twenty feet below. It was still frothy on the surface from the boat traffic. The turquoise of winter had faded into a murky, almost putrid green from the summer rains. He could see fish swimming near the surface but not the sandy bottom he knew was down there somewhere. Cap and the others had told him with some certainty that the area under the bridge was at least eight feet deep but now he was wondering why he hadn't confirmed that figure with the office.

Too late. This is it. Thirty-six years of living a shit life is coming to an end today.

He opened the small gate in the railing and stepped onto the concrete ledge. He took several deep breaths, positioned his feet and arms as he used to when he was on the platform, rose onto his toes, and did a perfect swan dive off the bridge. He entered the warm water with barely a splash. The instant he hit, he thought of his high school diving experiences and wondered what Coach Billingsley would have said about his form.

CHAPTER 3

Reporter Wes Avery was still smarting from the first and second rejections of his proposed series about problems with local security when his boss doubled down.

"Wes, I told you we aren't doing it. There is no crime problem on this island." Sara Fortune punctuated her remark with the kind of look his mother gave him as a kid when he brought home a bad report card or tracked mud into the kitchen.

Wes smirked in response and headed outside for the peeling blue bench by the door to the weekly newspaper, the *Island Sun. If she thinks I'm giving up on this, she's crazy* was written all over his face. He'd dealt with recalcitrant editors before at other, bigger newspapers. He was mulling the strategy he'd use with the female publisher when Randy Long, the paper's graphic designer and photographer, slid into the space next to him on the bench.

"Still no luck with the lady in charge?" Randy observed. It was more a statement than a question from the man with the ponytail and crooked smile who had worked at the *Sun* longer than anyone. When Wes arrived about eight months ago, he had been told that Randy could recall every story ever published but seldom volunteered information unless he liked you.

"Naw," Wes said. He reached for the cigarettes in the pocket of his pink golf shirt. He lit one up and took a big drag, inadvertently enveloping both him and Randy in a cloud of smoke. "Explain to me why she had to float my idea around town. Who does that? The Chamber didn't like it. The sheriff was insulted at the suggestion that he and his deputy couldn't handle any problems —especially in the summer when most everyone was gone. That's two law enforcement people to protect several thousand during the season and four hundred in the summer, including some celebrities, a bunch of millionaires, and several billionaires. All soft targets."

Randy nodded. "Bruce Webster and his new deputy, Alex Pendry. Not exactly your idea of the A-Team, eh? You do know that Bruce isn't really a sheriff."

"What?" Wes said, his eyes widening. "I saw him get sworn in."

"Technically, he's the senior deputy in charge. The tradition of calling the head law enforcement person on the island the *sheriff* started maybe sixty years ago. It stuck. The rich people here liked it. Made them feel important. So . . . "

Wes nodded as if to say he understood, then shifted in his seat so that his hazel eyes were focused on his coworker. "'What's the worst that can happen?' Sara asked me. Oh, I don't know. Since I moved here, there have been at least two major storms, five murders, the bust-up of a drug ring, and—"

"Little Chicago," Randy interrupted. He chuckled and stroked his wispy beard.

Wes didn't respond to Randy's humor. He knew Chicago, loved Chicago, and hated the crime that plagued many big cities these days. He didn't want anything like that, even on a smaller scale, happening to this island, and he wished Chicago would fix its problems soon so that he could feel comfortable returning to its fabled blues bars.

He took another drag on his cigarette. "At least the fire department was able to step in and help with the storms and their aftermath. Sara said those were anomalies. No big deal. Can you believe that?"

Randy cleared his throat and adopted a serious expression that Wes understood to mean he was about to impart vital information.

"You're talking about security? A couple of years ago, there was a plan floated to put an emergency communications system on the south end of the island with a dual repeater and backup power. For some reason, it never took off. Guess the powers that be were focused on planting trees in the median of the road that skirts those beachfront mansions. County didn't want to spend more money than they had to on this island. Those good old boys in charge never do. So that was that."

Wes ran his hand through his close-cropped brown hair and frowned, accentuating the character lines on his face. "You're telling me that the only reliable means of communication on this island is that cell tower next to the flower shop?"

"Even the firefighters use cell phones to communicate with each other during an emergency. That's what one of 'em told me not long ago," Randy said. "And I've heard that sheriffs in the surrounding counties don't talk much to Bruce. They were all tight with Sheriff Fleck. Their deputies also stopped coming into our county to help, but I don't know why."

Wes shook his head and poked his cigarette into a nearby bucket of sand. "I'm not giving up on those stories, Randy. We gotta let people know. Promote change. That's our job. If we piss off someone in charge, too bad."

Wes cared about his newly adopted community, especially the welfare of another of its year-round residents, a woman named Leslie Elliott. She had been in charge of public relations for the big-city electric utility Wes had reported on when he worked for the *Daily News*, a midwestern newspaper. They spoke at least once a week and occasionally had lunch. After she quit her job and moved to the island with her mother a little over a year ago, she sent Wes a text with her new phone number and followed up with a casual email about the advantages of living in Florida.

No worries here, she wrote. *The big news this week is who won the local tarpon fishing tournament, what the ladies' club is doing to raise money for charity, and my mother's progress in the hunt for a sexy senior citizen she can, ahem, hang out with. By the way, my career as a mystery writer has—sorry to say—not taken off yet.* She followed her message with a string of laughing emojis.

When Wes was offered a buyout during a round of layoffs at the afternoon paper to which he had given a big chunk of his life and gotten little in return, he decided to head south and snap up a job opening on Leslie's island. At the time, he pegged it a happy coincidence that she was an inhabitant.

Wes knew from hearing property owners talk when he first arrived that they believed they were surrounded not just by turquoise waters but also a cocoon of safety. Life on the island mirrored the 1950s, with a quaint village where the shops sold mostly ice cream, beachwear, Florida trinkets, and fishing equipment. The favored form of transportation was by golf cart. A swing bridge controlled access to this ten-mile-long strip of land, creating the illusion that anyone who committed a crime could be easily captured as they tried to escape across the causeway and head into the next county. But Wes soon discovered that the perception was not necessarily reality. He was getting plenty of big-city, crime-related material to report on whether he liked it or not.

As Wes mulled over his coworker's comment about the backup communication system that never was, Randy got up and leaned over the balcony of the second-story newspaper structure to converse with someone in the parking lot below. When he finished, he returned to his seat and shared a new piece of information.

"J.T. says today's the last day for fresh fish at the market—they're closing for ten days next month—in case you want to stock up on anything, like cigarettes."

Wes nodded and reached into his shirt pocket for another smoke, then hesitated, remembering his pledge to Leslie to cut back.

As if reading Wes's mind, Randy grinned. "So, how are you and Leslie getting along?"

Wes flashed a goofy smile in Randy's direction. His face reddened. "I'm taking her to dinner tonight in Sarasota. Thinking about popping the question."

Randy nodded and tugged at his beard. "You got a ring?"

"A ring? Do I need one? This isn't the first time around for either of us. She's in her midforties. You think that's a deal-breaker?"

Randy got up and stretched. "You don't know much about women, do you?" he deadpanned as he reached for the door handle and went inside, leaving Wes to ponder if there was any truth to his coworker's comment or if it was just a playful jab at the reporter's bachelorhood.

ꝏꝏ

Wes bounded down the steps from the newspaper office to the street below with Randy's words nagging at him. What *did* he know about women?

He knew his first wife had left him for a younger man, a stockbroker she met in a bar. He didn't mourn her departure, but savored the freedom his independence provided for full immersion in his job. He knew that Leslie was one hell of a public relations expert. The way she responded to his pointed questions used to drive him up the wall. Never a lie, but she could tap dance around the answers better than Ginger Rogers, the classic movie star from the 1940s. And he knew she was a damned attractive woman, with that wispy, reddish hair, pretty face, and slim figure. She was always watching her diet—and, lately, his, too, although he thought they both drank too much wine for their own good. Leslie had been first a source and then a respected friend until several months ago when—during a fact-finding trip he took to Panama that involved partaking in ayahuasca, a self-enlightenment potion—he had realized he was in love with her. Now this ring thing. If that's what it took to make her happy and say yes, he would do it.

He headed for the jewelry store across from the newspaper office, arriving at the four-way stop at the same time as a purple golf cart. Normally, Wes would have flashed a polite smile and nodded to the driver as he strolled to the other side of the crosswalk. Today, he didn't move; he was intrigued by the two people in the front seat.

The woman behind the wheel, who was looking in his direction and waving him across the street, was wearing a straw cowboy-style hat over a long blonde braid that rested on her right shoulder and extended to the top of her cleavage. Wes focused on her ample breasts—he couldn't help himself—then allowed his eyes to travel south to her white shorts and long, muscular legs. *Lots of workouts to get that definition,* he mused. She resembled one of those female kickboxers he'd seen on cable TV.

His gaze wandered reluctantly from the woman to the beefy man sitting beside her, smoking a cigar. *Definitely no stranger to weight lifting and maybe steroid use,* Wes speculated. On the bulge of the man's right bicep was a menacing tattoo: a skull wearing a Special Forces beret that incorporated a big knife with a fat, black snake coiled around it. Wes shuddered. It was the knife more than anything that made him uncomfortable. He wasn't crazy about snakes, but the sight of the big blade gave him the willies.

When he settled on the man's face, he realized the stranger was glaring back at him. Wes read the look to say that any second the guy was going to launch off the cart and coldcock the reporter for checking out his girlfriend, or wearing a pink shirt, or not walking when he had the right-of-way, or whatever he found bothersome. It was obvious this man had a big chip on his shoulder.

As the man's dark eyes burrowed into him, Wes felt a jolt as if Florida lightning had struck out of nowhere and traveled from the top of his head to his sneakered feet. He had seen those eyes and that look before. He couldn't remember where or when, but he was sure it wasn't on the island. He was also positive that the encounter hadn't been a good one.

Wes managed a weak smile, gave a hesitant wave, and mouthed, "Go ahead." As the cart moved on, the male passenger's scowl and the smell of the cigar stayed with Wes. He crossed the street slowly, all the while watching the cart proceed two blocks east, then stop across from the flower shop. He noticed the pair seemed in no hurry to go anywhere but remained in the cart, talking. He thought he saw the man turn to look in his direction but decided it was his nerves getting the better of him.

When he reached the jewelry store and opened the door, he was hit with a blast of air-conditioning, the sound of steel drums playing Caribbean music, and the glare of lights strategically focused on diamonds, rubies, emeralds, and pearls to enhance their luster. He felt nauseous.

"Whoa," he said and grabbed a seat in a nearby chair. "Do you have water?"

"A jewelry store often makes men weak in the knees," a red-haired lady in a colorful print dress said. A much younger woman in shorts and a halter top scurried to the back room and emerged with a plastic bottle.

"Here you go."

Wes lifted his head and gratefully accepted the liquid, gulping it down like a man who had just emerged from the desert.

"It's hotter outside then I thought. I'm Wes Avery. I work at the newspaper across the street and am here to buy a present for a friend," he managed to say. His voice sounded shaky to him. The penetrating eyes of the man in the golf cart lingered, but no name surfaced, which surprised Wes. He prided himself on being able to remember people. Had he blocked recognition of this face from the past?

"I'm Cheryl. This is Dede, my daughter," the older woman said. "How can we help?"

Wes knew the words *looking for an engagement ring* were the correct answer, but he was having trouble getting them out. He had the momentary worry that he might be as tongue-tied when it came to asking Leslie the all-important question.

"A ring, I guess."

"Engagement?"

He winced. "Sort of. More like a friendship ring."

Cheryl giggled. "A friendship ring is often a simple, filigreed band. Is that what you have in mind, or do you want something with precious stones?"

"Stones," he said, acknowledging Randy's not-so-subtle hint about stepping up his game. Deciding he really was okay with the idea of marriage, he now worried about Leslie's reaction to his proposal.

What if she says no? There's a good chance she will. She's divorced from a cheating husband, had a relationship with a wealthy utility executive that didn't end in marriage, and had a thing for that fisherman who was found shot on the beach. She seems to have moved on from his death but how can I be sure? And why would she say yes to someone like me who's older, lives in an apartment above the bank, and has nothing much to offer?

Cheryl pulled out a tray of rings from a glass case and signaled Wes to join her. "Perhaps one of these would meet your needs? They're quite lovely. And I can give you a nice discount, seeing that it's summer and you're only our second customer today."

Wes stood up slowly to steady himself, not wanting to create any more of a scene than he already had, and was heading for the jewelry tray when his cell phone rang. He was relieved to see it was Leslie. Hearing her voice might calm his nerves.

"Hey," he answered. "I was just thinking about you and our dinner tonight."

"You can forget about that," she said, sounding rattled. "It's chaos on the north end. Something's happened to the causeway bridge. It's stuck open for boats. Cars and pickups are lined up for as far as I can see, and people are plenty pissed. Something about a guy jumping off the bridge. I'm looking for an eyewitness. I'll take pictures for the paper and call you later." And then she was gone.

Wes clicked off and glanced awkwardly at Cheryl. "Uh, maybe I should wait on this."

"We're here when you need us, Mr. Avery," the saleswoman said. Wes could hear her and Dede snickering as he hurried out the door.

CHAPTER 4

First one, then a second shot rang out, breaking into the rhythmic whine of a nearby gas-powered leaf blower. The unsuspecting target was launched a foot into the air and then dropped lifeless among sprigs of newly planted periwinkle.

Gene Miller, a Ruger .22 now perched over his left shoulder, heard a scream from inside the white cottage with green shutters, followed by the sound of hasty footsteps. He steeled himself for what was to come.

"You idiot! What are you doing? I'm calling the sheriff," came the not-unexpected barrage of complaints from behind the screen door at the front of the house. The voice was followed by the appearance of a petite woman with disheveled gray hair, wearing a light-blue bathrobe. The look on her face said that if she had the rifle, Gene would be on the ground motionless, not a spiny-tailed reptile.

"Shooting iguanas, like the county pays me to do. Sorry, did I wake you?" He didn't feel apologetic, and it was a strain to sound respectful. But he'd been cautioned about overreacting when confronted by an unhappy homeowner. His goal was to protect himself and his paycheck.

"Wake me from my nap? Yes, you did. And who gave you permission to bring that weapon onto my property?"

She hustled down the front steps and ended up too close for Gene's comfort. He stepped back. He outweighed her by at least a hundred pounds and was thirty years younger, but she was intimidating for her size—like a pygmy rattler when threatened.

"Ma'am, you came to the office and filled out a form that gave me permission to shoot iguanas on your property," he said, producing a piece of paper that identified him as a county employee. "They were eating your hibiscus plants, and you wanted them gone."

She put her hands on her hips and let out a sigh that radiated exasperation. "That was a month ago. I'd forgotten all about it. Why didn't you come then? As you can see, the creatures destroyed my bushes. That's why I replaced them with ground cover. I mean, really, how much does the county pay you to do so little?"

Gene winced. He tried to sound understanding, but he worried that his growing anger would register with the woman. "These big boys aren't all that visible until summer," he said, walking over to the dead iguana and picking it up. *About five pounds—perfect for dinner.*

"You see, ma'am, I try to wait until there are fewer people around. Less chance of someone getting hurt. I thought you were gone for the summer. Most folks are."

"Well, I'm here, and I don't want you shooting those things around me. You understand?" she croaked as she turned to go. "Come back when I've left."

"When will that be, ma'am?"

There was no response from her as she disappeared into the house.

There was a time not that long ago when the island had been overrun with tens of thousands of iguanas in what some characterized as a plague of biblical proportions. They were eating anything that moved, including protected species and their eggs, and devastating the flowering vegetation. Worse, their population was doubling every couple of months. In answer to an ad, Gene left his low-paying security job and the cold weather in Michigan and brought his hunting rifle to the island. In short order, he eliminated—by his count—fifteen thousand of the prolific creatures and became a hero. Now that the reptile's numbers were manageable, those glory days were gone. People had forgotten how much of an issue the iguanas had been before Gene showed up. The reaction from the lady in the cottage was, sadly, typical.

He didn't care if he set foot on her property again, but he didn't want her calling the county and saying that he had been insolent. That was the word Victor Clerk had used a couple of weeks ago: *insolent*. Gene considered it a hateful term with unspoken connotations. Equally frustrating was the reaction of Gene's boss. Instead of standing up for his employee, he had lectured Gene on being more deferential to the island residents—especially the ones in the big houses. Bigger house, more money. More money, more clout with the county officials.

Gene was offended by any implication that he was of lesser value as a human being than someone who had a bank account with millions in it, but he kept his feelings to himself. He wanted to retain his nearly six-figure job, as trying as it could be sometimes. Patrolling the village and south end of the island in ninety-degree heat and humidity, not to mention contending with mosquitoes and blinding summer rainstorms, wasn't easy. It was made worse by people like the lady in the cottage and Victor Clerk.

Victor's mansion on the east side of the island sprawled across several prime waterfront lots and was the topic of much local gossip. A McMansion, some called it; others said it was a monstrosity that didn't fit the neighborhood. Nonetheless, county officials had stamped approval of the plans, even as they salivated over the enormous property taxes Victor would have to pay.

That was three years ago. By the time Gene stepped foot on the property to round up the offending reptiles, it was fenced and heavily landscaped, secluded and shut off from the rest of the island community, just like its owner. Gene tried to contact Victor several times before trespassing—another word the iguana hunter didn't care for. He even had his boss send a letter saying he would be eradicating the iguanas at Victor's request on such and such a date, and if that was a problem, Victor should let Gene know. There was no response.

On the designated day, Gene was on the property fifteen minutes and had bagged about ten big ones when Victor emerged with a towel wrapped around his waist and a mouthful of venom for the man disturbing his peace.

"You fucker! What the bloody hell are you doing?"

Gene had never seen Victor Clerk before. He was a lean man, maybe six feet two, and extra pale for someone who lived in the Sunshine State. He appeared to be in his early to midfifties, with black hair in the style of the *Peaky Blinders* series Gene was watching on cable: skinned on the sides and thick and longer on the top. The man was not dripping water as if he'd been in the shower, so Gene could only guess what he had been doing while the iguanas were being felled.

"I'm killing igu—"

"Yes, yes, I know what you're doing, but you scared the hell out of my girlfriend!" he yelled. It was downhill from there as Victor berated the county employee on every personal topic imaginable, including his manhood.

Gene left seven minutes into Victor's rant, not even bothering to pick up the dead iguanas on the patio, and said something to the effect of "You'll never see me again, asshole." He believed it was that comment that prompted Victor to call his boss and toss out the i-word. Or it could have been the middle finger Gene flashed Victor's way as he departed.

All the anger and humiliation Gene had felt at the hands of Victor Clerk now resurfaced at the cottage with the green shutters. This time he kept it contained, congratulating himself as he put the rifle on the front seat of his golf cart, stashed the iguana in the cooler in the back, and checked a second Styrofoam container to see if there was any beer left over from yesterday. When 4:00 p.m. rolled around, he was off the clock. A couple of hours later, he would be sitting down to curried iguana with his wife, Stephanie, and eight-year-old son, Liam. Yes, it tasted like chicken, he would tell anyone who asked.

He started for the next residence on his list, then made a sudden U-turn and headed for the ice dispenser at the village grocery store. He was done dealing with ingrates for the day.

There was a small oasis with a cluster of date palms and giant rush grasses where Gene liked to relax in the late afternoon. He parked his golf cart in the shade and welcomed the breeze blowing off the water. He had a full view of the Gulf of Mexico in front of him. The beach was empty save for a few umbrellas and the occasional sunbather down by the old lighthouse to his left. He stepped out of the cart, pulled off his XXL golf shirt with a county emblem on it, and draped it over the passenger's seat. He did a few toe touches because he still could and then reached into the cooler for a beer. He popped the top and took a swig, savoring the cold liquid and its ability to tamp down the frustrations of the day.

Not far away, closer to the road, he could see gopher turtles munching on grass, bearing traces of sand on their shells. They had been in danger of disappearing from the island as hordes of iguanas devastated their numbers, raiding their nests and gleefully devouring their eggs. He believed he alone had saved them. Now he enjoyed watching them thrive.

If the temperature dropped a couple of degrees, he and his boy could play catch in the backyard after supper. This weekend, he might borrow his buddy's boat and take the kid fishing. Bonding with Liam at an early age was important to Gene. He didn't want the boy to end up like his neighbor's seventeen-year-old: coddled and uncommunicative and, in Gene's opinion, the kind of person whose mugshot would be on TV one day for committing some horrific crime.

His gaze went to the water and the forty-foot Sea Ray dropping anchor about fifty yards offshore. He wondered why someone would choose to fish there—if that's what they were doing. During his first couple of months on the job, he had learned that this time of year the sport fish were in the South Pass on the end of the island. These guys must be rookies with a big boat, fancy gear, and no sense.

He was thinking about heading home when he noticed an inflatable raft, commonly called a RIB, being launched off the back of the boat into the gentle swells of the Gulf. When he saw two men in T-shirts and long pants transfer from the Sea Ray to the raft, carrying something that didn't look like a fishing rod, Gene grabbed his binoculars. He quickly confirmed that one had a military-style precision rifle. It reminded him of the Bergara Premier he'd been drooling over ever since he saw an article on it in *Field & Stream*. He was less enthusiastic when he found out it retailed for $3,500.

Whatever the guy has in mind, if he's trying to be subtle, he picked the wrong weapon, Gene thought. The Bergara made a hell of a noise when fired. He checked out the other man and discovered a holster on his waistband. It was a worrisome sight. Only Gene, Sheriff Webster, and Deputy Pendry were expected to open-carry weapons on this peaceful island.

He surveyed the area to see if the Florida Fish and Wildlife Conservation Commission boats were in the vicinity, knowing that the rangers were always switched on to potential problems. When he saw no other boats, he concluded they were likely in the South Pass, ticketing fishermen who had a bunch of out-of-season snook in their ice chests or chasing down speeders on the Intracoastal Waterway.

Gene grabbed his shirt, pulled it back on, and did a quick spin with his cart, spewing sand and bits of rock as he raced off the beach toward a grove of areca palms nearby. His cart hidden from beach view, he grabbed the binoculars and positioned himself so that he could track the men's movements without being seen. He watched them pilot the inflatable raft over a small sandbar just offshore like it wasn't even there, then roar onto the beach, disembark, and head north as if they knew exactly where they were going. When they passed the two historic homes closest to Gene and continued on, he knew their destination. It had to be the sprawling beachfront home of Hugo Clerk, Victor's billionaire brother.

CHAPTER 5

The big knife in the tattoo had bugged Wes since he saw it on the stranger's bicep. There had been an incident involving a knife in Wes's past, but it hadn't fully registered with him when he was in the jewelry store, surrounded by glitter and caught up in engagement-ring nerves. By the time he sprinted up the steps to the newspaper office, shared what Leslie had told him about the causeway bridge with Randy and Sara, and turned on his computer, his mind had zeroed in on the painful episode. He was convinced it involved the same man he had just seen in the golf cart.

About six years ago, shortly before Christmas, an attorney named Nat Banda had called Wes. It was obvious that Banda wasn't interested in wishing Wes happy holidays, even though the two were friendly. He called to chat about a client he'd just gotten released from federal prison. The man, an ex-soldier, had served time for murder, and Banda was lobbying for favorable publicity on behalf of his client, Daniel Frederick White.

"The guy was a hero, and they gave him a bum deal," Banda said. "He got a life sentence for the murder of his commanding officer because he had a rookie judge advocate who didn't know his ass from a hole in the ground. I got him out on a technicality."

"Just like that?" Wes asked.

"Hell no," Banda squawked. "I've been working my butt off—mostly pro bono—for this guy. His mom's a nice lady, who knows my wife from mah-jongg. She said her son went into the military a sweet boy and came out broken and bitter, like what happens to so many of those kids. This is a human-interest story. A wrong has been righted. Your readers will love it."

Wes wasn't sure that White's story was the kind of feature the newspaper was looking for during the holidays: a convicted killer returned to the population, and a shattered young man at that. But he agreed to read White's background material.

The court documents Banda sent him said that White had been on a scouting mission in Afghanistan with four others when they were ambushed by a band of al-Qaeda terrorists who were operating in the country with the blessings of the Taliban. Three soldiers were killed and one was captured, likely to face torture and certain death.

White escaped the skirmish with minor wounds and found his way back to his platoon, where he pleaded with the commanding officer to let him lead a mission to rescue the survivor and bring back the bodies of his fallen comrades. All he needed was a few good men to help him. His commander balked, saying that the situation was far too dangerous to risk more lives. A heated argument followed, with the CO screaming at White that he was out of line and needed to follow orders whether he liked them or not.

Under cover of darkness, White loaded up on ammunition and headed out into the rugged, mountainous terrain alone. When he returned a week later with his half-dead fellow soldier—a twenty-five-year-old named Rick Howell—and the dog tags of the dead men, his CO told him that he should consider himself under arrest for desertion. As soon as the platoon returned to Bagram Air Base, White would be court-martialed.

A couple of nights later, an al-Qaeda force attacked White's outpost. When the skirmish ended and the enemy was fought off, the commanding officer was found dead, his throat slit. Because survivors of the attack believed no one from al-Qaeda had breached the perimeter where the command post was located, an investigation followed. White, the obvious suspect, was arrested for murder.

"White never pleaded guilty—never said much, in fact—and it was well known that many in the platoon hated the CO," Banda said. "There was plenty for me to work with."

The attorney obtained laudatory testimony about White's bravery from his fellow soldiers, including Howell. He appealed on the grounds that White's military lawyer had not represented the soldier's best interests. The evidence was inconclusive that White had killed his CO. There were also errors in the military proceedings that violated White's basic rights, Banda claimed. After four years in a maximum-security prison, White was released.

When he finished reading the material, Wes contacted Banda to say that he thought he could sell the story to his editor. It was timely since the number of critics looking for excuses to get out of Afghanistan was growing. The attorney said he would arrange for Wes to meet the veteran at his mother's house, where the young man was staying.

"I'll call him and let him know you'll be there in a couple of hours," Banda said, telling Wes he was leaving the office to go Christmas shopping for his wife.

The reporter had a mental picture of Daniel Frederick White when he approached the front door of the modest Indiana home. He was expecting a pimply-faced man in his early to midtwenties; clean-shaven, military-style haircut; polite. Likely browbeaten from his association with hardened criminals but still respectful and accustomed to calling someone *sir* or *ma'am*. What greeted him at the door was a well-muscled man well over six feet tall, the veins in his arms bulging. He had a firm jaw covered with a three-day growth and steely eyes so filled with contempt that it jarred Wes. Four years in a federal prison had done no favors for White and the society in which he now operated freely.

"Whaddya want?" he growled at Wes, who took a step back and briefly considered making a quick exodus.

Wes cleared his throat, assuming that Banda had forgotten to make the introductory call, and said he was a friend of White's attorney and was there to interview the veteran about his release from prison. He wanted to write a feature story about how White had saved the life of a fellow soldier and was later arrested following the murder of his commanding officer. Wes used the sympathetic voice he'd cultivated over the years. The one that said, "I'm on your side, brother. Now tell me your story, and I'll fix whatever wrong has been done to you." Sometimes he meant it. Usually, it was an entry to getting an interview. All reporters resorted to this trick at one time or another.

While he was doing his best to be convincing, Wes failed to notice White's right hand reaching for a large hunting-style knife in a holster on his waist. Before Wes could finish his spiel, the weapon was at his throat, pressing hard against the flesh above his Adam's apple.

"Listen carefully to what I have to say," White snarled as he moved his left hand around the back of Wes's neck and grabbed the collar of his winter coat to get more leverage. "I'll remove this knife and allow you to leave if you swear you will never return to this house. Or call. Or attempt to have any contact with my mother or me. Got it?" He emphasized the question by pushing the knife tip farther into Wes's neck and drawing a few drops of blood. "I said, 'Got it?'"

"I-I got it," Wes managed to whisper, even if he didn't completely mean it. When he returned to the office, he wrote a story about the encounter. He figured White might not like it if he saw it but wouldn't seek out Wes for retribution and risk going back to prison.

Wes had put the incident out of his mind until it came roaring back, triggered first by the steely eyes of the man in the golf cart and then by his menacing tattoo. *If it is the same guy, what the hell is he doing here?* Wes thought as he typed the name of his former newspaper into his computer and was directed to the website of the *Daily News* and a button that led to PayPal.

"I am not paying one damned cent to view the archives of my own story," he said aloud, causing the others in the small office to stop what they were doing and look at him. "They already got my blood and sweat for nothing. What else do they want, the bastards?"

"You got a problem?" Sara asked, chuckling. "Chill and try typing in what you're looking for. It's bound to be on the web somewhere free."

Wes's face reddened with the realization that he was not thinking clearly. He couldn't be sure if it was the stranger or the engagement ring. He shot a grin at the publisher. "Oh yeah. I didn't think of that."

There were plenty of Daniel Whites on the internet, the most famous being an American politician named Daniel James White, who assassinated San Francisco Mayor George Moscone and Supervisor Harvey Milk in 1978 at City Hall. But after a few minutes of digging, Wes discovered a blurry photo of Daniel F. White. He looked to be in his early twenties and was wearing a uniform—likely a photo a reporter obtained from a distraught mother. The picture accompanied a small story about him being charged with murder. The man in the golf cart was burlier, but there was no mistaking him; he and the young veteran had to be the same person.

The causeway bridge was stuck open for boat traffic only, and there was a convicted killer on the island. Wes's instincts went on high alert as the words of his publisher rang in his ears: *There is no crime problem on this island.*

CHAPTER 6

Daniel Frederick White watched over his shoulder as the man in the pink shirt and khaki slacks crossed the street and disappeared from sight. Then the ex-soldier turned to confront the woman next to him, who was fiddling with her cell phone.

"Remember what I told you, Lilith!" he barked. "Act like a tourist. Don't call attention to yourself. Just get the job done and get back here. We can't afford to waste time."

Lilith Krueger grimaced and opened her mouth to respond but appeared to change her mind. She got out of the cart and reached into the back seat for a large straw bag with a flamingo on it. "Who was that guy crossing the street? He acted like he knew you," she said. She grabbed her blonde braid, wrapped it into a chignon at the nape of her neck, stuck in a couple of bobby pins, and tightly pulled on her straw cowboy hat.

White definitely remembered the guy: a reporter named Wes Avery. He was surprised to see him on the island and immediately wondered if he was still working? He had to be in his late fifties or early sixties, although he looked older. Until he moved out of Indiana, White had read Wes's stories in the local paper and thought he was good at his job, even-handed. But White wasn't ready to share the truth of what had happened with him or anyone—not even his attorney, who had managed to get him out of prison despite his reluctance to talk.

"A reporter who tried to interview me after I got out of prison," he said. "I don't think he recognized me, but I won't forget him. He came to my mom's house with this phony sympathy routine. I convinced him to move on."

Lilith laughed. "I'm sure you did." She threw the bag over her shoulder.

"You got everything you need?" he asked.

She glared at him with what White read as exasperation. "I got lipstick, a hairbrush, a couple of tampons, clippers, and an IED. Not IUD, *IED*, in case you didn't understand. And a hell of a lot more knowledge about these things than you," she said, reaching over and slapping him a little too hard on the thigh.

"An IED? The idea is to disable, not devastate. That's what the boss wants. No explosives."

"I got your plan A and your plan B drilled into my head, honey—no big boom. I'll get the job done," she said. She started to walk away, then turned and said loudly. "Sweetie, I'm going to that store down the street. I'll be back shortly. Love you."

"Okay, baby," White said, pulling out his own cell phone in an attempt to look like many of the people milling around the village. *Here they are in paradise with their noses stuck in these stupid devices,* he thought. He glanced up to check out Lilith strolling across the street, her firm rear cheeks grinding against each other like two ball bearings, her thong outline visible through her white shorts. He never tired of watching her departures but wouldn't dare mention it to her.

He worried that Lilith's appearance would draw undue attention to the two of them in this village where many in the population were over sixty and appeared to like their carbs. She was thirty-two and fit, with a six-pack that rivaled his. Though it wasn't obvious from her appearance, she was the best damn demolitions expert he had ever met. That's what the boss had said when he ordered White to hire her. White didn't want to work with a woman but had to admit he was impressed by her résumé, which included several complicated explosions in South America where only property was destroyed and no one died. Still, he couldn't afford any screwups.

He sat back in the cart and took in the surroundings. Things were exactly as he'd imagined from the photographs he had studied over the last several months. Small shops, a few restaurants, a smattering of palm trees, and the feeling that nothing bad could ever happen here. A restaurant across the street with outdoor seating and piped-in music had attracted a handful of day-trippers wrapping up their afternoon with ice cream. Wouldn't they be surprised when they decided to call it a day and found out they couldn't leave the island because the bridge was busted? White smiled at the mental picture of the kids whining in the back seat of the car and the wife complaining to her husband about them being trapped forever on this once beautiful but now godforsaken island.

After about twenty minutes, he saw Lilith heading in his direction and watched incredulously as she stopped to pet a golden retriever and chat with its owner, a tall man with a gray comb-over. "C'mon, c'mon," he said. He checked his watch and slid over to the driver's seat. They had plenty of time, but Lilith was acting too much like a tourist for her own good. He didn't want anyone to remember her face if it could be avoided.

When she left the dog and its master and strolled into the flower shop, he almost jumped out of the cart. He checked his watch again and was contemplating going after her when she emerged with a bouquet of yellow roses. She climbed in beside him and grinned.

"These are for you. Now smile big if you can; try to act happy to see me."

"Let's go," he said, ignoring the flowers and the sarcasm.

"Just a minute," she said, putting her hand on his knee. "I'm waiting for something."

"What's that?"

"For the shopkeeper to flip the Open sign in his window to Closed and leave the building," she said.

"It's almost four. What's the problem?" He glared at her with the same steely eyes he had flashed in Wes's direction.

"The problem is that plan A and B you've been bragging about all these months didn't work. It was impossible to cut the cell tower and land-line cables, given their location and thickness, so I had to come up with a plan C. Not sure who fucked up on your end, but my plan now requires the shopkeeper to leave the building."

White grimaced. *Where does she get off criticizing me?* "He's leaving. Let's go."

"Give him a second."

They sat there watching the balding man with the white mustache exit the door, turn to lock it, and then walk gingerly to a parking area across the street from the shop. He got into a silver MINI Cooper and, in a couple of minutes, was on his way.

"Satisfied?" White growled.

"Nice old guy. His wife died last year. He can't find another salesper-son but isn't prepared to part with his shop. Said he's in a quandary. Guess I'm gonna help him decide," she said, pressing a series of buttons on her cell phone. "What the fuck? What's the deal with the cell service? I'm not getting any reception."

"Your Plan C hit a snag?" White gave her a smirk, which she ignored as she continued to press buttons on her phone.

"Finally. I suggest we waste no time getting outta here."

The sound of four small explosions followed the golf cart down the street. Seconds later, bits of debris hit the fiberglass top, causing both riders to duck. When the racket from the cell tower crashing to the ground and taking the flower shop with it reached their ears, White flashed Lilith a lethal look.

"That was your plan C? I told you, no noise," White snarled as he rounded the corner and steered the golf cart north on the village's main street.

Lilith laughed and poked him in the arm with her finger. "When you come up with another idea that would have done the job as well as this one, big boy, you let me know what it was."

White simmered in silence. She had eliminated phone service for most of the island but not the way they'd planned, not the way the boss wanted the job done. This was the first glitch. He hoped there weren't more to come.

CHAPTER 7

Gene Miller considered Hugo Clerk a friend. The billionaire in his late fifties had welcomed the iguana hunter onto his property a couple of months ago and given him a large tip and several bottles of champagne—the good kind, Gene noted—for cleaning out a nest of reptiles in the guest house. He'd seen Hugo a couple of times since then, and the guy was always cordial; he always had time to stop and shoot the breeze. Hugo was nothing like Victor.

When Gene realized that the armed men were heading in the direction of Hugo's waterfront home, he grabbed his cell phone and called the private number he had for the billionaire. The call went to voice mail, as did Gene's attempt to reach the sheriff and then 911.

Few residents and only a handful of businesses on the island still had landlines. Cell phones hadn't worked properly since the storm six months ago. People often joked about how everyone sounded like a robot before their phones went dead in the middle of a conversation. But it was no laughing matter—especially not today, Gene thought.

He had no choice but to leave his observation point and track down Sheriff Webster. He worried about Hugo but knew he couldn't handle two armed men by himself.

Here's hoping you're not at home, buddy, Gene thought as he raced his golf cart down the quiet streets. *Or that I'm wrong about where they're going.*

Lilith had not yet felled the cell tower when Gene arrived at the sheriff's office. He found the door open and the sound of a Tampa Bay Rays baseball game blasting forth from a big-screen TV. Deputy Alex Pendry, the newest addition to the island's law enforcement team, was seated at his desk and talking on the phone. His face was flushed, and his pale-blue eyes were watery. Gene could tell he was frazzled.

"The sheriff's not here," Deputy Pendry moaned after hanging up and muting the TV set. He looked at Gene like he'd lost his last dollar in a slot machine. "This place is going crazy. The causeway bridge isn't working, I can't reach anyone there, and people are calling me like I'm supposed to know what to do about it. I don't even know what happened, Gene." He let out a heavy sigh and pushed back from his desk. "Besides, that bridge is in Sheriff Tom Lake's county. He should have a couple of guys there by now. There's nothing I can do. Nothing."

Gene felt uncomfortable for him, like the twenty-four-year-old with the marine-style haircut was just managing to hold it together because there was someone he knew in the office.

"I'm guessing you're not here to discuss iguanas," Deputy Pendry said. He took a deep breath after speaking, as if trying to calm himself.

"Nope. Where's the sheriff? We might have a problem at Hugo Clerk's place. Two guys with guns arrived in a RIB and were headed toward his house—the big one on the beach just off Laurel," Gene said. He'd brought his rifle with him and now propped it against the wall by the TV.

"Two armed men in a rubber inflatable?" Deputy Pendry went even paler than he had appeared when Gene first entered the office. "On this island?" He grabbed the office phone and punched in a number. Gene could hear it ring a couple of times before Sheriff Webster's voice mail kicked in: "This is Sheriff Bruce Webster. Leave a message. I'll get back to ya as soon as possible."

Deputy Pendry grimaced. "The sheriff's at a two-day emergency preparedness conference in Tallahassee. Fire chief, too. He could still be in a meeting or having a drink with some of the guys. I've already left several messages for him about the bridge. Guess I better check out Mr. Clerk's place. If it looks bad, I'll call for reinforcements from the neighboring county."

Gene held up his hand to reassure the deputy. "I'm a county employee. licensed to carry a gun, and a good shot. I was a scout sniper in the marines and got plenty of practice in Iraq. I'll go with you."

Deputy Pendry looked relieved. He reached into the lower drawer of his desk, pulled out a .45-caliber SIG Sauer handgun in a holster, and strapped it around his waist. "Technically, I can't ask for your help, but given the circumstances, I sure could use it. Please don't fire your weapon unless I give you permission."

"You're the boss," Gene said, and for the first time since he had arrived in the office, he managed what he hoped was a comforting smile for the rookie deputy whose island territory appeared to be under siege.

Deputy Pendry was reaching for his aviator sunglasses when the office phone rang again. "Sheriff's office," he said, sounding exasperated, as though he expected this to be another bridge complaint. "Clerk . . . you said your name is Clerk? . . . Yes, sir, we are aware that there are two men with guns on your property. We're on our way . . . Did you say your address is 24 First Street West? I thought your property was on Laurel?"

Gene's mouth dropped open. "That's *Victor* Clerk's property. Hugo's brother!"

Deputy Pendry was nodding, his eyes getting bigger. "Yes, sir, I'm gonna put you on speaker. Please try to remain calm so we can understand what you're saying."

". . . the dogs barking, and when I checked out the back window, I could see these guys. Two of them carrying rifles, big ones, and coming from the mangroves toward the house. This is no fucking joke. You've got to get here now!"

"Stay inside and don't confront them. Do you have a place you can hide?" Deputy Pendry reached into his desk for additional magazines as he spoke. Remembering his days in Iraq, Gene wondered if the deputy was preparing for a gunfight on peaceful little Anibonie Island—and if he should do the same.

"I sent Billie to the secret closet in the main bathroom. It's where I keep my safe. Fuck me—they're headed for the sliding doors downstairs. They're locked, but the alarm isn't set. Shit, I can hear them banging something against the glass."

"Sir, you need to head for your safe room immediately," Deputy Pendry ordered. "Lock yourselves in and remain quiet. We'll be there in a few minutes."

"What the fuck? Looks like they attached something to the door. My God, they've blown it!" As he spoke, the sound of an explosion reverberated through the phone.

"Go to the safe room now, Mr. Clerk! Now!" Deputy Pendry slammed down the phone and jumped up from his chair.

Gene could feel the hairs on the back of his neck stand at attention. This was not the surly Victor Clerk who had ordered him off his property. This was someone who was terrified that at any moment, he would be shot dead by intruders.

"Let's go. No time to waste," Gene said as he saw Deputy Pendry hesitate and reach for the phone again. "We can call for backup on the way."

Outside, they stopped briefly at Gene's golf cart for more ammunition and were headed to Deputy Pendry's SUV when they heard four small explosions, followed by the sound of metal buckling and breaking. For Gene, it was an eerie reminder of bombed buildings collapsing in Fallujah. He turned toward the direction of the noise and saw the cell tower, half a short block away, shifting and shaking as if being manipulated by a puppeteer, then toppling in slow motion toward the flower shop and the street. He gasped and dove under the SUV, scraping the left side of his face on the gravel as he yelled to the deputy, "Take cover!"

The image of his neighbor's car flattened by a falling tree during the recent big winds flashed before him. As he tracked the tower's slow collapse toward the SUV, he said a prayer for his wife and son and wondered what their life would be like without him.

CHAPTER 8

Wes was on his way to the sheriff's office to talk about White and his appearance on the island when he heard the explosions and saw the hundred-foot cell tower collapsing. He took cover in the post office's recessed entryway and stuck his phone out at arm's length to capture video of the dramatic event.

When quiet had settled over the village, Wes rushed to the site of the fallen structure, making sure that no one had been trapped in the flower shop. He stared in disbelief at the pile of rubble, then took a few photos.

To his right, he saw the iguana hunter, Gene Miller, emerge from underneath a county vehicle, his face bloodied. He watched the man stand shakily, holding on to the SUV as if trying to get his bearings. Coming around from the other side was Deputy Alex Pendry, his uniform dirtied by gravel dust and his face covered with bewilderment. He joined them, relieved that both men appeared to have only minor scratches.

"This is crazy," Wes said, reaching for a pen and pad of paper in his back pocket. "Any idea what happened?"

Both men shook their heads and offered no further information. The reporter thought they seemed anxious to leave the scene.

"Can you rope off this area and keep these people back?" Deputy Pendry asked three firefighters from the nearby station who were running toward the group after checking the flower shop. "What's left of this structure could collapse at any minute. We have a situation on the east side of the island, and possibly one on the west, involving weapons. Gene and I can't stick around, so we're counting on you."

"Do you need some of us to go with you?" The question came from Ray Santiago, a dark-haired firefighter who looked to be the deputy's age and brimming with eagerness. "I can help."

Deputy Pendry paused as if considering the offer and then shook his head. "I need you to maintain order around this tower and in the village. The sheriff's gone, and now there's no way to contact anyone off the island for help. Keep things under control here as best you can."

Randy Long, who'd arrived with the paper's official camera in hand— an older-model digital Nikon—approached the group and directed a quizzical look at Wes, who shrugged as if to say he had no information.

"You got a problem with armed men on the island? The bridge and the cell tower are both disabled. Seriously, what's going on?" Wes pressed, figuring they wouldn't want to share detailed information but hoping something useful might slip out in the confusion of the moment. "Have you called for backup?"

Gene jumped in, gesturing with his hands as he spoke, trying to capture the urgency of the situation. "There were a couple of guys with guns headed for Hugo Clerk's place about twenty minutes ago. Then Alex got a call from Victor Clerk saying *his* house was being invaded by two men with guns. They blew open a locked sliding door. The last we heard was that Victor was headed for a safe room. I don't see how it can be the same guys, but whatever it is, it's not good—especially with the cell tower down and no way to call for outside help."

Wes scribbled *Four armed men* on his notepad. "I also saw something strange. A man in a golf cart who I recognized as a former soldier convicted of murder. I watched him and a woman park by the flower shop. Obviously, they aren't there now."

"Well, crap," Gene said, tugging at his ear and surveying the others. "Why are we standing here jawing? Why not have one of the firemen go with the deputy to Victor's? Wes and Randy can ride with me to Hugo's place."

"I'm not sure the sheriff would support civilians getting involved," Deputy Pendry said, looking at Wes and Randy and shaking his head.

"Tough times call for desperate measures, as they say." Gene responded. "I'll tell Bruce it was my doing."

Deputy Pendry continued to appear uncertain as to how to proceed. Meanwhile, Ray had raised his hand and was looking eagerly at the others. "Count me in. I've got my gun locked up in my truck, and we can get another pistol or two if we need them, I'll get radios from the station."

Wes shook his head. "No gun for me. I'm out of practice and not a fan. Probably shoot myself in the foot." He noticed that Randy was also declining the offer of a weapon. Ray gave Wes a thumbs-up and took off for the station, returning a few minutes later with two short-range communication devices.

"I may get in trouble for this, but let's go," Deputy Pendry said as he and Ray headed for the SUV. "Try to stay in touch."

Wes glanced over at Gene after joining the iguana hunter in his golf cart. "These radios have to be fifteen years old. If they don't work, I guess we'll have to resort to what—tin cans and a string?"

"Give the kid a break," Gene said, shaking his head. "Situations like this don't happen every day on this island. He's doing the best he can with his boss gone and unreachable."

Wes nodded. He knew all too well how ill-equipped the lone deputy was to handle an island that was giving all indications of becoming a war zone, with no means of outside communication and only a small and haphazard militia for defense.

Leslie Elliott was walking Newton, the year-old rescue corgi Wes had given her, when she noticed the line of cars waiting to cross the swing bridge. Some traffic backup was normal this time of year. Even though many residents were gone, the number of boats on the Intracoastal Waterway was still high, plus construction workers flooded the island daily, grateful that every time a home changed ownership, a costly remodeling project followed. Today, the line of vehicles waiting to cross the bridge was longer than usual, and Leslie could hear the drivers griping to one another about the delay.

Dissatisfied with Newton's pace, Leslie picked him up, cradling him under her arm, and raced back to her condo. Her neighbor had offered his golf cart to her in the past; she hopped in and was glad to see the key in the ignition. She would explain to him later why she didn't have time to ask if she could borrow it.

After a brief phone conversation with Wes, she drove at a fast clip toward the head of the line, which had grown to include about fifty vehicles, mostly pickup trucks. Once there, Leslie was glad to see Joe, a man she knew only by his first name from the work he'd done rebuilding the bell tower at her church after the recent big storm. He was sitting in his black pickup truck with a *Trump/Pence 2016* sticker on the rear window and reading the *Island Sun*—the nose of his vehicle almost touching the traffic crossbar.

She snapped a few photos of the scene with her phone, then strolled closer to the open window on the driver's side. "Joe, hi; what's the deal?"

"Hey, Leslie. Beats me. I watched a sailboat and a speedboat go through. There was nothing else coming, but the bridge stayed open for boats. Then I seen this guy come out of that house on the bridge and take

40

a header into the water. That was thirty minutes ago, and the bridge is still closed to cars. I called my wife and told her I'd be late. Now I can't get hold of her. As soon as this crossbar goes up, I'm outta here."

Joe motioned toward a man three trucks to the south. "My brother, Adam, still has roaming sometimes. He was able to reach his girlfriend and tell her to pick us up by boat if we aren't home in an hour. We're thinkin' of runnin' a ferry service. Pickin' up guys and takin' 'em home. Fifty bucks each. Maybe a hundred."

Leslie laughed. "Aren't you the enterprising ones. Someone jumped off the bridge? You think it was a suicide?"

"Nope." The look on Joe's face was studied. "He came up real quick, and then I seen a speedboat, a big one, pick him up. The funny thing is that they didn't go under the bridge. They turned around and took off for the west side of the island. I seen three men on board—two others and the jumper. It was crazy."

"You think anyone else saw them?"

"I can't be sure. I mean, no one from the bridge office showed up for at least five, maybe ten minutes. I don't think they realized the bridge wasn't gonna close so that cars could cross. Guess they didn't see the guy jump. He must've been on drugs or somethin'."

Leslie thanked Joe, took a few more photos, and then tried to ring Wes again, with no luck. From her vantage point, she could see a handful of people standing near the bridge tender's house. The group looked to include sheriff's deputies from the neighboring county. She wished she was part of the conversation. She had plenty of questions. Did the diver sabotage the bridge? If so, what was his reason? Perhaps, as Joe had observed, he was mentally unstable or on drugs. But if he had been picked up by a waiting speedboat, there might be more to this than the actions of a deranged individual. Frustrated by her inability to cross-examine someone on the other side of the bridge opening, she hopped back into the cart and headed for her condo.

"Time for an early dinner, buddy," she told the dog when they arrived home. She reached for Newton's kibble under the sink, poured him a bowl, and headed for the bedroom, where she took off her shorts and T-shirt, slipped on a pair of slacks and a linen top, and ran a brush through her short hair.

"I'll be back soon, sweetie," she said when she returned to the kitchen and grabbed her purse and car keys off the counter. "I don't know what's going on, but I'm not going to sit around this condo waiting for your friend Wes to show up and tell me. I'm going to find out for myself."

CHAPTER 9

Deputy Pendry and Ray Santiago sped down First Street, slowing only slightly when they turned into a shell driveway that meandered through a parklike area shaded by lush olive trees and Florida oaks. After several hundred yards, their progress was halted by an eight-foot-tall iron gate.

"Any chance you know the code?" Deputy Pendry asked when he pulled up next to a small box with a keypad.

"I remember this place," Ray said. "We paid the owner a visit after he got his certificate of occupancy and asked him for the gate code for our files. He had a strange reason for not giving it to us. He said he was insured and if the place caught fire, we should let it burn. He'd just tear down what was left. He didn't really give a fuck. That last part's a direct quote."

"Crazy," Deputy Pendry said. "Who thinks like that? Guess he won't mind if I drive over his landscaping to get around the gate."

He backed up and pointed the vehicle toward a row of decorative grasses that appeared to be newly planted. He worked his way through them carefully, flattening only a few, and was soon back on the driveway and racing toward the home that he judged to be about a quarter of a mile away.

"Jeez, this place is huge," Deputy Pendry said when they reached the contemporary-style mansion with stucco siding and a flat roof. "I'm going to park behind that banyan tree over there. When we get out, let's approach the house from the south side. That's where Victor said the intruders entered."

"You think they're still here?" Ray asked, his eyes widening. "Should we have our guns in our hands? I'm not used to police work."

"I'm hoping we don't have to use them," Deputy Pendry responded, patting the weapon in his side holster.

The two men moved cautiously toward the back of the home, working their way through pitch apple and weigela bushes. When they stepped out into the open by a large pool that overlooked the Gulf waters, the damage done during the break-in was obvious. Two panels of a sliding door lay in pieces on the pool decking. Fragments were also on the tile floor inside. Three windows were shattered by what appeared to be the blast Victor had described. The casings had been ripped off and now hung like vinyl tinsel from the window frames.

"Victor Clerk wasn't kidding about how determined these guys were," Deputy Pendry said as he glanced through the opening into what appeared to be a large gathering area with a bar, an expansive gray leather sectional, and a TV screen that covered the north wall. The lower level was quiet except for the electrical hum from a large wine cooler and a nearby refrigerator and a faint whooshing noise from the air conditioner. He put out his arm again as if to caution Ray to stay behind him.

"All clear here," Deputy Pendry whispered when they'd examined the six rooms on the lower level and found nothing. "Let's check the next level."

Halfway up the staircase, they stopped. A clicking sound was headed their way. Both men froze, then chuckled when they identified the potential threat.

"Well, hi there, big boy," the deputy said. "You alone?"

The black lab standing on the landing wagging his tail was soon joined by another, a slightly smaller lab with a graying muzzle.

"Where's your master, boy? Where's Victor?"

The larger of the dogs whimpered and gazed over his shoulder, then back at Deputy Pendry, and then over his shoulder again. He barked and took off, scampering across the living room, past the kitchen, and down the hallway, with the deputy and the fireman not far behind. He led them through double doors to a massive bedroom, where they were met with signs of a struggle: furniture askew and a broken lamp on the floor. There was a fist-size patch of blood on a bedsheet and a fifteen-inch wooden stick with a knob that looked like a warrior's weapon lying on the floor. One of the pillowcases was missing.

Deputy Pendry turned to say something to the fireman when he noticed Ray was staring at the ceiling. A large mirror was affixed over the bed, giving its occupants a clear view of what was happening below.

"This guy must lead an interesting life," Ray said, looking at the deputy and grinning, then growing somber. "If he's still alive."

The lab had moved from the bedroom into the bathroom and was standing in front of a row of shelves with folded towels, whimpering. The older dog had also joined the group and taken a seat next to her companion.

"The safe room," Deputy Pendry said quietly. "This could be the place where Clerk told his girlfriend to hide. Hello! Sheriff! Is there anyone in there?"

There was a muffled but unintelligible response. Deputy Pendry hit the wall next to the towels three times. A like number of weak knocks could be heard from the other side, as well as a loud click that sounded like a door unlocking. The older dog whined.

"How are we gonna get in there?" Ray asked. "Is there a switch? Whoever is on the other side must have a way out. Why aren't they using it?"

Deputy Pendry shrugged and started pulling the towels off the shelves. When nothing was evident on the empty wall, the two men scanned the ceiling, the baseboards, and adjoining surfaces.

"Look at those three hooks on the piece of white trim. There's something odd about them," Ray said.

He put his hand on one of the silver pegs and tried unsuccessfully to twist it. He thought for a second, ran his finger over the trim piece, and gave it a push.

The panel that had once held the shelves swung open to reveal a woman in her midtwenties with long brown hair, wearing only a bra and panties. The skin around her eyes was black as if her makeup had been smeared from crying. She was shivering.

"They killed him. I heard his screams. My poor Victor," she said weakly and slumped forward into Deputy Pendry's arms.

CHAPTER 10

As the golf cart belonging to Gene traveled along the village streets with Randy in the front seat and Wes in the back, the reporter kept up a running commentary on the wealthy brothers whose homes were under attack.

He shared the story of his recent flight in the Clerk brothers' jet, a well-appointed Gulfstream G650ER, which was in a hangar at the airport just off the island. In earlier times, the landing strip had been small, poorly lit, and rumored to be used for drug trafficking. Several years ago, the Clerks and a consortium of wealthy property owners who liked the idea of having a proper landing strip nearby for their weekend getaways had purchased it, kicking in millions for its expansion. These days, it was well used.

Wes explained how Hugo, the elder of the brothers by several years, was an unassuming man interested in the community's well-being. When a storm had taken down the church bell tower six months ago, the billionaire had footed the bill for cleanup and repair. He also kicked in $500,000 to a fund he started to help local businesses damaged by the hurricane-like winds.

Wes had never met or even seen Victor. Rumors were that the brothers had not spoken to each other for some time and had only recently reunited.

"It could be because of Victor's divorce from his first wife," Wes speculated. "I heard the ex-wife's settlement put a strain on the brothers' finances, which I'm told are closely linked through their late father."

"How do you know all of this?" Gene asked.

"Cocktail parties," Wes responded, chuckling. "I don't go. I just hear about it afterward. I'm not saying they always get it right, but you know the adage: Where there's smoke, there's fire."

"And art shows," Randy chimed in. "Any place that people gather, there's bound to be talk."

When they arrived at Hugo's property, Gene parked by the opening in the pink stucco wall that separated the waterfront mansion from Laurel Street and grabbed his rifle. He instructed Wes and Randy to go to the front door and proceed with caution. He would check out the pool area in the back.

"If someone broke into this house and is still there, you think they're gonna answer the door?" Randy commented as Wes prepared to knock.

Wes had to agree with his friend's observation. Two men with guns wouldn't be inclined to greet unwelcome visitors with tea and cookies. He wished he'd accepted Ray's offer of a weapon. The idea of having something to brandish, like in those old crime novels, was suddenly appealing.

"How else you suggest we get in?" Wes asked, then rapped loudly on the ornate wooden door.

There was no sound of footsteps approaching or someone calling out that they'd be right there. Instead, the voice they heard sounded like it was coming from the back of the property.

"Help! Dammit! Help!" It was Gene. His shouts were followed by two shots from a rifle.

Wes and Randy took off running along the shell path to the back of the house. As they came closer to the source of the cries, they could see Gene leaning over the bloody body of a woman in a lounge chair. Wes couldn't be sure if she was dead or clinging to life. She was definitely not moving. If she was alive, it was obvious she needed medical attention.

He turned to Randy. "Take the golf cart. Go to the clinic. Get whoever is available!"

Randy took off for the island's only medical facility. Wes moved quickly to Gene's side. "It's Mrs. Clerk, right? Can I help?"

"Get some wet towels."

Wes headed for the door of the guest cottage next to the main house and quickly found the bathroom. He grabbed the hand towels off the rack and stuck them in the pedestal sink, turning on the hot water and wringing out the excess. On the way out, he saw an envelope on the floor marked *Sheriff*, picked it up, and stuffed it in his pocket. This was worse than he could have imagined: Patricia Clerk badly wounded and no sign of her husband. Where was he? In the main house, dead?

He handed the towels to Gene, then stood back to give him space. He felt helpless and was glad the iguana hunter was not shy about taking charge.

"Did you fire the shots?" Wes asked, remembering the sound that had accompanied Gene's cries for help. "Or was someone shooting at you?"

"It was me. I needed to get your attention."

Wes nodded. "Randy's gone to the clinic. I'm gonna check the cottage first and see if Hugo's in there. Maybe he needs medical help, too, or maybe . . ." *No need to finish the sentence,* Wes thought as he returned to the guest accommodations.

There was a fireplace and a living room filled with overstuffed furniture. It had a beach-like feel, with shell wallpaper, paintings of tropical birds, and wicker baskets that resembled the ones that Leslie had purchased from one of the scores of catalogs she received every month. Off the living room were two bedrooms and two bathrooms—but no sign of Hugo. When he decided that nothing was out of place in the guest cottage, Wes headed next door.

He had been in the main house before. In exchange for the use of the Clerks' private jet and with the blessing of his publisher, he had done a freelance piece for *Architectural Digest* on the historic home that had stood on the beach for almost a hundred years and been carefully restored. The magazine hadn't responded to his inquiry yet, but Hugo had seemed happy with Wes's work, which was all that mattered to the reporter. Wes considered this a puff piece—a favor for a favor—not real journalism.

He entered cautiously through the French doors on the porch, letting himself into a living room with a fireplace and a ten-foot ceiling with beams made of pecky cypress. He checked the living and dining rooms and the kitchen and found a few dirty dishes in the sink and a newspaper turned to the financial section on the coffee table. Nothing else appeared disturbed.

Upstairs in the spacious main bedroom, a black-and-white cat was asleep at the foot of the bed. When Wes entered the room, the cat lifted his head, meowed loudly, then watched Wes check out the closet and adjoining sitting room. As he was leaving, Wes noticed the cat had returned to its afternoon rest, unaware that one or both of his owners could be in serious trouble. He made a mental note to fill the cat's food and water bowls before he left and find someone to check on the animal.

Unless he'd been murdered and his body stuffed in some out-of-the-way part of the house, Hugo was nowhere to be found. If the men with guns had planned on robbing the Clerks, it didn't appear they had taken anything. If they'd wanted to kill both of them, why was Patricia the only one he and Gene found?

Wes bounded down the steps and out the French doors and saw Gene on a deck chair, sitting next to Patricia and pressing on the towel that covered her wound.

"You try to call 911?"

"Yeah. No luck. When do you think someone from the clinic will be here? I don't know what else to do for her. Her pulse is really weak."

Wes surveyed the scene. The lounge chair next to Patricia was over-turned. A nearby stand and silver bucket were upended. A champagne bottle had survived the fall, but there were small shards of glass everywhere. The only blood was on and around Mrs. Clerk.

Even under trauma, Hugo's wife was a striking woman. The reporter had heard through the grapevine that she was his second wife, but Wes didn't know for sure. He guessed her to be in her midforties—at least ten years younger than her husband—with a slender nose and full lips. Her skin, smooth like porcelain, reminded him of Leslie's flawless complexion. There was no sign of pain or distress. It was as though she were asleep. A young child with the face of an angel taking an afternoon nap.

Wes knew little about gunshot wounds, but it appeared the bullet had passed through her right shoulder, exiting her back. He remembered hearing from a doctor that shoulder wounds were usually not fatal if the bullet avoided hitting a major artery when it traveled through the body. He hoped Patricia would be lucky in that regard.

He was relieved to see Randy rounding the corner, followed by two women in aqua-colored scrubs, one carrying bags of liquids, the other pushing an IV stand. Behind them was a shortish man with a name tag that Wes read when he got closer as Dr. Louis Sandburg.

"What've we got here?" Dr. Sandburg asked. He took Patricia's pulse and checked her eyes, then directed the other women to start an IV. He pulled back the towels, emitted a few "Ums," and then lifted her gently to check her back. "She's in shock. Lost a fair amount of blood. Let's get this wound cleaned and dressed." He turned to Gene. "You her husband?"

"Hardly," Gene responded with an embarrassed laugh. "I'm the iguana hunter. Was checking on the house when I found her. Don't know how long she's been here or exactly what happened—"

"We need to get her to a hospital," Dr. Sandburg interrupted, then scowled. "With no means of contacting the outside world, that's not going to happen anytime soon, so we're going to have to do the best we can here."

"There's a bedroom in the guest house," Wes offered. "We can take her there."

Under the doctor's direction, Wes, Gene, and Randy lifted the lounge chair, with a nurse handling the IV pole, and carried Patricia into the guest cottage and the larger of the two bedrooms.

"Guess you don't see many gunshot wounds in your practice here," Gene said when Dr. Sandburg emerged from the bedroom and instructed one of the nurses to arrange for the patient's care until they could get her off the island.

"I was in Iraq," Dr. Sandburg said. "I saw plenty."

"Me, too," Gene responded.

Wes saw Gene looking at Dr. Sandburg as if he expected a further explanation. When he got none, he remained quiet, joining Wes on one of the couches upholstered in a tropical fabric. Wes wanted a cigarette badly but thought twice about smoking in someone's house without first asking permission.

"This is one of the craziest things I've ever seen. Where do you think Hugo is?" Wes asked Gene without really expecting an answer.

"We can only hope wherever he is, he's safe. But I've got a feeling that isn't the case."

CHAPTER 11

R ay sat down on the bed, waiting patiently for Victor's houseguest, Bilyana Tsvetkov, to shower, dry her hair, dress, and put on makeup. Except for his mother and two sisters, he'd been too involved in his career to focus on having a woman or serious girlfriend in his life. Now he remembered one of the reasons why: it took them way too long to get ready to go someplace. He fully expected to marry someday and have children, but for now, he was content to put those responsibilities on the back burner. His father was his role model, and he hadn't married Ray's mother until he was in his midthirties.

Deputy Pendry had given the fireman his assignment: "Try to keep her calm. Reassure her that we will do everything we can to find her boyfriend. I'll talk to her when we get to the station. I can record her there. If she has any questions, don't answer them." Meanwhile, the deputy was searching the property, looking for anything that would help locate Victor Clerk or discover what had happened to him.

"You can call me Billie," she said when she finished getting ready and was standing by the bathroom door. Everything about her was voluptuous: luxurious, black hair that fell to the middle of her back; large, brown eyes; perfectly shaped eyebrows; long eyelashes, thick, red lips. Her figure filled every spare inch of fabric in the low-cut, red sundress she was wearing. She wore high-heeled sandals that exposed bright-white toenails. Around her neck was a solitary diamond the size of a dime. When she spoke, her accent was a mix of German and Russian with a touch of honey added for sweetener.

"What's your name?" she crooned.

"My name? Raul Santiago." He swallowed hard but couldn't immediately pinpoint why. "Ray."

"You a deputy?" she asked, easing closer to him.

He glanced up at the ceiling mirror and could see her black hair draping from the crown of her head and cascading around her alluring shoulders. He took a deep breath.

"No, ma'am. I'm a fireman." He started to tell her that he'd volunteered to help Deputy Pendry because Sheriff Webster was gone, the cell tower was down, and there was chaos on the island, but he stopped. His instructions were to keep mum.

"You think your friend will find Victor?"

Ray shrugged. "We, uh, I don't know. But he's looking for him, and I'm sure he'll turn up."

Her lips formed a pout. "You think so? I was in the bathroom getting ready to go out to dinner when I heard him yelling at me to get in the safe room. I knew where it was and how to get in there, but not how to get out. You have to believe me. Then I heard what sounded like an explosion and Victor screaming. How can you tell me he's going to be all right? He's dead. I know it."

Her face crumpled. Ray jumped up from the bed. Assuming he was going to be blamed for her state of mind when Deputy Pendry returned, he tried to comfort her. When he put his right arm around her, she turned into his chest and nestled against him, crying softly. Both of his arms instinctively surrounded her. *"Todo ira bien,"* he said, resorting to his native language.

A few minutes later, Ray was relieved to see Deputy Pendry appear in the doorway, even though comforting this beautiful woman who smelled like rain on a spring day was not an unpleasant task.

"I guess we're ready to go," the deputy said. He held up an envelope with writing on it to indicate that he had found something important and then pushed the button on the radio he was holding. "We're headed to the office. Over."

There was a crackling response and a voice that sounded like Gene's saying, "We'll meet you there. We found the missus and an envelope and . . ." The radio faded.

While Deputy Pendry was talking, Billie slipped into the bathroom, telling the fireman she needed to check her makeup. She returned a few minutes later with two Louis Vuitton suitcases, which she set in front of Ray. She hurried back into the closet and brought out a large, black duffel bag clutched tightly under her arm. The weight of the bag caused her to tilt slightly to the left. "What are we going to do with the dogs? We need to take them with us. I'm not coming back here. I couldn't."

"Okay. I'll think of something. What are their names?" Deputy Pendry asked.

"Victor never bothered to name them," she said. "Dog One and Dog Two. That's all I know. They answer to that."

When Billie started for the stairs, leaving the suitcases for the two men to carry, Deputy Pendry leaned toward Ray and whispered, "Don't say anything to her. I found this letter downstairs. It says they kidnapped Victor and his brother and are holding them for ransom. A hundred million each."

"Who has that kind of money?" Ray asked, shocked.

"They've got seventy-two hours," Deputy Pendry said, shaking his head. "And get this: There were no instructions on how to get the ransom to the kidnappers, and they're planning on burying the Clerks alive until it's paid."

Both men groaned simultaneously. Could there be anything worse than being buried alive?

CHAPTER 12

Cell service was always spotty on the island, but not like this. Shortly after the bridge had been disabled, Leslie discovered she had no bars and no service. When she arrived in the village, she found out why. The fallen cell tower lay on the ground like a defeated creature from a *Transformers* movie; the flower shop beneath it was a pile of smashed bricks, shattered glass, and squashed blossoms. Mr. Cavendish, the owner, was standing on the street, wiping his eyes and being comforted by a waitress Leslie recognized from a nearby restaurant. She stopped to offer her sympathy.

"So sorry for your loss," Leslie said, patting him on the back. "I'll miss your place. So many nice things. Do you have any idea what happened?"

Mr. Cavendish shook his head. "May would be heartbroken," he said. "Not sure I'll rebuild. I still have my home on the island. I hope that's enough to keep me busy."

"Thank goodness you weren't in the shop," Leslie said. Keeping a business going on an island with seasonal customers was a challenge. If she owned the flower shop, she would take the insurance money and open a place on the mainland. Or if she were in her seventies, as Mr. Cavendish appeared to be, she'd retire. That's if the insurance paid off. So many companies in Florida didn't come through after a disaster.

"Yes. Lucky for me and the young woman who came in to buy roses," he said. "She seemed to be in a hurry. A lot of folks are these days. She even suggested that she was probably my last customer and that I could close early."

"Um, that's odd," Leslie said. "What did she look like?"

"Blonde hair in a braid fastened into a bun in the back. May used to wear her hair like that. Straw cowboy hat and sturdy. Not the kind of woman you want to get in an argument with." He perked up. "But very sweet and interested in what I had to say."

"You should share that information with the deputy," Leslie said, squeezing Mr. Cavendish's hand before moving on toward the sheriff's office.

It bugged her that she didn't have an answer as to why the cell tower was on the ground. It had survived strong winds, and it wasn't as though the structure was historic and had collapsed under the weight of age. She wondered if there was some link between the bridge and the tower, then shook that off as a ridiculous conspiracy theory. Still, the presence of the blonde who had been eager for the shop owner to close early was intriguing.

She hurried up the ramp to the sheriff's office and found the door closed but not locked. When she opened it, she was surprised to see the room was empty of people. The TV was on but with the sound muted; the coffeepot was simmering and dangerously close to running out of liquid. *Not good,* she thought as she turned off both devices. Whoever had been there before her must have left in a hurry.

Since Bruce Webster had been appointed sheriff to take the place of the late Harry Fleck, the area had been arranged to accommodate desks for two deputies. She wondered if Deputy Alex Pendry would be getting a coworker. She had lobbied Wes to write a column about the need to expand the island's law enforcement presence. He hadn't done it yet but kept assuring her it was in the works.

She sat down at the empty desk. *No cell tower, no phone, no cable, no internet, no roaming. No nothing. A return to the 1970s.*

She was thinking about leaving when a small crowd that included the deputy, Gene, Wes, and Randy came through the door, one after the other. Bringing up the rear was a good-looking, dark-haired man Leslie surmised was a fireman from the emblem on his shirt. He was trying to corral two rambunctious black labs and a woman who Leslie thought could be a model. All seemed surprised to see Leslie, but only Wes and Randy mumbled hello.

As she watched Deputy Pendry head for the refrigerator and begin handing out bottled water, Leslie cleared her throat. "Is someone going to tell me what's going on?" she asked, scanning the room.

Wes took a drink and sat down in the chair by the sheriff's desk. "It's complicated," he said, sighing. The others nodded. "This is Ray Santiago, who is new to the fire department. The woman with him is Billie. Sorry—I can't remember your last name. Anyway, the lady and the dogs go with Victor Clerk, who's been kidnapped, along with his brother, Hugo. We have two letters addressed to Sheriff Webster, seeking two hundred million dollars in ransom. If the money isn't transferred to a designated account within seventy-two hours, it's curtains for the Clerk brothers, who are going to be buried alive until the ransom's produced. Mrs. Clerk has been wounded and is being treated by a clinic doctor. Even if we wanted to help ensure the ransom is paid, we have no way of contacting anyone about it. We don't even know where to start."

"Buried alive?" Leslie shivered and started to say something, but Wes shushed her.

"The sheriff's gone, and there's no way on God's green earth that we can immediately contact him or anybody else. We should be getting help from Sheriff Lake in the next county or the state police, but as you saw when you came in, someone blew up the cell tower, and for some fucking reason, there's no backup communication system. No one can get on or off the island except by boat. Also, a convicted killer is running loose. He has a woman with him."

Leslie interrupted. "A blonde with a cowboy hat?"

Wes appeared surprised. "Why, yes."

"The flower shop owner, Mr. Cavendish, had a conversation with her. The deputy should talk to him."

"Thanks for that," Wes said. "Anyway, the catastrophe you've been predicting for the last several months—since those hurricane-force winds hit the island—has come to pass. I don't know whether to laugh or cry. Where's the emergency response plan for our little slice of paradise, which is now in deep shit?"

Leslie's mouth had dropped open in the middle of Wes's story. "You're joking, aren't you?" she asked when he finished speaking. "About the burial?"

"What do you think?"

The room was silent.

"Our hands aren't completely tied," Leslie said, standing up and turning to Deputy Pendry. "The bridge is still intact, and I'm guessing it will be fixed soon because I saw deputies and other official-looking people at the site not long ago. My friend Joe, who's stuck there, said he and his brother have called their friends with boats to get people off the island. We can get word out through them. And it's not like there aren't plenty of boats at the marina, including the one used by the fire department. It's our best link to the outside world."

Ray, looking embarrassed, handed the dog leashes over to Billie. "The boat! Why didn't I think of that? I can get word to the deputies at the bridge, and my cell phone's gonna work the minute my roaming picks up the tower in the next county."

"Don't bet on it," Wes said. "You know how bad the cell service is around here."

Deputy Pendry was nodding as if sold on Leslie's and Ray's ideas. "We need a helicopter to get Mrs. Clerk to the hospital, then bring reinforcements onto the island. We could use police boats and Fish and Wildlife rangers to start the search for the brothers. I'm working on a plan. The kidnappers couldn't have gone far. How long will it take you to get to the bridge, Ray? They can hook you up with reinforcements."

Ray glanced up at the ceiling as if doing mental calculations. Leslie watched his lips moving. "Under an hour," he finally said. "Does anyone want to go with me?"

"I will," Randy said. "As long as I can take photos for the newspaper."

"This will be all over the news at some point," Deputy Pendry said. "Go for it. And tell Sheriff Tom Lake's guys we sure would appreciate their help."

Billie was standing off to one side, twirling a strand of her hair and looking like any minute she could burst into tears. "What's going to happen to me? I can't stay at Victor's house. I have no place to go."

Leslie took a deep breath and began explaining that her daughter, a college student, and her mother were gone for a couple of weeks, and she had the space to accommodate a guest. "But I'm sorry—I can't keep the dogs. My corgi would have a fit if another animal intruded on his domain. Besides, the condo association has a one-dog rule."

Billie sighed and flashed a provocative look at Ray that made Leslie grin. "Don't fire stations always have dogs?"

Ray blushed and reached out to take control of the leashes again. "I'll take them with me now. You said they're called Dog One and Dog Two? The guys are crazy enough to think those are cool names."

Wes turned to Deputy Pendry. "Leslie's right about the boats. It's too late today, but I think we should join the search for the brothers. It can't hurt to have as many people looking as possible. Who's with me?"

Gene and Leslie raised their hands. Randy nodded. Billie checked her nails, then stared out the window as though she hadn't heard a word Wes said. The deputy shook his head and said, "I can't be gone all day. I think you'll be wasting your time, and it could be dangerous. If you see any sign of the kidnappers, you need to back off and contact me."

The deputy may be right, but it feels like we have to do something, Leslie thought as she, Wes, and Billie headed out the door for her car. Billie had the black duffel secured under her arm. The reporter was carrying her two suitcases.

"I can't bear to think of those two men somewhere under the sand, trying to stay alive and not go crazy. I couldn't do it. We have to find them," Leslie said, looking at Wes with pleading green eyes.

"We'll do our best," he responded, glancing over his shoulder at Billie. She was falling farther behind as she tottered along the shell-covered roadway in heels, listing as she walked. "Keep an eye on her. I'm not sure any outsider associated with the Clerk family can be trusted."

CHAPTER 13

As Victor Clerk and his captors skimmed over the water, he thought back to what had happened when the intruders broke into his home. It had taken only seconds for him to realize he'd grossly underestimated them. When they charged through the door like a pair of wild boars, he was quickly overpowered. They grabbed him and tossed him around like a cat playing with a mouse. Their brutal blows left him bleeding from the nose and mouth. Within minutes of their arrival, he felt himself losing consciousness. The last thing he was aware of was someone putting something over his head. When he came to, he was on the boat.

His mind went to the first time he and his brother and their wives had visited the island. It was five years ago. Hugo was eager to invest in property and encouraged Victor to join him in this exciting venture.

"You won't regret it," Hugo said. "It's the safest place in the world. My boys will be able to play outside until dark without me worrying about them. If you decide you don't like it, you can double your money in a couple of years. It's the strangest real estate market I've ever encountered."

Following his older brother's advice, Victor bought three lots on the east side of the island and tore down two old structures to build a stunning, ten-thousand-square-foot contemporary home designed by his wife, Sheila, and an exclusive New York architect. He saw it as the gem of local architecture and thought others would agree. He wasn't prepared for the public outcry and the stories the local newspaper wrote about this travesty: the destruction of beloved fishing shacks by a wealthy outsider.

Even before he could move into his new place, the island's cocktail-party circuit had labeled Victor a pariah.

The animosity extended to Sheila. In Greenwich, Connecticut, where the childless couple had a summer home, Sheila was known for her work on several not-for-profit boards. While those organizations existed on a much smaller scale on the island, there were no invitations forthcoming to this newest monied property owner. This ostracization grated on both husband and wife. Victor, who spent the majority of his time managing the substantial wealth his father had left him and was used to Sheila being gone most of the day, found her constant presence annoying. A day didn't pass without Sheila whining that she was bored to tears and asking what Victor was going to do about it. The strain on their marriage was palpable.

As he sat there on the boat trying not to think about his uncertain future, he remembered the day at Hugo's when he finally realized it was over for him and Sheila. Instead of following in Victor's failed footsteps, Hugo had purchased a 1930s waterfront home on the opposite side of the island and was painstakingly remodeling it. The contrast between the brothers' approaches had been noted in the community, and Hugo declared a hero.

On this particular weekend, even though the house wasn't completely finished, Sheila and Victor were guests of Hugo and his wife, Patricia. Victor was lounging by the pool, thinking about how good Patricia looked, when Sheila emerged from the guest house in what she declared was a new bikini in a colorful fish print designed by a beloved local artist.

"What do you think?" she asked, sucking in her diaphragm and presenting her body in an exaggerated pose.

Hugo and Patricia glanced up from their magazines and nodded. "I'm so envious," Patricia said, even though Victor was sure she wasn't. How could she be? She was ten years younger and didn't have a wrinkle anywhere on her size-two body.

Victor also smiled and gave his wife a thumbs-up, but his internal, unspoken response was, *My God, what's happened to you?* He wondered if this was something new or if he hadn't noticed the small differences over thirty years of marriage. After all, Sheila was fifty-something. He couldn't remember if it was fifty-two or fifty-three. She'd always been slender. Now her waist had a certain flabbiness about it. Years of excessive tanning had left her skin leathery. Fine lines paired with deeper crevices around her mouth. Her eyes were crinkly. Her thighs were dimpled and fleshy. The spotlight cast on her by the intense Florida sun prompted Victor to grimace. It was a moment of inner ugliness that he acknowledged and regretted but couldn't shake.

During the next several weeks, Victor used this moment of revelation to examine the question: If he really loved his wife after all those years, would he be obsessed with the superficial flaws that came with aging? The answer, which was obvious to him, led to a cocktail-hour confession.

"I'm so sorry. I don't think I love you anymore, even though you are a wonderful person. It's me, not you," he told Sheila.

She was shocked, devastated, then angry and on the phone with her attorney in less than an hour after Victor presented her with the news. He had expected and was willing to go through counseling, but her reaction was swift and final. The divorce left him with a paltry $250 million, a much lesser figure than he had anticipated. He never had his brother's wealth, but with no prenup to protect his assets, he ended up feeling like a pauper.

He used his new freedom to act on an infatuation he'd had for years. The affair lasted a couple of months and left him feeling guilty and despondent. He had a few flings afterward, then sought solace through travel. It was in a bar in Madrid where he met Billie, a former beauty pageant contestant from Bulgaria, who said she was celebrating her twenty-sixth birthday. It was a whirlwind courtship with no thought of marriage on Victor's part. Still, during the six months they'd been together, Billie told him almost daily how much she adored him.

If that's so, why didn't she unlock the fucking safe room door? he asked himself more than once as he pondered his fate.

"Mr. Clerk, I'm going to take the pillowcase off your head."

The sound of the voice trying to be heard over the boat noises caused Victor to jump. He squinted against the reflection of the late-afternoon sun and welcomed a cooling breeze against his battered cheek.

"What's going on? Where are you taking me?"

"You've been kidnapped." The man speaking to him must have been one of his muscular abductors. His face was obscured by sunglasses, a baseball cap, and a COVID-19-style black mask. His muted English was understandable but heavily accented.

"Why me?" His mind went to the money Sheila had taken from him. Would they want five million or ten million? More? "I don't have much money. If you were going to kidnap someone, you should have taken my brother. He's worth over a billion."

"We have him," the man said.

"Kidnapped Hugo? Both of us? You'll never get away with this!"

The man ignored Victor's comment and continued. "Let me urge you to cooperate—fully. If you follow our instructions, you'll be home in three days. If you don't, I can't say what will happen. Don't test us. Can I get you some water?"

"Yes," Victor said. He was aware his eyes were stinging and tears were traveling down his cheek. He didn't want any of the three people on the boat to see this reaction. He took the short-sleeved shirt he was wearing and pulled it up to wipe off his face. When he let it drop, he saw it was covered with blood. He felt the tears flowing again. *Oh God. Help me.*

CHAPTER 14

The Sea Ray carrying Victor and his kidnappers cruised into the shallow waters by a small island and dropped anchor. Victor watched two of the men gather up what appeared to be camping equipment, then slip over the side of the boat into knee-deep water, slogging toward the shore with their gear over their heads. The third man, the one who had talked to him earlier and given him something to drink, touched Victor on the shoulder.

"It's time to go. You need my help?"

The words Victor wanted to say—*You think I'm a wimp who can't get over the side of a fucking boat by myself?*—turned into "I'll be okay."

As he trudged through the shallow water and stepped onto the sandy shore, he saw the men set up two large tents, lay out fishing equipment, and gather kindling for a fire. He marveled at how efficiently they worked, as though they'd done this hundreds of times.

"Are we camping here?" he asked.

When the man with him nodded, Victor experienced a feeling of relief. *These guys are fools. Someone will spot us immediately. They'll have the sheriff here in no time. You can't hide me in plain sight.*

"They are. You're coming with me," the man clarified.

Victor's hopes shrank as if someone were letting the air out of his balloon. *Maybe they aren't so dumb after all. These monsters are the first line of defense if someone gets nosy. They're just fishing and spending the night and haven't seen anything or anybody. The sheriff wouldn't give them a second thought.*

The sun was setting; the air was still warm, sticky. When Victor reached down to smack at the no-see-ums biting his ankles, one of the men near the tent yelled at him and tossed a small bottle his way. "Try this," he said.

Victor murmured thanks, then sprayed his ankles, legs, and arms with liquid from a bottle with an *X* imprinted over a mosquito-like creature on the label. *They beat the shit out of me but haven't treated me badly otherwise,* he mused.

He briefly wondered what their names were, then decided it didn't matter. They were masked goons whose physiques and bearing resembled Gregor Clegane from *Game of Thrones.* He had watched that series with Billie, never imagining that one day he would be pummeled and kidnapped by some TV scriptwriter's fantasy bad guy. Even though he couldn't see their faces, he wouldn't soon forget these lookalike thugs and the tattoos and scars on their rugged builds.

When the man with him motioned for Victor to follow him into a jungle of wild peppers and scrub brush, he was shaken. This wasn't some dream from which he would awaken and feel instant relief. This was a stomach-gripping, heart-pounding nightmare. He had the brief thought that the words *died peacefully in his sleep* would not appear in his obituary.

One of the men said that Hugo had also been kidnapped, but there was no sign of his brother. Did these men plan on going back for Hugo? And where was this place? There were so many small islands in this part of Florida, the police could search for days and never find them. Never find him. He bit his lower lip to keep from crying out in despair.

The farther they walked from the shore, the thicker the vegetation became until the scrub brush turned into something Victor recognized as more formal—the work of humans, not nature. Plantings of trees and flowering bushes, though not well tended, surrounded a two-story structure, a house on stilts shadowed in the gathering darkness. Victor guessed it and the neighboring landscape would look even more neglected in daylight.

"Up there," the man said, pointing to stairs that led to a porch and a door. "Better hold on to the railing. Toward the top, the steps are rickety."

More kindness from the devil men, Victor thought. *I must be worth more alive than dead.*

Victor plodded up the sixteen stairs, cursing the federal government's flood-level building mandates with each painful step. "We're here," the man called out behind him. In response, the door was opened by a large individual wearing a long-sleeved fishing shirt and the requisite kidnapper's uniform—a Covid-style mask and baseball cap.

"Let's have some light," the man who opened the door said as Victor entered the house. At his command, brightness from a battery-powered lantern illuminated the room.

"Victor! My God, Victor! They have you, too?"

It was the voice that had called to him so many times. As a child, when he had gotten locked in the closet and thought the darkness would swallow him alive, it was Hugo who had saved him. When the crash of thunder had driven him from his bed, seeking comfort, it was Hugo who had protected him. When their father had passed away, it was Hugo who said, "You were his favorite." Today, especially, Victor loved the sound of his brother's voice.

"Hugo!" he cried out. "Why is this happening to us?"

The room in which the Clerk brothers were reunited had no furnishings except for a few chairs. Using a stone fireplace and rusted chandelier as guides, Victor could see where a family room had at one time adjoined a kitchen and dining area. There were kitchen cabinets but no appliances. He assumed the two doors off the living room led to bedrooms and one or more probably nonfunctional bathrooms. Victor imagined his own sprawling mansion on this site and wished this was where he had built it: away from people and their petty criticisms.

When the two men from the campsite arrived with brown paper bags, the smell of cooked food made Victor realize how hungry he was. Fried fish and potatoes were spread out on paper plates on the kitchen counter, and the man who had opened the door and appeared to be in charge motioned to the brothers to queue up with the others. As the group helped themselves, Victor counted the number of kidnappers. There was the one woman, who also wore a mask but did nothing to conceal what Victor considered to be a highly identifiable blonde braid. There was the man in charge, five of the thugs, and a smaller man with a bit of a gut. Victor speculated about which of these eight was the mastermind and concluded it was the man who had opened the door and told the others what to do. Regardless of who was in charge, he recognized that none of these people was to be trifled with.

Victor and Hugo were shuttled off to a small room with one of their captors and told to eat quickly. When he finished and was feeling better, Victor licked his fingers and tossed his paper plate into a plastic bag. If this hadn't been the worst day of his life, he might have enjoyed the camaraderie of people who seemed to rely more on brawn than brains for their livelihood. He admired their self-sufficiency.

"You need to take a piss?" the man in charge asked.

The brothers nodded.

"Take them out. When you come back, put them in the lower level," the man in charge said to one of the goons.

As they descended the stairs, Victor saw lights off in the distance and felt a surge of excitement. He had thought he was in a remote location in the middle of the Gulf. But now he was recognizing signs of civilization not that far away. He didn't know the area well, but he could remember Hugo taking him on a boat trip and showing him this part before. What was it called? He focused on the name. *Paraiso Island* came to him. Hugo had talked about the lots that were available and mentioned an abandoned home. Unfortunately, the only way on and off the island was by boat and an unreliable strip of dirt that might pass for an access road at low tide but was not built for routine car traffic. No more than a spit of land, he had said.

With food in his stomach and the main island so close, Victor contemplated making a run for it. It was dark, and there was plenty of vegetation to use for cover while he escaped. He would have to swim a quarter of a mile or so to the houses on Anibonie Island. He did laps in his pool every day, so swimming a short distance wouldn't be a problem. But what would happen to Hugo? Would his brother take the butt of the kidnappers' fury, or would they keep him alive to ensure payment of the ransom money? Within seconds, he had made his decision. He loved Hugo but had to put himself first.

"I gotta take a dump," he said to the guard. "I got a constipation problem, so it will take me a while. I'll be right over here."

"Be quick about it," the man growled. He lit a cigarette. The smell of marijuana wafted through the humid night air.

"You got toilet paper?"

"Are you stupid? Use a leaf," the man responded.

Victor moved close to and then behind a large date palm and coughed loudly. The man didn't even look in his direction.

Here I go.

He sprinted toward the distant lights, dodging the branches of large bushes and clumps of underbrush as he ran. It would be a few minutes before the goon realized he was missing. He had time, plenty of it. He wondered if Hugo would try to make a run for it, too. *Maybe that's what he did.* He must have seen the lights and known where they were. Maybe they would meet up along the way.

I can do this. I can make it.

He reached the shore and gazed across the water to the island. He definitely knew where he was. The moon was a waning crescent that provided enough light to help him see but not so much that he could be easily spotted. To the right was a row of deteriorating boat docks that Hugo had shown him previously. Beyond the docks was the dirt road that connected Paraiso Island with Anibonie. Since the big storm, its viability was questionable. Still, it was a familiar landmark.

A few more steps and he'd be in the water. The insects were feasting on him. His mouth was dry. His heart was pounding with a mix of exertion, fear, and anticipation. *Can't stop. Can't even think about stopping,* he told his weary body. He could hear the waves lapping against the shore, calling to him to keep coming, keep coming. He wanted to scream with joy at the sense of liberation.

He didn't know what caused him to stumble and fall. It was as if someone had pushed him, then put a heavy weight on his back. He turned his head to the side to see the muscular legs of the woman with the blonde braid. She was sitting on him and flashing a gun low so that he could distinctly see it pointed in the direction of his head.

"Where do you think you're going, sweetie?"

CHAPTER 15

Newton the corgi welcomed Leslie and Wes home and gave the dark-haired newcomer and her black bag the once-over. Leslie was relieved that the dog didn't jump up and go for Billie's crotch, as many do. Trained by its former owner to detect drugs, Newton was more interested in doing his police work than in sniffing out the visitor's pheromones. When the dog finished his search and moved on without indicating there was something of street value in Billie's possession, Leslie was surprised. Since the two women had met in the sheriff's office, Billie had been clutching the black bag as though her life or someone's addiction depended on it.

"You'll be sleeping here," Leslie said, directing Billie to the room with a daybed, a desk, and an adjoining bathroom. "There's not much space in the closet, but there are a few empty hangers."

"I don't plan on sticking around," she said. "Even if they find Victor alive, I'm gone. Things haven't been good between us recently, and I know he will hate me for not opening the door to the safe room."

Leslie was trying to think of a sympathetic response when Wes appeared with a bottle of red wine in one hand and a bottle of white in the other. "You ladies ready for a drink? Leslie has plenty of alcohol, Billie, but she's a little low on the hard stuff."

"Cristal?" Billie asked.

"No Cristal," Wes said, chuckling. "Not even any Brut."

Leslie, who was standing behind Billie, rolled her eyes. "I'll take the red and don't be stingy. This has been one hell of a day."

"I'll have white," Billie said, then strolled out toward the lanai as though expecting Wes to bring the drink to her. "Nice view. Maybe even better than Victor's, but not Hugo's."

"You know Hugo and his wife well?" Leslie asked, sitting down on the camp stool so that Wes could have the other Adirondack chair. "Patricia, is it? I don't remember ever seeing her."

"She's very kind. Hugo's always kidding her about how standoffish she is, but he says that as a joke, I'm sure. She's the opposite. She's been nice to me," Billie said, taking a sip of the wine Wes handed her. "The whole thing is terrible. I pray she'll be okay."

"I guess you're anxious about all three of them," Leslie said.

Billie nodded with no further comment, then reached for a piece of the cheese Wes had set out. His interest in the newcomer revived, Newton appeared from the far corner of the lanai and sidled up to her, drooling in anticipation.

"Sweet little dog," Billie crooned. "Okay if I give him some?"

"Just one," Leslie said. "He's picked up a couple of pounds since he came to live with me. Someone's been spoiling him." She directed a look at Wes, who chuckled and reached for a handful of peanuts on the table next to him. "You're from?" Leslie asked Billie.

"Bulgaria. Sofia, the capital. I lived there with my mother and father until I was fifteen. We were middle class but didn't have money for extras. They sent my brother to college but couldn't afford for me to go. I entered a beauty contest and was first runner-up. I took the prize money and left."

"Where'd you go?"

"Lots of places. I got jobs but was always looking for something better. In France, I met a man who owned a bakery and was his assistant for six months. His wife ordered me to leave, which was okay because I was getting fat on his pastries."

Wes chuckled. "Is that when you and Victor hooked up?"

"It was a couple of years later. I was working as a hostess in a restaurant and bar in Madrid. He came in and ordered the most expensive thing on the menu. He was good-looking and seemed rich, so I told him it was my birthday. It wasn't, but he liked the idea and asked me out. Can you blame me?" she said, slipping Newton another piece of cheese. "He told me he'd had an affair with a married woman who broke off their relationship and was in Europe to mend his broken heart. I tried to help him forget her with my special talents."

Wes gulped down the rest of his wine, got up, and headed for the kitchen without saying a word. Leslie was amused by his sudden departure and wondered if he was envisioning what Billie's special talents might be. When he returned with a second bottle of white, Leslie asked if he and Billie would mind taking Newton for a quick walk while she started dinner.

"I need to get my bag first," Billie said.

"We'll only be gone for ten minutes," Wes said. "You'll look after it, won't you, Leslie?"

"Your luggage is safe with me," she responded.

Billie seemed hesitant but got up and followed Wes as he retrieved Newton's leash from the peg in the hallway, fastened it to the dog's collar, and then opened the screen door. The three of them sauntered down the steps and onto the asphalt parking lot before turning the corner toward the seawall that separated Leslie's condo from the Gulf of Mexico. When Leslie was sure they were out of sight, she slipped into the spare bedroom.

Billie's suitcases were in the middle of the room. Leslie found the black bag stashed in the closet behind a bed pillow. Newton had done most of the work for her. If there were no drugs in the bag Billie guarded so zealously, there was only one other possibility: money. Leslie pulled the bag out of the closet to check its heft and confirm that the amount of cash Billie had taken from Victor's home must be significant.

Unable to curb her curiosity, Leslie reached for the zipper and opened the container, revealing stacks of $100 bills. Lying on the bundles of cash were photographs of a man Leslie assumed was Victor and a beautiful woman with golden hair and a dazzling smile. On top of the photos was a black jeweler's box. *Who can resist looking into one of these?* she thought as she reached for it and flipped open the lid. Inside was a ring with the biggest diamond she'd ever seen. Maybe the size of a quarter.

Given Billie's description of their current rocky relationship, Leslie assumed the ring had been meant for the mysterious blonde. Maybe that was why Billie was leaving. Victor had kept the photos and the ring—an indication that Billie wasn't as successful as she had thought in helping him get over his broken heart.

CHAPTER 16

"You should have seen the poor guy lying there, broken like a rotten twig. A part of me wanted to let him get away." Lilith stretched her legs out in front of her, brushed traces of sand off them, and gazed over at White. He was sitting next to her on a decaying palm tree trunk, sipping a beer.

"If they pay the money, your wish will come true," White said matter-of-factly.

"And if they don't?"

"The boss is confident they will. No final instructions yet. I'm supposed to ask the brothers who their financial contact is," White responded. He pulled a cigar out of his shirt pocket, tossing the gold-and-red band off to one side, biting off one end, and lighting the other.

"I signed up to disable the cell tower and help look after these poor wretches. I don't do killings. I made that clear from the start when I answered the ad in the magazine.," Lilith said. "And this burying-them-alive shit. Who does something like that? Since you're the only one among us who knows who he or she is, I guess the boss's state of mind is something only you can determine."

White said nothing. Lilith shuddered, reached for a nearby stick, and drew two oblong boxes with crosses in the sand.

"I don't mind elevators or MRIs, but I remember hanging out with a guy who was into cave rescues," she said. "On our fourth date, he talked me into going into a cave with him. Not to save anyone, just to go exploring. The entrance was a hole in the side of a hill. I wondered how anyone could find it, let alone crawl into it. He said the kids from the nearby college took booze there and partied. Sometimes one or two would go a little farther in and get lost. The others, sobered by the disappearance of their friends, would go to the police, who'd call my friend and his buddies to drag the lost kids' asses out of there.

"The guy tells me the only way to get into the cave is to lie on your back and scootch in. After about eighteen feet, the cave widens, and I can flip over onto my hands and knees, but I still can't stand upright, he says. Turns out I can never stand in this cave, except in a small room that leads to something called the corkscrew. I don't even ask what that is because I know I'm not going there.

"He gives me a helmet with a light on it, and away we go. Thank God I'm in good shape. I don't know how drunk college kids navigate the entrance, but I'm finally in and staring at a ceiling that is about ten inches above my nose with rock on either side of me, maybe twelve inches from my shoulders. It's like a tomb from some horror flick. It's cold and damp, and there are five or six bats clinging to the rock above me. They are little guys, but what if they have rabies? I'm telling myself not to think about the bats, the walls, and the fact that my arms and knees are getting weird on me. I'm trying hard not to freak out as I keep scooting forward. It wasn't my bravest moment.

"The guy's a minute or two ahead of me, and when he gets to what he calls the bigger section of the cave, he reaches in and pulls me out like I was a breech birth. He says, 'That wasn't so bad, was it?' He flips me over on my hands and knees, and I lift my head to respond, and my helmet hits the top of the cave. He laughs. Not cool.

"Then he tells me we're gonna rest a minute before we go on. Go on? I'm thinking this guy must have cracked his head one too many times because I am not going on. They'll find me one day, dried up and dead. Go on? Hell, I'll never make it back through that skinny limestone tunnel to see daylight again. I take a couple of deep breaths. I don't want to go, but I can't stay there by myself. What if he gets hurt and I'm stuck there in the dark?

"An hour later, after I've crawled through muck and dirt and hit my head on the cave ceiling a dozen times, I decide I detest the guy who brought me in there, and I hate nature for creating this cave from hell. If I make it out alive without my mind exploding from the sheer terror I'm feeling, I will never step foot in a confined space again. Even if someone points a gun at my head. I'm telling you, Dan, that only a sicko would want to bury these two brothers alive. As tough as I am, the closer we get to this part of the plan, the less I like it."

Lilith had been up and pacing as she recounted her experience. Now she reached over and grabbed the beer White was holding and chugged it.

"Oh, and another bad part was how those college kids ruined the cave by painting graffiti all over its walls," she said with a grunt. "And the little shits want us to believe they care about the planet."

White took a draw on his cigar and slowly nodded as he let the smoke filter out between his lips. "Don't get any funny ideas, Lilith. The mercenaries wouldn't have any problem killing us if we screw up. The boss insists on burying the Clerks. If we do it right, it'll work. I'll show you in the morning."

Lilith turned to face White. "Those goons don't scare me, but this situation is starting to feel loosey-goosey. It was pretty clear-cut to begin with. Now I'm getting bad vibes. What if this kidnapping isn't about money but some statement against society and the seven hundred billionaires in this country? Maybe this boss you talk about is an Antifa member who hates profits and rich people or is part of some right-wing group that wants to make it look like it's Antifa. Or its someone with a grudge against the Clerks."

White shook his head. "As long as I'm getting paid, I don't care about someone's motives."

White turned quickly from Lilith toward the house, put his hand up to silence her, then reached for the large knife in the holster around his waist. She followed his glance to see a dark figure approaching through the brush.

"Relax—it's only Foxx. Man, you're jumpy," she said.

She'd only seen Mark Foxx with White once before, and that was during a planning session a couple of months ago. This evening in the house, she'd noticed him sitting off by himself in a corner. She knew nothing about him except that he had been in charge of disabling the bridge and had concocted an elaborate plan that seemed like overkill. Still, it had worked well, which was more than she could say for White's scheme to cut cell and landline service to the island.

"Everything okay?" White asked, relinquishing his grip on the knife handle.

Foxx mumbled something and sat down cross-legged on the sand in front of the other two. Lilith couldn't read his face; the twilight had faded into night. But his body language said he was physically and mentally exhausted—like his heart was no longer in this mission.

"You missed Lilith's cave rescue story," White said and chuckled. "Why don't you tell her yours?"

Foxx smiled. "Maybe some other time."

"Yeah. Some other time. What's the brothers' status?" White asked, getting to his feet.

"Hugo's asleep. Victor's at his wit's end. When are we supposed to bury them?"

White stared off into the distance and didn't say anything for a few minutes. "I'll talk to the boss in the morning to get the timing. We have to be ready for anything," he said, looking once again at Lilith. "Whether we like it or not."

CHAPTER 17

"You awake?" Victor's voice reached out through the darkness to his brother about ten feet away.

"I am now," Hugo said.

"I don't know how you can sleep."

"It's not the Ritz-Carlton, I'll give you that," Hugo said. "It's important to get as much rest as we can. This is a fluid situation. You never know when we'll be tested."

"Tested? You mean we might get a chance to escape?" Victor replied. "I don't know if I have the strength to make a run for it again. I was so close, H. So close—and then that blonde tripped me.

"I can't figure this out," he continued. "Someone broke into my fucking house and kidnapped me. Then you told me they went to your place, shot Patricia, and took you. Then they brought us here. I think we're on Paraiso Island. You know, that island you showed me several years ago—the one you talked about buying and developing?"

"Did I? I don't remember."

"Maybe I was wrong. You think Patricia's dead? Why would anyone want to hurt her?" Victor felt tears forming again. The recent events had sent him into an emotional tailspin. He was vulnerable, weepy; it was a struggle to keep his feelings in check.

"I love Patricia. I would never want any harm to come to her," Hugo said.

"I know you did, brother."

"Let's not talk about her in the past. In my heart, I know she's alive."

"You're right. We have to keep thinking that way," Victor said, rubbing the tears from his eyes. "So how long do you think we'll be here? Is there a deadline for the ransom?"

Hugo hesitated. "On the boat, they said they expect to release us in seventy-two hours. That's the deadline they gave the sheriff."

"They talked to the police?" Victor was surprised. Kidnappers usually instructed the victim's family not to communicate with anyone. Then he realized that with both Hugo and himself captured and Patricia's condition unknown, the only other individual with authority to transfer funds on their behalf was their attorney in Tampa. If given the attorney's contact information, the police could be helpful.

"They said they left letters addressed to the sheriff at your place and mine."

Victor groaned. "I don't want to give them the money, but I don't want to die, H. Afterward, when we're free, you'll help me get back on my feet, won't you? Maybe give me some more of Dad's money if I need it?"

"There's something else you need to know," Hugo said, his voice barely above a whisper. "One of the guys on the boat told me. I would have said something earlier, but I was afraid to tell you. Now you have to know because it could happen soon. Can you take it?"

"Take what, H?" Victor laughed nervously. "They beat the shit out of me. We're stuck in a room with army cots, a little pot to piss in, and no light. What could be worse?"

"They're going to bury us alive, Vic."

There was a gasp, followed by silence. It hung as heavy as the darkness around them. When he finally spoke, Victor's voice was childlike. "That's not funny. Why would you say something like that?"

"I'm so sorry, little brother. They said their boss wanted it done that way. Until the ransom's paid."

"But buried alive? Why would they do something that terrible … that cruel?"

There was no answer from Hugo. The silence returned. Victor could hear himself breathing as though it wasn't him but someone very close. His mind was processing what his brother had just told him. He pictured himself in a box under the sand, looking at it from several angles, like a schematic. He was lying there in total darkness, unable to move, struggling to get enough air, feeling like everything was shrinking around him and slowly squeezing him into oblivion.

When a feeling of panic started to set in, he diverted his thoughts to a short story by Edgar Allan Poe that both he and Hugo had read in high school English class. It was about a man in the 1800s obsessed with the idea he would be buried alive because of a medical condition that caused him to pass out and appear dead when he wasn't. He took precautions to protect himself in case he was misdiagnosed, including rigging the family tomb with a bell so that he could alert passersby of his plight. One day, the man had an attack and woke up to darkness, panicking when he thought he couldn't escape. He soon discovered he'd fallen asleep in the bowels of a boat and was awakened from a nightmare by fellow passengers. The episode cured him of his fear.

Hugo liked the story, but Victor didn't care for it. He thought it strange that a Poe tale should have a happy ending. Back when he was fifteen, Victor had wished for a gruesome death for the poor man. Now he longed to be saved and released from his fear, just as the Poe character had been.

"H, you can offer them more money. However much these people were paid to kidnap us, you can give them more to set us free. We won't survive being buried alive. You have to pay them. Anything they want."

"I don't think that'll fly, Vic, but I'll make the offer. That's all I can do."

White was outside the door listening to the Clerk brothers' conversation as he waited for Lilith. He wasn't sure why he'd asked her to join him. He thought the presence of a woman might be comforting to Victor, who was obviously less stable than Hugo. White had never been involved with a kidnapping before and was surprised to find himself torn between greed and a nagging, uncomfortable feeling of compassion, especially for the weaker of the two brothers.

Involving Lilith was risky; she was not your average female. She could be empathetic. The flower-shop owner was a good example. She was okay with destroying his livelihood but didn't want to endanger his person. Then there was that conversation about the burial plans and her own feelings of claustrophobia. Still, when it came to tracking down Victor, she had been ruthless, like a big cat on the hunt. She had been so pissed when he slipped away that she laid into the mercenary whom Victor had given the slip, blackening his eye. White believed she had more testosterone running through her veins than the average eighteen-year-old male. Would she be soft or hard? She could be counted on to follow orders most of the time, but how Lilith would react to a spontaneous circumstance was always a question mark.

"How are they doing?" he heard her ask.

He turned to respond and was momentarily at a loss for words. Her waist-length hair fell freely about her shoulders. Her nipples and the outline of her breasts was visible through the white V-neck T-shirt that clung to them. The moon shadows played temptingly about her, softening her features. He thought of the other mercenaries and how they might react and was instantly angry. He'd worried about something like this when he hired her. Looking the way she did could put their mission in jeopardy.

"I just took a quick swim and feel much better," she said.

White wondered if she was unaware of the impact of her appearance or if she was dressed seductively for a reason. He didn't want to go there. This was business, not pleasure.

"Let's get this done," he said, pushing himself to move on to the task at hand and slipping on his mask and baseball cap.

When they opened the door and entered, White turned on the flashlight he was carrying, first illuminating Hugo, who was lying down, covered with a light blanket. Then he shined the light on Victor, who was sitting on the edge of his cot, his head bowed. Both men looked up, squinted, and put up their hands to shade their eyes from the high-powered beam.

"I need information from you. Who has power of attorney to handle your money?" White asked, directing his comment to Hugo and tossing him a pen and pad of paper.

"Both of our funds are under an umbrella trust created by our father," Hugo said, scribbling as he spoke. "Our family attorney is Farrell Rogers of Rogers and Van Zant out of Tampa. I can give you his cell number and email. He will handle the, uh, ransom payment. I understand that you've given us seventy-two hours to get the money. That was some time ago. I hope you're willing to be patient. We have every intention of paying, but getting that amount out of the hands of our bankers and investment firms could take time."

He looked at Victor and continued. "And, uh, I'm not sure who's in charge here, but I'm willing to authorize the payment of an additional hundred million if you agree to let my brother and me go now. I'll authorize the payment of two hundred million in ransom, plus the additional funds. If not the both of us, please at least set my brother free."

White didn't hesitate. "Your offer's tempting, but I'll have to run it by the boss. I'm not authorized to make those kinds of decisions."

"It wouldn't be for your boss," Hugo said. "It would be for you and the others to split. I don't know what you're getting paid for this job, but this bonus for setting us—or him—free would amount to about ten million apiece."

Victor had been watching Hugo and now turned to White, pleading, "I'm not a good person. I've made a lot of mistakes. My brother says you are going to bury us alive. I wouldn't survive. Don't you understand? This money would be all yours if you let me go."

White shook his head, feeling embarrassed for the man whose face was already swollen with self-pity and who was only pleading for his life and not his brother's.

"The sooner the ransom's paid, the sooner you'll be free. We've set this up so you won't be uncomfortable. You'll have plenty of air, water, and food. You'll only be a foot below the surface in a waterproof box. It will have a battery-operated light and radio you can use for music. There are bathroom provisions. Not great, but you won't be lying in urine or shit if you're careful and follow our instructions. We'll check on you every couple of hours."

"Why? Why do we have to go through this—this torture—when we're willing to give you more money than you asked for? I don't understand," Victor whined, shaking his head.

Lilith touched White on the shoulder as if to say she would take care of it. She walked over to Victor and sat down on the cot next to him. White directed the light onto the kidnap victim's face so that the temptations of Lilith's flesh would remain in the shadows.

"Those bites on your legs. They bothering you?"

He reached down, scratched a series of red bumps, and nodded.

"I'll get some ointment."

"Thank you," Victor murmured.

"Taking off showed a lot of guts. I wouldn't have guessed you had it in you," Lilith said, putting her arm around his shoulder.

"The desire to survive is great even among the lowest forms of life," Victor said. "Have you ever seen a ghost ant scurry like crazy to avoid being squashed by some human looming over it?"

Lilith chuckled. "Don't demean yourself. The thought of being in a box covered by a foot of sand is scary as hell. I couldn't do it. It creeps me out just thinking about it. What we're going to do is give you a sedative that puts you into twilight for about twelve hours. You won't exactly be asleep, but you won't care. Hell, when the sheriff finds you and digs you up, you'll be able to write a best-selling book about it. Get back some of the money you're going to give us. You're a good-looking man. Maybe you'll end up with a movie career."

Victor laughed and reached out to touch a strand of her long blonde hair as if curious about it. White cringed.

"That's better. My partner and I are going to leave now," Lilith said. "Try to get some rest. In the morning, we'll come back and give you an update and go from there. Okay?

"One more thing," she continued. "Man can live about forty days without food, about three days without water, about eight minutes without air, but only for one second without hope. Darwin said that. Don't give up, honey."

White watched incredulously as Lilith ran her fingers through Victor's dark hair, smoothing it into place like a mother readying her child for an outing. All the things she had said were lies concocted to make Victor feel better. White couldn't fathom why she cared. There was no guarantee that Victor would be free in twelve hours. At this point, there was no plan for a sedative. Lilith could say what she thought Victor needed to hear, but in White's opinion, he would be lucky to survive without going mad.

CHAPTER 18

Tuesday, July 13, 8:35 a.m.: Day Two

When Leslie emerged from her condo the next morning en route to the sheriff's office, she was relieved to see vehicle traffic flowing across the causeway. She contemplated stopping by the bridge office but decided an update on the kidnappings was more important. She left Billie a note indicating she was welcome to stay in the condo as long as she needed, though she was sure the woman's residency would be brief. Billie had the money and the ring, and she didn't seem too concerned about Victor. Now that the bridge was open, Leslie figured the young woman wouldn't want to stick around.

Then there was the question of whether Leslie should report the suspicious bag of cash to the sheriff. She decided against it, figuring that Billie would say that Victor had given her the money. Who was around to dispute that claim? When she mentioned it to Wes as he was leaving, he agreed that it was the right thing to do for now but cautioned she might have to tell the sheriff at some point to protect herself from being arrested as an accessory to theft.

Wes, Gene, and Deputy Pendry were already at the sheriff's office when Leslie arrived. "Isn't it great the bridge is open?" she enthused, greeting the trio and taking the seat next to the sheriff's desk. Deputy Pendry looked like he'd slept in his clothes. Leslie guessed he had an apartment off the island, where rents were more reasonable. Since he couldn't get home, he had probably grabbed a bunk at the fire station. "What's the latest on the Clerk brothers, and have you been able to contact the sheriff?"

"No cell service yet, but Ray told me about an hour ago that there's a temporary tower on the way, and the state police and feds have been alerted and have started searching for the Clerks," Deputy Pendry said, taking a sip of coffee. "Ray also contacted Sheriff Webster when he was on the fire department boat. The sheriff's counting on me to handle the situation here until he returns. Didn't say when that would be. No further word from the kidnappers."

Some progress, just not enough, Leslie thought. She noticed a box of doughnuts on the credenza by the TV set. Wes and Gene had coffee cups. There was something about a law enforcement office in the heart of a tiny community that was comforting and old-fashioned. She thought of the black-and-white TV show her parents had watched about a small-town sheriff and his bungling deputy in the 1960s. With Sheriff Webster away, the presence of Gene and Wes had to be helpful to the rookie deputy. He was no bungler, but she presumed he was feeling overwhelmed and hoping no one noticed.

"I think I got a boat lined up. We can leave in a couple of hours," the iguana hunter said, refilling his cup. "We'll take Randy with us. He told me yesterday he thought they'd be someplace obvious. Not sure what that means, but Randy will know."

"Uh, hello?" A boy of ten or so with a buzz cut was standing at the door with an envelope in his hand and an expression of uncertainty on his sunburned face. "I'm looking for the sheriff."

"He's not here. Can I help?" Deputy Pendry responded.

The boy stared at the young man, then moved on to Wes and Leslie. When his gaze settled on Gene, he spoke. "I'm supposed to give this to the person in charge," he said and handed it to Gene, who grinned at the others. "The man who gave it to me said it's about someone named Clerk."

"Thanks," Gene said. "You want a doughnut? I picked these up at the bakery."

The youngster studied the box of pastries, carefully selected one, and took a bite. Powdered sugar cascaded from his mouth and settled in white patches on his navy shorts. He mumbled thanks and turned to leave.

"Hold on," Gene said. "Who gave you this?"

"Some guy on the street. I was with my dog, Buster." The boy pulled a $50 bill out of his shorts, showed it to Gene, then quickly stuck it back in his pocket. "And this."

"How long ago?" Deputy Pendry asked.

"I had to take Buster home. I'm not sure."

"What did he look like, honey?" Leslie asked, offering him a napkin so that he could wipe the crumbs off his face as he reached for another doughnut.

He pointed to Wes. "Like him. 'Cept he had on sunglasses and a baseball cap. It was blue. And a funny-looking beard."

"The bridge tender had a beard," Leslie said, looking at the others. "Although I guess a lot of young guys around here have them."

"Where did you say he gave you the envelope?" Deputy Pendry inquired.

The boy, his mouth full, pointed toward the post office. "Buster and I were getting the mail," he said after swallowing. "He was by the door when I went in. Asked me if I knew where the sheriff's office was, and I said yes. I told him I rode on the fire truck when I was little and met the sheriff."

"Thanks for delivering this," Leslie said. "Why don't you take the rest of the donuts with you."

A big smile crossed the youngster's face as he accepted the box and walked out the door.

"Whoever gave the boy that note is probably gone by now," Leslie said. "But if he was around here not that long ago, that means the kidnappers didn't go far. Maybe they're holding the brothers in one of the houses on the island. Wouldn't it be ironic if it was somewhere on Hugo's or Victor's property?"

"Unlikely," Wes replied. "I searched Hugo's place thoroughly. There was no one there but a cat, who's now with a neighbor."

Deputy Pendry reached for the envelope Gene was holding. "Let's see what this says before we jump to any conclusions." He used a letter opener, then unfolded the piece of paper inside. "The contact for the money is Farrell Rogers of Tampa. They've got a couple of numbers for him and bank transfer information. We have two days to get the deal done."

"What happened to the seventy-two hours?" Wes asked. "And how are we supposed to contact the attorney with the cell tower and landlines down?"

"You and I can drive off the island to get service," Leslie said. "After we've talked to the attorney, we can stop at the bridge office and see if they know anything about the saboteur. Can you wait for us with the boat, Gene?"

The iguana hunter nodded but appeared troubled. "They didn't say anything more about the brothers being buried. Is there a chance they've changed their minds?"

"Don't count on it," Leslie said. "There are plenty of wealthy people on this island. Why they picked on the Clerks is a mystery in itself. I don't know anything about their pasts, but it feels like someone wants to inflict pain on them. What better way than sticking them in a box underground? It would do me in."

CHAPTER 19

The minute they crossed the bridge, Leslie was able to get cell service on her phone. She parked by the bridge office next to an old Kia hatchback and punched in the numbers on the piece of paper the boy had given them. She received a quick response from the company's switchboard. Farrell Rogers was out of the office, but his secretary could assist the caller if needed.

Leslie's expression reflected her frustration. "The attorney's not there. Should I tell his secretary what this is about?"

"All she needs to know is that it's an emergency," Wes said. "Unless the guy is one of the kidnappers or has turned off his phone, we should be able to get ahold of him. Lawyers who earn a thousand dollars an hour like he probably does don't usually make it difficult for their clients to reach them."

"There's a thought," Leslie said.

She told the switchboard operator to transfer her call to his secretary, whose voice mail indicated she, too, was not in the office. Her referral number was also unable to answer the call. Leslie left terse messages for both individuals.

"I'm on the verge of losing it, Wes," she said, throwing her phone down on the car seat. "Valuable time is slipping away. While we're waiting for someone to call us back, let's see if we can learn anything from the bridge people."

They exited Leslie's SUV and climbed the outside steps to the gray, island-style bridge office. Once inside, they waited at the countertop that separated three efficient-looking female workers and several desks from the public. The delay lasted only a few minutes but still annoyed Leslie, who felt her mood worsening with each passing moment. Finally, a middle-aged woman approached the pair and sat down at a computer, readying herself to type. "Do you need to renew your bridge pass?" she asked, glancing over the top of her glasses and smiling.

"I'm Wes Avery from the *Sun*. Is there someone I can talk to about the incident with the man who jumped?"

All three women stopped what they were doing and stared at the reporter; the two in the background whispered to each other. Leslie was sure they'd been prepped on how to respond to any inquiries about the topic.

"I'm sorry, but we aren't allowed to talk to the press, and our supervisor is away at a meeting. She won't be back until later this afternoon." The woman at the computer appeared nervous and kept glancing back at her coworkers.

"Okay, thanks," Leslie said cheerily, figuring the supervisor didn't know any more than the other workers. And if she did know something, she'd guard it as closely as everyone else in the chain of command. That's how bureaucracy worked, even at the county level.

"Let's go, Wes. We'll come back later," she said, directing him down the stairs and toward one of the three small gatehouses where bridge tolls were collected. He appeared content to let Leslie take the lead.

Although the toll takers' names were no longer posted on nameplates outside their booth windows during their shifts, Leslie remembered many of them from previous encounters. "Bill, how's it going?" she said to the man with the thick crop of gray hair. He looked hesitant but returned her smile. He wouldn't know her name, but her face must be familiar to him. She remembered him not just for his friendly manner but also because he gave Newton a biscuit every time Leslie stopped at his booth with the dog in her vehicle.

"I have a quick question," she said, recognizing that she could be putting his job in jeopardy just by speaking to him. "Anyone here know anything about the, um, incident? The guy who dove off the bridge?"

Bill took a minute to respond as if weighing his answer. "We all knew him. He's been here for several months. I wasn't on duty that day. I heard about it later."

"Is there someone who can say what happened?"

Bill sighed, scratched his head, and pointed toward the bridge tender house. "Cap Collier's on duty. He'd just finished his shift on the day it happened, and I think he knew the guy better than most of us. Mark Foxx was his name. Sad."

"Yes, but also fortunate he didn't die when he jumped off the bridge. I talked to a man who watched him get into a speedboat, and this morning, someone in the sheriff's office reported seeing someone we think was him," Leslie said.

"That's a relief," Bill said, shifting his gaze from Leslie and looking up at the bridge office. "I'm gonna get in trouble if you don't move on. If you want to talk to Cap, he'll be on break shortly. You can hang out by that bench over there, but don't walk out on the bridge. Rules, you know."

"Sure thing—and thanks, Bill," she said.

"Did I tell you I think you have good newspaper instincts?" Wes asked as they took a seat on the concrete bench, which was conveniently out of sight of the office workers. "I like a woman who takes charge."

"You'll say anything for a home-cooked meal and the chance to hang out with that dog." Leslie laughed and gave him a nudge with her elbow. She let the conversation drop. She knew there was more to his feelings for her than that. She wondered why she hadn't been able to sort out hers for him after all the time they had spent together lately.

With what's going on, now isn't the time, she thought as she gazed fondly at the man sitting next to her.

CHAPTER 20

Cap shut the door to the bridge tender's house, stepped outside, and immediately felt the heat. He had a routine for his breaks in the summer when the temperature and high humidity could drain the life out of him. He would get his sandwich out of the cooler in the back of his car, sit on the nearby bench where the breezes from the water were the best, have a soft drink, read the sports news on his cell phone, and then return to the bridge house when his thirty minutes were up. There was comfort in predictability.

But nothing had felt the same since that day. The sense he had of being needed when he pushed the switch to open the bridge for boat traffic. The joy at reading that his Cincinnati Reds had notched another victory. The banter with his coworkers about who was the greatest figure in sports history. All had lost their luster. His world had been shaken to the core less than twenty-four hours ago.

He hadn't seen his coworker and friend dive off the bridge. When he had heard about it a couple of minutes after the fact, he had rushed to look for any sign of him in the waters of the Intracoastal. There was nothing. When Foxx didn't return to work to assure everyone it had just been a lapse, Cap wasn't sure if he was alive or dead. The feelings of disbelief and loss continued to gnaw at him, even as he tried to focus on other things.

It wasn't just the jump that disturbed him. It was the thought that Foxx had purposely disabled the bridge so that cars couldn't get on or off the island. Keeping the traffic flowing was a bridge tender's duty and not to be taken lightly. Cap was positive that Foxx appreciated and understood the gravity of that responsibility. No, sir. Pete Rose hadn't really bet on his own baseball team, and Mark Foxx hadn't intended to sabotage the bridge. No matter what others said, those violations of sacred trust didn't happen.

As he lumbered off the walkway, he noticed two people on the bench where he usually sat during his break. He wondered what they were doing there and where he might now find some relief. Even though it was only midmorning, it was almost impossible for him to be outside for any length of time unless he was in the shade. He'd resigned himself to sitting in his car and turning on the air conditioner, wasting expensive gas, when he saw the couple stand and approach him.

"Mr. Collier? Hi, I'm Leslie Elliott, and this is my friend, Wes Avery. Could we speak with you a minute?"

"What about?" His usual smile—an expression of openness and trust—was gone. It had disappeared when his friend hit the water.

"Mark Foxx," Leslie said.

"I got nothin' to say," Cap said, wondering how to get rid of these people without creating a scene or making them mad. He never liked to offend others. He glanced first at the tollbooths and then in the direction of the office. He didn't want the others to see him talking to strangers whose names he had forgotten the minute they spoke them.

"We have reason to believe that Mr. Foxx is still alive and is involved in the disappearance of two brothers from the island," Wes said. "You may know something that could be helpful in resolving this police matter."

Cap was surprised to hear the words *alive* and *police matter*. He still didn't know what these two strangers had to do with Foxx; they hadn't identified themselves as law enforcement. But they seemed official and appeared to know what they were talking about. "You undercover police?" he asked.

Wes laughed. "I'm a reporter for the *Island Sun*. Ms. Elliott is my, um, assistant."

"I don't want to be quoted," Cap said, removing his handkerchief from his back pocket and wiping his face and neck. "I could answer some of your questions if it will help Mark. He's a nice guy. An Afghanistan vet. Suffers from terrible PTSD. I thought that was what happened to him. That he had a flashback or something."

Leslie directed him to the shady bench. He'd been on his feet. It felt good to sit down.

"So, you'd be surprised to learn that he was involved with these kidnappings?" Wes asked.

"No, sir, I wouldn't believe it. Maybe it's a coincidence. You see, Mark was a hard worker; never sick a day. Didn't take vacation time. He gave most of his money to his dad, who lives in Tucson. The poor guy was injured at work, but his disability payments don't cover a lot of his medicine, and he's not old enough for Medicare. He's a widower, and I know Mark really worries about him." Cap paused and wiped his eyes. "A lot of vets have internal wounds that never heal—not physical but emotional. Most folks can't begin to appreciate the sacrifice or understand that for many of us, the war never ends. It was that way for Mark. I wouldn't have been surprised if he committed suicide. But you tell me he's a kidnapper? I'm not buying that one."

"You wouldn't happen to have his father's name and number?" Leslie asked.

"Guess it wouldn't hurt to share it with you," Cap said, thinking about his sandwich and cool drink. "It's in my car." *What harm can it do?*

The couple remained on the bench while Cap walked to his car. He checked his watch. Still seventeen minutes left in his break. He'd give them the number and hope they'd leave straightaway so that he could have a few minutes to relax. He was tearing up again—not just for his friend but for the thousands of soldiers like Mark who were never able to get their lives back on track after serving their country. If he thought about it too long, he would realize he always counted himself as one of those people who would forever be disenfranchised—who'd given up the chance at a normal life on a battlefield far from home. He reached for his cooler and let the tears flow freely, if only for a few seconds.

"Mr. Foxx?" Leslie asked when a male voice answered. She put the phone on speaker so that Wes, who was sitting beside her in the car, could hear the conversation.

"Sorry, you have the wrong number."

"My name's Leslie Elliott. I live in Florida, and I'm looking for the father of Mark Foxx, who works as a bridge tender on Anibonie Island. A man named Cap Collier gave us this number."

"Bridge tender, you say? My son works for a bridge authority, but his name's not Mark Foxx. It's Rick Howell."

Wes and Leslie exchanged looks of surprise as the reporter leaned closer to the phone. "Mr. Howell? Hi, I'm Wes Avery, and I write for the island newspaper. Is your son the same Rick Howell who was held captive in Afghanistan and rescued by another soldier, a man named Dan White?"

"Why, yes, yes. My boy was a prisoner in Afghanistan in a cave. Those bastards tortured him nearly to death. They wrapped barbed wire around his face, burned him with cigarettes, starved him and violated him in inhuman ways. Corporal White saved him—twice, in fact—and ended up going to prison. Rick said he got out several years ago."

Wes stared at Leslie in disbelief and mouthed the words, "Holy shit."

"Mr. Howell, have you spoken to Rick recently?" she asked.

"A couple of days ago, I called and told him I needed money for medicine. He sends me something every month—a part of his check. But these medical bills are eating me alive. The pharmaceutical companies invent stuff to make you feel better but price it so high that you don't have enough money for food. Sometimes I think I'd be better off dead."

"You haven't heard from your son in the last day or so?" Wes pressed.

"No," Mr. Howell said, his voice suddenly registering concern. "Is he okay? He's all I have."

Leslie was shaking her head. "Don't tell him," she whispered.

"As far as we know, he's fine. We wanted to question him about a bridge problem, but no one here has his cell number," Wes said, not wanting to lie but realizing that Leslie was right. Rick Howell's father didn't need to know about his son until the Clerk brothers' situation was resolved one way or the other.

"I guess I don't feel right about giving you my boy's number. You can always reach me, and I'll let him know you called," he said. "You mentioned something about Dan White? There's no finer man alive. He went through hell and back for my boy. Fought off his captors in that cave in Afghanistan, carried him to safety, and nursed him back to health. Since that time, he's helped Rick in so many ways. My son would do anything in the world for him. Anything."

"Okay, well, thanks for your help," Wes said. "We'll stay in touch."

"I just want to say one more thing," Mr. Howell said, his voice trembling with emotion. "If there were more men like Dan White, the world would be a better place."

CHAPTER 21

Patricia Clerk felt a dull ache in her left side and wondered if she'd fallen asleep in an odd position on the lounge chair. She opened her eyes and looked up, expecting to see the fan overhead and the last few purple blooms from the wisteria bush dangling from the top of the pergola. Instead, she saw the face of a young woman with dark-brown eyes and braided black hair leaning over her.

"Well, hello!" the young woman said, then reached into the pocket of her white blouse, pulled out a thermometer, and held it about an inch from Patricia's forehead. "Let's get your temperature." A ding sounded, and the woman read the device and smiled. "Ninety-eight point six. Very good."

Patricia tried to speak, but what came out surprised her. Not the words she wanted to say—*Who are you and where am I?*—but a croaking sound that made no sense, followed by an unsettling full feeling in her throat.

"Aww. I bet you want water, but the doctor said only ice chips for now. Would you like some?"

Patricia nodded, watched the woman reach for a paper cup, then felt her head being lifted and a sensation of cold touching her lips. When the chips reached her tongue and began melting, she sucked greedily at the liquid in hopes it would provide relief to her throat. It felt like a glob of phlegm was stuck there, threatening her ability to breathe. When the first drops of water reached it, she summoned what energy she had, swallowing vigorously until it felt like the passageway was clear.

"Better?" the nurse asked.

"Yes," Patricia said in what sounded more like a whisper than her normal voice. She wanted to sit up and check out her surroundings, but when she put weight on her right arm, the pain shot through her shoulder, prompting her to cry out.

"Please don't try to move. The ambulance will be here shortly. And then we'll get you to the hospital and have you fixed up in no time. Have a few more chips."

As the glass reached her lips again, she surveyed the area, recognizing it as the guest room in the cottage. She was home. Where was Hugo? Were her sons still at camp, and were they okay? The last thing she remembered was sitting on the patio with her husband, drinking champagne and waiting for Vic and Billie to show up so that the four of them could go to dinner.

Since their teenage sons and usual crowd of friends were gone for the summer, they'd seen a lot of Hugo's brother and his girlfriend. It had been uncomfortable at first. Billie was so beautiful. Patricia liked her but felt lacking when she compared herself with the young woman. Sometimes she would catch Vic looking at her and wondered if he, too, was sizing up the twenty-year differences. That's what he told her he'd done to his ex-wife. Patricia never liked thinking about Victor's cruel side.

As stunning as Billie was, the recent body language between the couple foretold that she wouldn't be around much longer. Since his divorce, Vic had gone through several girlfriends before hooking up with Billie. The minute they started talking about settling down and having a beach wedding, they were gone. Billie didn't ooze domesticity, so she'd hung on longer than most. But Patricia knew her brother-in-law well enough to recognize the signs that Billie was soon to be history.

"My husband?" she managed to ask.

"Your husband?" the young woman repeated as if confirming Patricia's question. "I don't know anything about him. I'm sorry. The doctor will be here any minute now. Maybe he can tell you something."

She thought about how attentive Hugo had been since the boys left for camp. She missed them and enjoyed their twice-a-week texts and photos. She'd sent them a care package a couple of days ago and hoped they were having a good time but couldn't be sure. They had wanted to stay on the island for the summer and hang out with some of the locals, but Hugo would have none of it. He had gone to Camp Winaukee when he had been a boy, and his sons would follow in his footsteps. "I was happy there. They will be, too," he told her. Patricia remembered thinking at the time: *Was that the only time in your life when you were truly happy?*

She felt a desperate need to switch positions in the bed but was constrained by the pain in her shoulder and the hovering presence of the nurse, whose silver tag announced her name as Tyonna. *What a caring person,* Patricia thought, remembering that it was Tyonna who had drawn her blood about a year ago when Patricia thought she was pregnant and was relieved to get a negative test result.

"You're awake." She heard the constrained voice of Dr. Sandburg coming through the bedroom door. "That's a positive sign." She managed a smile as he examined her shoulder, instructed Tyonna to take her blood pressure, and then pulled up a chair by the side of her bed so that he could listen to her heart and lungs.

"Stroke?" she asked, thinking that she was in good health and not overweight, but strokes could happen to anyone.

The doctor's face grew solemn. "You were shot yesterday, Patricia. Do you remember anything about it?"

She shook her head. She had been drinking champagne and feeling like she'd had too much, but that wasn't unusual. Drinking was the favored late-afternoon pastime on the island. You could hear corks popping and ice clinking in glasses any time after 5:00 in almost every household. It was a social place, and that's what people did. She tried not to become too dependent on the popular ritual. Her mother was an alcoholic, and she needed to be watchful.

Her thoughts focused on Hugo. She recalled that he hadn't been in the best of moods yesterday. Had he been angry with her for some reason she couldn't now pinpoint? They hadn't been arguing, just drinking too much. She'd felt woozy, as though she'd been drugged. She remembered Hugo leaving to get more champagne, but when he came back, he didn't have a bottle in his hand. It was something else; she couldn't recall what. The afternoon was now a jumble of disconnected events. But shot? She and Hugo didn't have any enemies that she knew of. She felt sad and suddenly uneasy.

"Who did this to me?"

Dr. Sandburg shook his head, removed the stethoscope from around his neck, and tucked it back in his bag. He put his hand on hers as if to comfort her in the presence of bad news. "We believe it was kidnappers who took your husband and his brother and are holding them for ransom. The police are looking for them and hope to have them home in the next several days."

"Kidnappers! Hugo and Vic! My God, they took Vic, too?" She closed her eyes in an attempt to shut out the painfulness of the doctor's words.

CHAPTER 22

Leslie and Wes followed a Verizon truck into the village and watched as the driver maneuvered his load into a spot not far from the post office. She wondered how long it would be before a temporary cell tower was up and operational. Any effort to restore island communications would be helpful in the search for the missing brothers.

Back in the sheriff's office, Deputy Pendry greeted the couple with good news about Patricia Clerk. A nurse from the island clinic had stopped by to say that Hugo's wife had been transported to a Sarasota hospital and was expected to be all right. Dr. Sandburg had ordered plenty of rest and no visitors until tomorrow.

"Did she recall anything about the kidnapping?" Leslie asked.

He shook his head and checked his watch. "Nothing yet," he said. "I'm supposed to tell you that Gene and Randy will meet you at the marina after lunch. About 1:30. Randy has some places he thinks you should check. It's my opinion that this search party thing's a bad idea. If something happens to any of you, I—"

"Don't worry," Wes said, reaching for a coffee cup and filling it with the dregs from the pot near the TV set. "I, for one, don't want to test Gene's ability to protect us from a bunch of kidnappers. Or mine."

As the two men talked, Leslie chewed on her thumbnail and focused on the ransom payment. It was nearly noon, and it had been almost two hours since she had called the Clerks' attorney, Farrell Rogers. She fretted about the messages she left. Had she been emphatic enough? She hoped that at least one of the unavailable assistants had listened to her voice mail and understood the urgency of the matter.

"We should probably have some lunch before we go. You want us to bring you back something, Alex?"

"Maybe a sandwich," he said, appearing grateful for her offer. "All I've had today is three doughnuts." He reached for his wallet, but Leslie waved him off, indicating she would pay for his food. It was the least she could do for the young man who was performing with such dedication in the absence of his boss.

She and Wes headed out, past the temporary cell tower that was being erected and across the street to the outdoor restaurant with the colorful sun umbrellas and wrought iron tables where Wes liked to eat breakfast.

After giving the waitress their orders, Leslie decided to ask Wes about something that had been bugging her all morning. "Maybe I shouldn't say this, but I'm surprised the sheriff is letting Alex handle this by himself. The state police and Fish and Wildlife rangers are involved in the search for the Clerk brothers on the neighboring islands. But going back to when he was a deputy, it's unlike Bruce to relinquish any of his authority. I wonder if something's going on with him?"

Wes nodded. "Maybe trouble at home. Plus, he has a lot of pressure on him in his new job. You forget, he's only been the head guy since January and, according to Randy, isn't getting much support from the other sheriffs in the area. Or maybe his apparent lack of concern is a vote of confidence in Alex."

"If so, it's well deserved," she said, making an *umm* sound as the waitress set a large plate of fries in front of her, along with a turkey wrap. Wes had a burger and a small salad.

Leslie grabbed the ketchup and squirted it on her fries, then popped one in her mouth. "I'm worried that the pieces aren't falling into place yet and we're working against a burial clock. We can assume the bridge tender was involved because he had the boy deliver the message about the ransom yesterday. At least, we think it was him. And if it was, that means your friend with the knife and the blonde are part of this, too. Remember what Mr. Howell said about Rick being loyal to Dan White?"

"Yep. And we have a motive: money," Wes said, rubbing a spot of mustard off his chin.

"Two hundred million is a lot," Leslie responded. "Reason enough to kidnap someone. But why complicate the crime by taking both men? You still think money's the only objective?"

"It has to matter in this kidnapping, or they wouldn't have demanded so much," Wes said. He was scanning the crowd at the restaurant as he talked. Now Leslie could tell by the expression on his face that he was zeroing in on one diner in particular.

She turned to look over her shoulder and saw a sandy-haired man with a plate of half-eaten food in front of him. His hair was slicked back, and he was wearing a smartly tailored beige suit that looked out of place on an island where shorts and T-shirts were the unwritten dress code. On his table was a leather briefcase. She watched him type something on his cell phone, then throw the device on the table in apparent frustration.

"Does that guy over there remind you of anyone?" Wes asked.

"You mean the one who looks like he could be Central Casting's version of an attorney for some drug cartel?"

Wes laughed. "I don't know about the cartel, but I think you have the attorney part right."

The reporter got up and approached the table, pulling a card out of his shirt pocket and handing it to the stranger. The two men talked for a few minutes, and then Wes waved Leslie over.

"I'd like you to meet Farrell Rogers."

The attorney for the Clerk family had received not one but three messages from his assistants and then listened to Leslie's voice mail as he was preparing to board a plane for New York. He'd been in the area visiting another client, so he had use of his own car. On his way to the island and the sheriff's office, he made a few phone calls to the banks and investment firms that managed the Clerks' fortune. All were reluctant to commit to a quick turnaround on the ransom funds, he told Wes and Leslie.

"Once they have your money, they're not so eager to give it up." As he spoke, he ran his finger down a scar that went from underneath his eye to just below his lower lip. Leslie was at first intrigued, then annoyed with this habit and relieved when he stopped and reached for a glass of water.

"Did you explain the gravity of the situation?" Wes asked. "And what are your thoughts about it?"

Rogers cleared his throat and told the story of his relationship with the family, which, for him, had started after law school. He had gone to work for the Clerks' father, Joseph, who had made it big in oil and gas. He set his sons up for life but didn't want them to become unproductive members of society like so many trust-fund babies.

"He worked them hard," the lawyer continued. "It paid off—especially with Hugo, who, by virtue of being the oldest, took over the management of a great portion of the family funds even before their father died. Joseph had to rein Vic in every now and then, but underneath it all, he's solid. He sometimes forgets that about himself."

Rogers stopped speaking and seemed lost in thought, his finger returning to the scar. Leslie watched him stroke it thoughtfully and wondered what he wasn't telling them.

"But the burial thing?" Wes said. "I just can't understand why the kidnappers would want to do something like that."

"Oh, it's happened before," Rogers said, "to a family that lived not far from here. A twenty-year-old woman named Barbara Jane Mackle was the target of kidnappers in the late 1960s. Her father was a wealthy real estate developer in Florida. After the ordeal was over, she wrote about it in a book called *83 Hours Till Dawn*. Compelling. I came across the book a couple of years ago in relation to a case I was working on. If you want to know what Hugo and Victor could be going through, she nails it in her book. She was buried for more than three days and survived. It's comforting to think about that positive outcome."

Leslie wondered which of Rogers's cases would have led him to the Barbara Mackle story. She wasn't born when it happened, but she remembered her mother talking about it and later saw more than one made-for-TV movie with Mackle's story as the premise. It had left an impression on her when she was a college student, although she hadn't thought about it recently—not even with what was happening to the Clerks.

"You say she was buried for three days. When was she discovered?" Wes asked.

"After a massive search by police, the perps were arrested. A female was convicted, served time and was deported to Honduras. The second kidnapper was sentenced to life in prison but was out after ten years. He's led a checkered life since then," Rogers said.

"And you know so much about this because?" Wes probed.

Rogers laughed. "Listen, friend, I'm not involved with this kidnapping, if that's what you're thinking. Like I said, the case was something that came up a couple of years ago. Not so much for the crime but what happened to the kidnappers afterward." He removed his suit jacket and hung it over the back of the chair next to him. "It sure is hot here."

Out of habit, Leslie checked her phone for the time and saw it was still not working. She glanced over at Wes's watch to confirm they would be meeting Gene and Randy in less than thirty minutes. She wondered why she was feeling uncomfortable with Rogers and decided that underneath the outward concern he was attempting to convey, he seemed nonchalant about his clients' dire situation.

"Do you have a plan for the ransom money?" Wes inquired.

Rogers sighed and checked his cell phone again. "Still no bars. If you tell me where the sheriff's office is, I'll head over there. I saw them working on a cell tower. Once it's up, I'll start dealing with the banks again."

Leslie gave Rogers directions, then signaled the waitress. "Would you mind taking a sandwich to Alex Pendry, the deputy? Poor guy has hardly had time to eat."

Rogers nodded, paid his own check in cash and grabbed his suit coat and the carryout. "Nice to meet you folks. Thanks for your help. I know that when this is all over, the brothers will want to show their gratitude."

Leslie watched him cross the street and head past the post office toward the sheriff's office. "What did you think of him?" she asked as they left the restaurant and headed down the sidewalk toward the marina a few blocks away.

"I'm not sure," Wes said, shaking his head. "I give him credit for responding quickly to your message, but he didn't seem panicky or even nervous for the Clerks. The fact that he knew about the earlier kidnapping was odd but still plausible. Attorneys come across a lot of unusual cases, just like reporters."

Leslie reached into her purse for a Kleenex and dabbed at the perspiration that was gathering on her forehead. "At least he was right about something. It's bloody hot today."

Wes chuckled and looked at Leslie with an impish grin. "You know what the problem is when you bury six attorneys up to their necks in sand?"

Leslie's expression was blank. She shrugged.

"Not enough sand," he said, chuckling.

"Funny but totally inappropriate," Leslie said, flashing a reproachful scowl in Wes's direction. "Please, no more burial jokes until the brothers have been found alive."

CHAPTER 23

Sunlight was filtering through the cracks of the walls, filling the lower level with welcome light. Hugo was lying on his cot, staring at the ceiling. Victor was pacing back and forth on the far end of the room, wondering what was going through his brother's mind. Was he formulating a plan to escape? Was he hoping that his offer to spare Victor would be accepted, or did he regret making it?

Although he had been a loving and supporting sibling when they were boys, as an adult, Hugo was often difficult for Victor to read. He tried to act as though nothing Victor did was so bad that it transcended their blood relationship. "Family comes first; that's why it's easy for me to forgive and forget," Hugo would say when Victor did something thoughtless or hurtful, like abandoning his wife after all those years of marriage. There was never a situation when Hugo didn't act that way. But in the back of his mind, Victor always worried that one day, he would go too far, and his brother would turn away from him forever.

The door opened, and the blonde and the smallish man entered, both still wearing masks.

"It's time," the man said, looking at Victor.

The brothers, the two of them now sitting on the cots, glanced at each other and then back at their captors but said nothing.

"Here's what's going to happen," the woman said. "My friend and I are going to take you one at a time—Victor first—to the boxes we've put together. They're state of the art, solar-powered with the latest ventilation system. Air is what you need more than anything, and you'll have plenty of it." She hesitated and studied the man standing next to her. "The others have gone. There are only three of us now. As long as we're here checking on the batteries, you'll be fine. Once we get the ransom money, we'll notify the sheriff of your location. If they fuck up and don't get to you in time, that's not our problem."

Victor stood and moved deliberately toward the kidnappers like a man resigned to his fate. He tried to focus on what the woman had told him last night. He was still alive. He would have air. All that gave him hope. When he came closer to her and stumbled, she reached out and steadied him.

As if triggered by rage at the sight of his brother being taken, Hugo jumped up from the cot, screaming, "Hit them! Kick them! Dammit! Don't go without a fight, Vic!"

At Hugo's command, Victor broke loose from the woman's grasp and attacked the man, toppling him onto the ground. He climbed on top of him, pummeling him with every bit of strength he could muster and shouting with each blow, "Fucker, you are not going to bury me! I'll kill you first, you son of a bitch!" The man seemed too surprised to fight back and instead covered his face with his hands.

Hugo grabbed one of the cots and swung it at the woman. She ducked, wrenched it from him, and lunged at her assailant.

"You're making a mistake!" she yelled, connecting a right jab to Hugo's jaw that sent him sprawling onto the dirt floor.

"Bitch!" he cried. He scrambled to his feet and tried to headbutt her. She grabbed his shoulders and delivered a knee to his groin. He fell to the ground, clasping his legs together and whimpering.

When it was obvious Hugo wasn't getting up again, she grasped the back of Victor's T-shirt and pulled him away from the man on the ground. "Get off him, you idiot. Even if you manage to escape, which is laughable, my partner's out there waiting for us. You've seen him. He's a tower of trouble."

It was over quickly. Victor briefly wondered how movie fight scenes seemed to go on forever. Even this small exertion had drained him, and he was in relatively good shape.

Hugo was on his feet again, tears traveling over his flushed cheeks. "Please take me. Let my little brother go. I'll offer you anything." When he started sobbing, Victor went to Hugo and wrapped his arms around him. He'd only done this a couple of times in their adult lives, and it felt good.

"Didn't you hear her, H? She said everything will be all right. We have to believe her. To have hope." He put his hands on either side of Hugo's face and kissed him firmly on the lips. Then he turned to the woman and said, "I'm ready."

The first thing Victor noticed when they left the house was the heat. It hung in the air, waiting to be stirred by the breezes from afternoon storms that hadn't yet materialized. Would they bury him in the shade? The woman had talked about him having plenty of air but had never mentioned a fan or something to keep him cool. Would the sand insulate him? It was always cooler in an underground structure like a basement. He wondered if that would be the case with the box. A waterproof container was what the big man had said. The woman had mentioned a sedative last night, but there was no word of it today. He wanted her to fulfill that promise to him, that she would knock him out and he would remember little of the ordeal.

He wasn't sure how far they'd gone when he heard the woman say to the man, "You go back for the brother. Dan will meet you there. I'll take it from here."

"You sure?" the man asked.

Victor honed in on the man's face as they stood in the bright sunlight. There was blood around the top of his mask. He felt bad for having beaten on this poor fellow. The woman was tough, but this one didn't fit in with the others. He didn't fight back.

When the man turned to go, the blonde motioned for Victor to keep moving.

"What's your name?" he asked. "I won't tell anyone."

"Lilith Krueger."

"German?"

"*Jawohl.* That's the only German I know. I came here with my parents as a baby. My dad was an engineer, and my mother a fitness trainer. Why do you care?"

"I was just wondering how you ended up, uh, how you came to be—"

"A kidnapper? My parents were killed in a car crash when I was eight. I got caught up in the foster system and learned to be tough. From an early age, I had an aptitude for survival. I joined the army when I was eighteen and learned about explosives. I'm very good at blowing up things but not people. When you hire me, you don't get a killer."

"But you're willing to kill me, Lilith?" He met her eyes directly for the first time and noticed they were a pale violet. Almost translucent.

"You haven't heard me. You're going to be buried and dug up still alive. That's the deal," she said as they continued walking. They were side by side now.

Victor laughed. "That's what you think? I thought you were smarter than that."

Lilith was silent as though considering his comment. They walked along a tree-lined sandy path another hundred feet to a clearing surrounded by Mexican fan trees and young sabal palms. There was a bird-of-paradise plant, like a beacon, among the native plants. Did the people who built the home on this remote island hope to civilize it but gave up when hurricanes battered their property every couple of years?

Victor zeroed in on two wooden boxes, tops off, positioned in holes that appeared to be about four feet deep. Between them was a battery-like contraption. He felt suddenly sick and swallowed hard to keep the meager contents of his stomach in place.

"Hop in," Lilith said.

"Wait, uh, you haven't told me how this works."

She shrugged. "I want to see how you fit and if everything is comfortable for you before the big guy gets here."

Victor obediently stepped into the box, sat, and then laid down, stretching his feet to within ten inches from the end. He could see her towering over him, hands on hips, examining his situation. There wasn't a pillow but a blanket on which he could place his head. There was also a flashlight, a package of batteries, and a box containing apples, energy bars, and what looked like two peanut butter and jelly sandwiches. There were half a dozen large bottles of water. A box and a couple of empty bottles were close to his feet.

"How is it?"

"It could use some padding." He flashed a wry smile her way.

She hoisted the wooden lid, which had a two-foot-long metal cylinder and black rubber hose attached, and placed it on top of the box. Victor was immediately encased in darkness except for the small amount of light coming through the cylinder. In a few minutes he could detect a hissing sound, like air from a leaky tire, traveling through the hose.

"Can you hear me?" Her voice resonated through the cylinder.

"Yeah, I can," he said, exploring for the objects he had seen when he first examined the box. With the lid on, there was enough room that he could prop himself on one elbow and reach the items he was supposed to use for his eliminations. It wasn't comfortable, but it worked.

Now that he was confronted by the reality of his situation, he realized that he did feel hopeful, as Lilith had suggested he should. But what was he going to do until he was found? Maybe he could spend the time searching for redeeming moments in his life—times when his actions had been meaningful and beneficial to others. That would take about five minutes, he estimated. The occasions on which he had been a failure as a human being would take longer to review, starting with the day he told Sheila he no longer loved her. And the betrayals—there were many, but one in particular. How could he absolve himself when so much that he had done was, in reality, unforgivable?

Where was the sedative Lilith had promised?

He thought he heard voices. Lilith's for sure. Were the smaller man and Hugo there? He couldn't tell. Then he heard a sound that nearly stopped his heart. It was like sleet pelting against a window during a winter storm. He recognized it as clumps of sand striking the top of his box. This hadn't been a test of his accommodations. No, his ordeal was beginning. Would it be his ending?

CHAPTER 24

Wednesday, July 14, Midmorning: Day Three

Leslie hadn't been on a boat since the celebration of life service six months ago for Frank Johnson, the fisherman with whom she'd had a brief and unfulfilling relationship. It was good to be on the water again, watching dolphins jump the wake, feeling the wind against her face—all with no sign of the seasickness she'd experienced on previous trips. This time, she was with Wes, Gene, and Randy on a mission that she hoped would not end with another funeral or two.

After problems with the engine in their borrowed boat yesterday, they had scrapped their search for the missing brothers, leaving it up to state and federal law enforcement to check the more remote areas. Today, Randy had a detailed plan that started with a nearby island. Gene had gotten his hands on a twenty-six-foot Grady-White with a center console. Because there was no head, Leslie vowed to drink water sparingly.

Following Randy's instructions, Gene skirted the shoreline of Anibonie Island, traveling at a speed that didn't create a wake. They saw several fishermen Leslie knew, giving them the traditional shout-out— "Catching anything?"—and got thumbs-ups in return. As they approached the shore of their destination, they passed a forty-foot Sea Ray with what Leslie observed was a group of toughies on board. No greetings, just stares. Leslie wondered if they were using the wrong bait or if someone had forgotten to pack the beer.

She had bent down to apply sunscreen on her legs when she heard Gene yelling and felt the boat take a quick turn, throwing her to one side. She grabbed the railing and held on as they picked up speed, swerving as if trying to avoid something. She looked past Gene and could see that the last boat they passed had circled back and was coming straight at them. When the driver began mimicking Gene's evasive actions, she heard Randy scream from the front, "Hang on!" Leslie braced herself for impact.

At the last minute, the boat deviated from the collision course and appeared to be headed north. Leslie breathed a sigh of relief. "Jerks. Are they drunk or what?" she said to Gene when he'd slowed the boat to idle.

"I can't be sure," Gene said, glancing over his shoulder at her. A worried expression remained on his face. "There were five men on that boat, and they didn't look like any fishermen I know from around here. Why did they come after us?"

Wes had joined Randy on the bow. The graphic designer was bellowing another warning. "Comin' back around!"

Gene pushed the throttle forward, putting maximum strain on the twin engines. Leslie grabbed the railing again, trying to remain calm as she watched the bigger boat closing the gap. Two of the men had moved to the bow and appeared to be pointing something in her direction. She heard a popping noise, muted by the wind and the sound of the boat engines, and felt a stinging sensation in her left arm. A wave of nausea hit her as she yelled to the others, "I've been hit!"

Wes scrambled to Leslie's side, pulled off his shirt, then yanked off his T-shirt and ripped it in two, tying one of the pieces around her arm. She thought he said she'd be okay, but she wasn't convinced that any of them would be all right. Not with a boatload of weapon-toting hoodlums bearing down on them.

Gene suddenly made a sharp turn and charged full speed past the enemy boat, heading for what Leslie assumed was the South Pass. Leslie admired Gene's quick thinking. Not only would there be plenty of boats in the pass fishing for tarpon, but rangers would be patrolling to make sure the big-game fish were being handled legally. When the chase boat slowed and turned away, Gene backed off the throttle and cruised in among the gathering of fishermen as though looking for a niche in which to cast his lines.

Randy, looking pale, joined the others near the back of the cuddy cabin. "Jeez, Leslie, you're lucky to be alive. Who in the hell were those guys, and what did they have against us?"

"They must have thought we were getting too close to someplace they didn't want us to be—like the Clerk brothers' location," Leslie said, trying not to think about the burning sensation that had settled into her upper arm. "We were minutes from Paraiso Island. Maybe they were trying to scare us off."

"We need to get you to the doctor," Wes said, fussing with the make-shift bandage.

Leslie protested, shaking her head. "I-I'll be okay. It's barely a scratch. We can't afford to stop now. I'm positive Randy is on to something."

Randy smiled. "Yep, like I said. They're hiding them in plain sight."

Wes was still insisting they get Leslie to the clinic when Gene pulled up to the shore and ordered Randy to drop anchor. Gene was quickly over the side of the boat, his rifle and ammunition pouch slung over his arm. He motioned to Leslie, who eased into his arms so that he could carry her to the beach. *The iguana hunter is plenty strong,* she thought as he set her down on the dark sand and shell fragments that made up the tiny island's beach.

"Let's get a move on," he said to the two men trailing behind. "We don't want those guys from the Sea Ray finding us here. We're sitting ducks."

As she did a quick scan of the area, Leslie noticed footprints in the sand and a scattering of charred logs. She couldn't tell how recent the fire was, but it was obvious that whoever built it knew how to extinguish it properly.

"Over here! A campsite, maybe!" she yelled to the others.

Gene was the first at her side, spreading the burned remains with the toe of his tennis shoe. "This is pretty clean. It could have been any group of campers. What do we know about this island?"

"I have some information," Randy said, holding up his hand as if answering a question in school. "Someone built a home here decades ago and cleared this stretch of beach for more development. There was a dirt access road built for the fire department. The developer thought he could create a permanent link to Anibonie, but the neighborhood that adjoined Paraiso didn't want the extra traffic, especially during the construction phase. To get permission to build a road, the developer had to obtain sign-offs from one hundred percent of the residents. There was no way that was going to happen."

"The development stopped?" Wes asked.

"Never got started. I heard someone bought the island not too long ago, including the house, which has been abandoned for several years. That was before you came, Wes, and we didn't have anyone to follow up on the tip. Must be someone who doesn't mind being cut off from the rest of the world."

While they were talking, Leslie had taken off for a patch of faka-hatchee grass. When she returned, she found the trio waiting for her. "Nature called," she said, grinning. "This place is definitely interesting. Let's take a look at the house."

The structure loomed large as it sat there on stilts with part of the lower level enclosed. Several windows were cracked or broken, but the Hardie board cement siding had survived the storms, its pale-green color only slightly faded. Leslie guessed the new owner, whoever he or she was, would tear it down and start over. Sometimes old houses were unfixable, especially in Florida where mold settled in and stayed like an unwanted relative—impossible to get rid of.

They climbed the steps and found the front door unlocked. Inside was the faint odor of fried food but no other evidence that anyone had been there recently. If someone had used the house for any reason, they'd left no trace of their presence. A check of the lower level also yielded nothing.

"I guess this is a dead end," Leslie said, looking at Randy, who was obviously disappointed.

"We're not done here," Gene said. "Why don't we split up and search the rest of the island? Randy, you come south with me. Wes, you and Leslie go north from the house."

The island wasn't large, but traversing it was challenging. The undergrowth was as thick as the mosquitoes. Leslie kept a wary eye out for snakes.

"I wouldn't mind stopping for a minute. Over there," she said, thinking about her arm. The wound was just a nick, but it felt like it was sapping her energy. She walked to a fallen palm tree in a small clearing. Wes joined her, taking a seat next to her on the trunk, and reached for his cigarettes. He stopped after she flashed him a look of disapproval.

"Those poor men. I feel like we aren't doing enough for them. Let's face it, Wes: This little search party of ours is pretty laughable. How can we hope to find them? We're not trained in these matters. Surely the state police checked this place straightaway. It's so obvious."

Wes nodded sheepishly. "You sure I can't smoke?"

"It's your lungs," she said, sighing. "I only want what's best for you."

Her eyes searched the space, examining the palm trees and native bushes. She thought about how much she liked Florida. It didn't have the northern oaks and maples that provided a carpet of shade for spring wildflowers to thrive, but it had its own charm. Best of all, there was no snow. She paused, took a second look, and reached over to pick up a shiny object not far from the tree.

"Is this a cigar band?" she asked, cradling it in her hand. It was red and gold and had the name *H. Upmann* on it.

Wes shot up like someone had touched his backside with a hot poker, snatched it from her, and began examining it.

"Dan White. The first time I saw him, he was smoking a cigar. This could be his. Cuban. Distinctive."

Leslie was also on her feet, sharing Wes's excitement at the discovery and wondering how someone like White would be so careless as to leave behind a cigar band. This was the only evidence they'd located that the kidnappers might have been there. A shout from Gene sent them sprinting in the direction of his voice.

"We found them!"

CHAPTER 25

Leslie later remembered the scene as otherworldly: two metal pipes sticking out of the ground with a solar-powered generator attached to another device that was pumping air into the cylinders. The sand was disturbed and slightly mounded. Randy was on his hands and knees, shouting into one of the pipes.

"Hello! Hello! Are you down there? We're here to rescue you." He struck the cylinder with his open hand as if to get the attention of whomever was underground.

"Careful," Gene said. "We don't want to dislodge the pipe or injure the person below."

Randy backed off. "Why isn't he answering? You think he's still alive?"

"My guess is that he can hear you, but maybe his voice isn't strong enough for you to hear him. We don't know where the pipes are in relationship to their bodies," Wes said. "Maybe they gave them a knockout drug."

Gene was on his cell phone to Deputy Pendry. By the look on his face, Leslie could tell the call was going through for a change.

"Alex, it's Gene," he said, breaking into a big smile. "We located the brothers."

Leslie felt her eyes tearing up. *What happens next?* she mused. She wondered why they hadn't brought shovels. She was willing to dig with her hands, even with her wounded arm. Four people could move a lot of sand, especially since the air flowing into the cylinders gave them time.

She paced, wishing that Gene would wrap up the conversation so that they could get started. Just because they'd found the burial site didn't mean the kidnapping victims were safe.

"Here's the plan," Gene said after hanging up. "The deputy's notifying Fish and Wildlife rangers, who should be here in thirty minutes or less. Alex is concerned that the guys who shot at us will be coming back to check on their captives."

"We're supposed to hang out for half an hour doing nothing while these guys are lying there helpless?" Wes asked, shaking his head.

Leslie desperately wanted to be on her hands and knees clawing at the sand, but she thought that Gene was making sense. "We don't want to jeopardize them, Wes."

"Okay. Do nothing. That's the plan," Wes said, kicking the sand next to one of the cylinders.

"I brought two rifles: this one and the another I left on the boat. I remember you turned down Ray's weapon, but the offer is open, Wes. Have you ever fired a gun?"

Wes nodded. "My dad used to take me hunting when I was a kid. I finally told him I didn't want to kill animals, and that was that. But I could take on these scum if I had to. Happily. Let's get the other rifle."

When Wes and Gene departed, Leslie focused on Randy, who was sitting on the ground near one of the cylinders. His eyes were closed as though he was meditating. Perhaps he was trying to communicate telepathically with the brothers. She didn't know Randy well. He seemed like a nice guy. Wes liked him, but even he had to admit that most newspaper people were—what did he say? Different. Not your run-of-the-mill folks. Leslie knew that Wes and many others in the profession liked the idea of being out of the norm. They even wore it as a badge of honor.

Randy's eyes popped open. "You hear that? Gunshots."

"Oh no!" Leslie cried out. "Wes and Gene!"

Randy hopped up, grabbed her hand, and pulled her into the over-grown brush nearby. They crouched down and waited for what seemed a lifetime before they could hear Gene calling to them.

"We're over here," Leslie said, noticing that Gene was alone. "Where's Wes?"

"You'd be proud of him," he said, looking at Leslie and grinning. "When we got back there, the thugs were all over our boat and fixin' to head on to the island to look for us, I'm guessing. Wes saw them, insisted I give him my gun, and started shooting like a madman. I'm calling him Rambo from now on. He just kept firing away. They got off a few. I don't think he was hit, but I can't be sure."

Leslie was in Gene's face in an instant. "What do you mean you can't be sure? Is Wes okay or not? And why did you leave him back there?"

Gene stepped back, appearing surprised that Leslie had lashed out at him. "Two other boats showed up almost right away. Our guys. The kidnappers—or whoever they were—hightailed it. Lucky, because Wes yelled to me that he was getting low on ammunition."

Leslie took off, running for the beach. Halfway there, she saw Wes walking toward her with two other men. All three were carrying shovels; one had a first-aid kit.

"Thank God, you're all right," she said, running up to Wes and hug-ging him. "We heard the gunshots."

"Everyone survived, including the bad guys," he said, putting his arm around her as they trudged on. "Meet Jerry and Basilio with Florida Fish and Wildlife. Today, they're gravediggers hoping to turn up two live bodies. We left the other two rangers behind to stand guard."

When the four arrived at the site, Gene grabbed one of the shovels and began digging, along with the two rangers. They worked with purpose, and in a few minutes, they'd removed enough sand to uncover a plywood box approximately eight feet long and three feet wide.

Leslie felt the anticipation growing in her. Which brother was it, and was he okay? She hoped it was Hugo; Wes had spoken highly of him. She didn't want anything bad to happen to Victor, but he didn't seem to be the man his brother was. At least, Billie hadn't spoken all that favorably about him, and Gene didn't care for him at all.

Jerry and Basilio pushed the lid askew so that they could get a better grip, then lifted it off, tossing it to one side in preparation for helping whoever had been buried emerge from his coffin. There was a gasp that passed from one man to the other, then from Leslie to her companions. It wasn't Hugo Clerk, and it wasn't Victor Clerk. Aside from apples, water, and a couple of sandwiches, the box was empty.

Without uttering a word, Gene and the others grabbed the shovels and began digging around the second cylinder. Their movements had a frantic quality, as if retrieving whichever brother was left was now an obsession. Leslie watched the sand fly through the air until another box, the same size as the first, was exposed.

As the two rangers reached down and removed the lid, the entire group of rescuers held their breath. There was another collective sound of surprise. The second box was also vacant.

CHAPTER 26

He had gone through a range of emotions when he had heard the sand hitting the top of the box. At first, Victor wanted to scream and cry, to bang on the lumber that enclosed him. As time passed and he envisioned himself powerless—encased in soil and sand—he grew silent and accepting. Maybe today was a good day to die. As he had realized often throughout this ordeal, he hadn't been a good person even though he'd been given every advantage in life. He was filled with shame and hoped he'd be forgiven if there was some higher being that doled out mercy in the end.

He estimated he'd been in the box for half an hour. Time was passing slowly. He reached for a bottled water and started to open it when he heard a noise above him. He cocked his head. It was muffled but ongoing. When it finally stopped, the lid was removed and sunlight filled his box. He wondered if he was hallucinating; then she appeared. Leaning over him was Lilith, maskless and with sweat dripping off what Victor thought was the most beautiful face he'd ever seen.

"Get out!" she ordered.

He sat up, then stood up and climbed out onto the sand, his legs feeling shaky.

"What's going on?"

"Shut up," she said. "Help me get this lid back on. We've got to get this covered up before they get back."

He dropped to his knees, taking in gulps of the salty air and thanking God he had been saved by this unlikely rescuer. He began pushing sand back over the box, remembering what it was like building elaborate castles with Hugo on the beach during family vacations in Naples. When he and Lilith finished, she tamped down the sand with her foot, then grabbed Victor and pulled him to his feet. She put her hands on his shoulders, looking at him resolutely.

"I want you to head in that direction," she said, pointing north. "When you get to the water's edge, stay put. Keep your head down. I'll pick you up later. If I'm not there by sunset, you're on your own."

"Why are you doing this?" he asked.

"You're going to die someday. I didn't want it to be this way. On my watch," she said and turned to leave.

"What about Hugo?" he asked, touching her arm and pointing to the cylinder next to the one for his burial box.

"He'll be fine. Don't think about your brother. Worry about yourself." And then she was gone.

Victor started running in the direction he thought was north. He couldn't stop picturing Lilith's face leaning over him, looking concerned. No, it wasn't concern; it was more like determination. As far as the others knew, he was still down there buried under the sand and would be until the ransom was paid. He remembered her saying it earlier: Once the kidnappers received the money, it would be up to law enforcement to find and save the brothers. The kidnappers would never know she helped Victor escape. If they did find out, he figured she'd put the finger on someone else. Maybe the smaller, weaker man. It would be his word against hers.

He thought of Hugo. He needed to go back and help his brother, but he was scared. If he returned, they were sure to see him, and then it would be all over for the two of them. With her help, he'd get off the island and do whatever it took to save Hugo. He realized that for the first time in a long time he felt optimistic about himself and his future. He was getting a second chance at being a decent human being.

CHAPTER 27

After a quick stop at the clinic to get a tetanus shot and have her wound dressed, Leslie and Wes headed home, stopping to pick up Mexican food on the way. En route, Leslie's thoughts turned to Billie. How would she react to the news? Did she have sense enough to let Newton out while they were gone? Leslie was ashamed that she hadn't given the dog a second thought while she and the others had been out on the boat. Her mother usually saw to Newton's needs when Leslie wasn't around, but that was no excuse.

Billie was lounging in the Adirondack chair on the lanai with the dog at her feet when Leslie and Wes arrived, shouting a greeting as they entered the condo. "We have dinner. Mexican," Leslie called out.

"I love Mexican," Billie enthused as she and Newton popped up and strolled toward the kitchen. "And I'm so hungry I could eat a dog."

"A horse, you mean?" Wes said and chuckled, looking at Newton.

"Oh yes. I get my sayings mixed up sometimes. I wouldn't eat this little puppy. We had so much fun today. We went for a walk a couple of times. There's a cute guy who lives three buildings over. Turns out he's married. Any news on the kidnappings?"

Leslie had left Billie a message telling her they were checking the nearby islands for signs of anything related to the brothers' disappearance. She hadn't provided any further details and wasn't sure how much to tell her houseguest about the empty pine boxes they found.

"No luck in locating Victor or his brother," Wes offered.

"I told you, Victor's dead. I don't know about Hugo," Billie said matter-of-factly.

"How can you be so sure?" Leslie asked as she reached into the cooler for a bottle of white wine. *And so detached about it?* She remembered Wes cautioning her when they had left the sheriff's office yesterday that no one outside the Clerk family should be trusted. Billie was an attractive woman—there was no doubt about that. Likable, even. But after discovering the money and the pricey diamond ring in her duffel bag, Leslie doubted she would win any prizes for honesty.

"You didn't hear his screams like I did. I think they took him somewhere and dumped the body. Of course, they aren't going to tell anyone. They want the ransom," Billie said. "I'll take red."

Leslie reached up in the cabinet for the wineglasses and dinner plates. When she set them on the counter, she noticed that Billie was staring at her bandage.

"What happened to your arm?"

"Oh, that. I scratched it on a bush when we were exploring one of the islands."

Billie nodded as though the story was plausible, picked up the dishes, and placed them on mats on the glass-top dining table. "Where's the silverware?"

Leslie pointed to a drawer in the small credenza, surprised that Billie was being so helpful. She hoped she would be as forthcoming when Leslie grilled her during the meal. She had a lot of questions for the young woman.

After the obligatory small talk during dinner, Leslie cleared her throat and looked intently at her guest. "So, how long have you and Victor lived here?"

Out of the corner of her eye, she could see a faint smile cross Wes's lips. He knew what was happening and seemed prepared to enjoy it.

"Eight months. Maybe longer. We came here after we met in Spain. I thought he was in love with me and would marry me. Otherwise, I wouldn't have wasted my time," Billie said, reaching for another fish taco. "At first, everything was perfect," she said as she bit into the crunchy shell. "We had amazing sex. Did you see the mirror over his bed? That was in the beginning. I even did some volunteer activities to get involved with the community. Then we started doing things with Hugo and his wife. Like I told you earlier, Patricia's a sweet woman. We had a lot of fun together. But I got the feeling that Hugo didn't like us being—what do you say—buddy-buddy? You know how women talk. Some men don't like that."

Billie took another few bites, washed them down, and held out her empty glass to Wes. "Do you mind?"

"Not at all," he said, grinning.

"How did Hugo and Victor get along?" Leslie asked, returning to the conversation she wanted them to have.

"Good, I think," Billie said. "I guess there was a time after Victor's divorce from Sheila, maybe after their father died, when they didn't speak much. Once I arrived, everything seemed okay. We started spending more time with them."

"Was that something you enjoyed?"

"Victor did. Me, I got tired of doing the same thing over and over. We never did anything fun. Never went on any trips. We just stayed in the house during the day and then went over to Hugo and Patricia's in the evening. Old people stuff."

"Why do you think Victor enjoyed that so much?" Wes asked, reaching into his pocket for a cigarette and then glancing at Leslie before returning the same hand to his water glass.

"Her. He wanted to see her. It took me a while to figure it out. Then I remembered that when we met, he told me about this married woman he had an affair with after his divorce. It was Patricia."

The room fell silent. Billie pushed what was left of her food around on her plate with her fork, sniffling. Newton was sitting off to one side, panting in anticipation of someone slipping him a morsel. A look of surprise was frozen on Wes's and Leslie's faces.

"Are . . . are you sure?" Leslie finally asked.

"I wasn't at first. Then one day, Victor told me about the safe in the closet and gave me the combination. We were making love, and I was using this technique I have"—Billie paused—"uh, and he was pretty drunk. Afterward, he said he wanted me to have the numbers to the safe in case anything happened to him. I don't think he remembered the next morning. But it was one of my better moments."

Leslie noticed that Wes's face was bright red and had to stifle a laugh.

"I'll be back," Billie said as she slipped out of the chair and scurried toward her bedroom with Newton following her as though she was his new best friend.

"You need to go outside for a smoke?" Leslie asked, grinning at Wes. "Or maybe you'd benefit from a cold shower?"

"I'm not missing the rest of this conversation," he said.

Billie returned with the small, black box and what Leslie recognized as the photographs of Victor with a beautiful blonde who she now knew was Patricia Clerk. Billie tossed the photos on the table, then presented the box, opening it with a flourish to reveal the large diamond ring.

"He was gone one day, and I tried the safe out of curiosity—to see if the combination he gave me worked. I found these. I knew the ring wasn't for me, or he would have given it to me a long time ago. The photos showed me he's still in love with her."

"How can you be sure? Did you ask him about her?" Wes inquired.

"How could I?" Billie replied, twirling one of the strands of her long dark hair. "He might change the combination. When those men broke into the house and dragged him off, I knew I had to get out of there and take these things with me. Along with the money he kept in the safe. Victor wasn't going to marry me or leave me anything in his will so I had to take care of myself. I've always had to take care of myself."

Leslie wasn't about to judge Billie, even though what she had done was questionable. "What if he's not dead?" Leslie asked. She could see Wes nodding in agreement with her question.

Billie shrugged. "I hope he isn't, but I'm leaving tomorrow anyway."

Leslie cleared the table and suggested the others go onto the lanai while she dished up ice cream and brownies she'd removed from the freezer. The sun was starting to set, its light reflecting on the voluminous late-afternoon clouds, making them appear a vibrant pink. It was still hot. Wes turned on the ceiling fan in the lanai. Billie scratched the dog's ears.

"This is vanilla, but it's the best. It's from Kappy's," Leslie said, handing a dish first to Billie, then Wes, and going back into the kitchen for her bowl. When she returned, Leslie said, "I'm sorry you had to go through the heartbreak of learning that someone you care about is in love with someone else. I wonder how Hugo felt when he found out about Victor and Patricia."

"He didn't know."

"Didn't know? I thought you said the brothers didn't speak for some time. I assumed it was because of that," Leslie said.

"Hugo didn't know," Billie repeated, scraping the bottom of the bowl and looking at Leslie as though she might want seconds. "I think the reason they didn't speak had to do with their father's death. He had billions, Victor said. But evidently, the dad left Hugo a lot more, even though Victor was supposedly the favorite son. Victor would have made a bigger fuss about the whole thing with that lawyer of theirs from Tampa, but I think he was feeling guilty about the affair. He was always pretty hard on himself, even though he liked to put up this front that he was a tough guy who didn't worry about anything."

"Did Victor have an opinion as to why his father didn't split the money evenly?" Wes asked.

Billie reached down to pet Newton. "He never said. He used to say he had all the money he needed, but it couldn't buy him what he really wanted."

"What was that?" Leslie asked.

Billie shrugged, then held out her dish. "Who knows? As long as what he wanted when we were together was me, I didn't ask. Could I have some more ice cream?"

CHAPTER 28

Thursday, July 15. 9:00 a.m.: Day Four

When Leslie woke up at about 8:30 and strolled into the kitchen, she noticed a thick envelope with her name neatly printed but spelled *Leslee*. It was a thank-you note from Billie, along with a stack of $100 bills that totaled $5,000. *For treats for your precious little puppy,* Billie had written, underlining the word *precious* and signing her name with a series of *O*'s and *X*'s after it.

Unusual woman, Leslie thought. It was obvious that Billie was a survivor and would be fine wherever she landed, especially with her boyfriend's money. Leslie was skeptical, though, that Billie loved Victor as much as she had insisted. If she really cared, she would have stuck around to find out what happened to him. She briefly pondered what to do with the money and decided she would return it to Victor if and when he surfaced. If he didn't, she would donate it to a local charity.

It was a surprisingly cool morning; a cloud cover was preventing the summer sun from fueling the oppressive heat that had hung over the island for weeks now. Even though the weather was favorable, Leslie decided to skip her morning walk in favor of finding out what she could about the new owner of Paraiso Island.

Online county records were helpful to a point. If you had addresses, you could easily look up the background for a parcel in a certain area. But there was nothing like a face-to-face chat with an underpaid county employee to obtain the real skinny. That was Wes's favorite term for information that hadn't been filtered through public relations or governmental spokespersons.

After a thirty-minute drive, Leslie arrived in the parking lot of the three-story county building. Before departing her car, she made a phone call to Wes, leaving him a message about where she was and telling him she planned on stopping by the sheriff's office when she returned. She estimated she'd be there about noon. "And tell Randy I said thanks for mentioning that the island has a new owner," she concluded, clicking off.

The property appraiser's office was on the second floor, and the employee at the front desk, a woman with short brown hair and glasses with rhinestones in the corners, was friendly enough.

"I'm interested in some information about a small island in the north part of the county. It's near Anibonie Island, and I think it's called Paraiso Island, although I can't be sure. I'm told it was purchased recently," Leslie said.

"Have a seat," the woman said.

Leslie recalled her last visit to the county government building nine months ago. She had waited an hour for property information about a house she suspected was involved in local drug trafficking. She'd used the time to check up on her twenty-one-year-old daughter, Meredith, through her Facebook page. Now that Meredith was spending most of the summer in Florida, Leslie had a better handle on what was going on in her life. When she returned from visiting her father up north in a couple of weeks, Leslie was confident Meredith would be reaching out to Deputy Alex Pendry. The two had gone out on several dates before Meredith left, and it was obvious to Leslie their attraction was mutual. The deputy would have plenty to tell Meredith about the kidnappings before she returned to Ohio State in the fall. Leslie hoped her daughter would be appreciative of what the young law enforcement officer had been through and how well he had performed.

"Phil over there will help you," the lady with the glasses said after about ten minutes had passed.

Leslie thanked the woman and took a seat at a desk across from a man wearing a white short-sleeved shirt that was tight across his stomach and a blue tie populated with tiny sharks. "I'm a little computer-challenged, which is why I drove here to ask you about this property instead of trying to get information online," she said.

Phil looked at her expectantly but said nothing.

"It's called Paraiso Island, I've been told, and is adjacent to Anibonie Island. In this county, I think."

He nodded and began typing on the keyboard. In less than a minute, he appeared to have accessed the information Leslie needed. "What do you want to know?" he asked.

"Let's start with when it changed hands and who the new owner is."

"It was purchased eight months ago by an LLC. Cain LLC," Phil said, looking up at Leslie.

"Good, good. And who is the person or persons involved with Cain LLC?"

"Can't tell you," Phil said. "It's an anonymous LLC, meaning that the state is not required to disclose information to the media or the public. Florida also has a double LLC program that allows you to keep your name off the public record by creating two Florida LLCs that manage each other. That, essentially, is what has happened here."

"That's sneaky. Why would someone want to do that?" Leslie asked.

"Your guess is as good as mine," Phil deadpanned.

"Well, it doesn't sound ethical to me. What's the other LLC?"

"Del. Del LLC," Phil responded.

Leslie sighed. "Neither of those names is helpful if I can't get any additional information. Can't you tell me something, give me a hint about who the owner is?"

"Even I don't know," he said, indicating that he had told her everything he could by reaching for the water bottle on his desk, taking a drink, and leaning back in his chair.

Leslie sighed and stood up, frustrated that her trip had been so unproductive. "Thanks so much. If you think of something else you can tell me, please let me know. Here's my card." *No real skinny today,* she thought.

She climbed into the car, feeling there should be a law against people who didn't want others knowing their business. She was more determined than ever to find out who or what Cain and Del were and if they had anything to do with the kidnappings. When she grabbed the steering wheel to head out of the parking lot, she noticed a twinge in her arm—a reminder of the dangers that can sometimes accompany an overly curious mind.

Sheriff Bruce Webster was sitting at his desk, alone in his office, when Leslie arrived shortly after noon. She had thought maybe Wes and Gene would be there. She had also expected to see Deputy Pendry. She hoped they weren't on a fact-finding mission without her.

"Bruce, how was the conference?" she asked, closing the door behind her. She cautioned herself against appearing critical of him for being gone when all hell was breaking loose and then dragging his feet about returning to the fray.

He glanced up from the paper he was reading and surprised Leslie by smiling. "Good. They have them every year."

I guess whatever you learned last year about responding to emergencies hasn't sunk in, was what she wanted to say. But in fairness to the sheriff, he'd only been on the job seven months, and this was probably his first crisis management conference. Sheriff Fleck had been the kind of man who would attend all such meetings and call all the shots. Back then, Sheriff Webster had been like Deputy Pendry—a follower of orders.

"Did you learn anything new?" Leslie asked, grabbing a paper cup, filling it with water from the blue cooler in the corner, and popping two aspirin into her mouth.

Sheriff Webster shook his head. "The world's getting more dangerous every day, and we gotta be prepared. Plus, there are a lot of folks out there who want to second-guess how we do our jobs—until someone's coming at them with a gun. Then they want us Johnny-on-the-spot to protect them."

"They had a seminar on that?"

"Nope. A bunch of us talked about it at the bar afterward," he said.

"I'm sure you've heard this from others, but Deputy Pendry did a fantastic job while you were gone. He was persuaded to let us help him and did the best that he could in a freakishly bad situation." Leslie worried that Sheriff Webster, a by-the-book kind of guy, would fault his deputy for relinquishing some of his responsibilities to what some might view as a citizen posse. But the sheriff was nodding and smiling.

"I couldn't have done any better myself," he said.

Leslie took a seat beside his desk, emboldened by his openness. She wondered what other information she could get out of him.

"Do you have any theories about what might have happened to the brothers or what the situation is with the ransom?"

Sheriff Webster's smile faded quickly. He shuffled some papers on his desk and got up, moving to the air-conditioning thermostat and mumbling something about the temperature in the office. Leslie wondered if he was thinking that this was police business, not hers. She had no standing as anything other than a very inquisitive private citizen who was always butting in where she didn't belong. The sheriff and his predecessor had both told her that on numerous occasions and had been chagrined when their admonitions were ignored.

"Nothing new since yer little search-and-rescue party discovered the empty boxes. Good work," he said, returning to his seat. "That air feels good. It's stuffy in here."

Leslie welcomed this softening in a sheriff who, more often than not, resorted to a tough-guy routine with her.

"We had a call from someone who lives in the neighborhood adjacent to Paraiso Island this morning. Said there were some lights on in one of the houses down the street from her, and she knew the folks who lived there were gone for the summer. I sent Alex to check it out. Probably someone put on timers before heading north. That's all today."

Leslie was silent for a moment, wondering how far she could push him. "I guess I'm surprised we haven't heard anything from the kidnappers about the ransom. Maybe they know the brothers aren't really buried and are keeping them hidden someplace else, like the house you just mentioned."

"That was my thought," Sheriff Webster said, shrugging.

He started to say something else when Deputy Pendry burst through the door, rushing to get a chair for the person trailing along behind him. Leslie gasped.

The man was dirty and haggard, and his clothes were torn. He had a three-day growth of beard and had aged ten years since Leslie last saw in church, but there he was. Hugo Clerk was alive and now safe. Even as she was eager to hear what he had to say, she saw Sheriff Webster giving her a sign. His look and nod toward the door were telling Leslie it was time for her to leave them alone.

CHAPTER 29

Sheriff Webster handed Hugo Clerk a bottle of water and the Kleenex he'd asked for, then turned on a tape recorder and placed it on the small table next to the billionaire, making a note of the date and time.

"We're gonna record what ya tell me, Mr. Clerk, starting with your name and address. You okay with that?"

Hugo gulped down half the water in the bottle, then nodded.

"My name's Hugo Clerk. I live at 12 West Laurel Street on the Gulf, not far from the church. Do I need to say Anibonie Island in southwest Florida? We all know where we are, right?"

Sheriff Webster scooted his chair forward until he was a couple of feet from Hugo and close enough to the table to periodically check the recorder. "Yes, we do. Can ya tell me what ya were doing on July 12, late afternoon?" he asked.

"My wife and I were relaxing by the pool, expecting my brother and his girlfriend to drop by around 5:00. We had reservations for an early dinner at that Italian restaurant. One of the few places you can get a good meal year-round. We were celebrating because our place and his had been damaged in that big storm a while back and have been repaired, thank heavens."

"Was it just the two of ya?"

"Yes, the staff, including our personal bodyguard, are on a two-week summer leave. I felt safe enough here to give them the time off. What a mistake that was. The boys are at camp, and I was missing them, but it was also a relief to have them gone for a couple of weeks. When you're in your fifties, teenage boys can drive you up the wall. To be with Patricia alone was, um, I can't even think of the word that describes how happy I was. *Ecstatic* comes close. Married eighteen years, and I can't keep my eyes off her . . . or my hands. Guess I shouldn't say that."

He laughed nervously, brushed flecks of dirt off his pant legs, and settled back in the chair. Sheriff Webster was struck by how calm he appeared. Even though he had asked for a tissue, he didn't appear to be emotional. Perhaps he was numbed by his horrendous experience.

"Is yer marriage a happy one?" Sheriff Webster asked.

Hugo sat up straight. "Oh God, yes. Why would you ask me that? That morning, we made love, and I brought her breakfast in bed. That's the kind of guy I am. I adore my wife. Has someone told you differently?"

The sheriff didn't respond to Hugo's question. "You were sitting by the pool. Did ya see or hear anything suspicious or out of the ordinary?"

Hugo shook his head. "We were under the pergola. The hum from the overhead fans drowns out most other noises, but you get used to it. In the summer here, you melt like butter if there's no fan. But you know that. The afternoon clouds were building; there was thunder in the distance. Maybe a speedboat or two in the Gulf. Usual stuff.

"Not that it matters, but we were drinking champagne, and I remember asking Patricia about my brother's girlfriend, Billie. We've been spending a lot of time with them. I wondered what Patricia thought of her. She laughed and called her the Bulgarian Bitch."

"She called her a bitch? How did ya react to that comment?" Sheriff Webster asked.

Hugo shifted in his chair. "I was a little surprised, but my wife was never one to hold back. Her parents encouraged her from an early age to speak her truth. She often offended people, but it never bothered her. Sorry to say that she seldom had a nice word to say about anyone."

"It sounds like yer wife might have enemies?"

"No, no. None. We were never involved in politics." Hugo shook his head emphatically. "If people didn't like us, they didn't have to deal with us, and vice versa. We kept to ourselves most of the time."

"I see. Go ahead with what happened," Sheriff Webster said as he got up and grabbed the cup of coffee on his desk before sitting down again.

"It was a little before four. We had plenty of time before Vic and Billie arrived, and I was hoping Patricia would join me in the bedroom. When the boys are around, you can't be as impulsive. I poured myself more Cristal and raised my glass to her in a toast to spontaneity.

"I heard a pop, and the glass exploded in my hand. I was showered with champagne and fragments. I couldn't make sense of it. I was expecting to hear Patricia's voice chastising me for breaking her Italian crystal, but she was silent. When I looked her way, her head was slumped forward like she'd fallen asleep. There was blood on her sundress. It was so red it didn't look real. I called her name, and then everything went black."

Hugo lowered his head into his hands. When he raised it a minute or so later, his cheeks were wet with tears. "I guess someone hit me on the head, Sheriff. I don't know how long I was out. I was confused when I woke up, but I knew I was on a boat. And then it came to me that my wife had been shot. Could you, uh, give me a minute?"

He reached for the Kleenex box Sheriff Webster had put on the table, wiped his eyes, and then blew his nose. The sheriff motioned for Deputy Pendry to get him more water.

"I'm sorry I didn't mention it from the get-go. I thought ya knew . . . although if I think about it, I'm not sure how ya would have found out. Yer wife is alive and being treated for a shoulder wound. The doctor says she's gonna be all right," Sheriff Webster said as he reached over and patted Hugo on the arm.

Hugo's face contorted, registering shock. "What? . . . Praise God! I didn't ask because I assumed she was dead. I can't believe it. Thank you, Lord! My beautiful Patricia is safe." Sheriff Webster and Deputy Pendry exchanged looks as Hugo's sobs filled the room. "Safe. I don't believe it," he kept saying.

After what seemed a respectful delay, Sheriff Webster cleared his throat and asked what Hugo remembered about the boat ride after the kidnapping.

"There were three men with me, all wearing masks and caps. The much smaller of the three seemed familiar, but I couldn't place him. He asked me if I wanted water and tried to calm me down. The other two—big guys, they were—didn't say much, but when they did, it was in a foreign language. They were obviously criminals, like the typecast bad men you see in the movies. Patricia's alive. My God, I just can't get over it. Why would they shoot her? It doesn't make sense. It had to be me they were after."

"How long were ya on the boat?"

"I couldn't say. At first, it felt like we didn't have a destination. Then the smaller guy got a call on a walkie-talkie or some device like that, and we took off and went through the Pass on the south end of the island. The place was packed with tarpon fishermen, so one of the big guys sat down next to me, pulled his hat low, and put a gun to my ribs. I saw a couple of people I know and waved to them like I was on a joyride with friends. It was surreal. I wasn't afraid for myself, Sheriff. I was thinking about Patricia and the boys and trying to hold it together."

Sheriff Webster nodded as if picturing the scene. "Once ya got through the Pass, did ya have any idea where they were going?"

"No. I kept asking them what they wanted from me. The big guys acted like they didn't understand. Finally, the smaller guy said my questions would be answered in due time. He said I shouldn't be afraid because no one wanted me dead. Alive, I was worth a hundred million dollars to them. Dead, nothing."

Sheriff Webster reached over and checked the small tape recorder before continuing. "What did ya think he meant by that?" he asked.

Hugo looked at the sheriff with an expression of disbelief. "Isn't it obvious? I was being kidnapped and held for ransom."

Sheriff Webster cleared his throat. "When did ya find out they had kidnapped yer brother?"

"They took me to an abandoned house on a small strip of land. I recognized it right away as Paraiso Island. Nobody lives there. I still don't understand why they wanted both of us. They could have gotten all the money they wanted from me, and it would have been a lot less trouble for them. After Vic arrived and we had something to eat, they stuck us in the lower area of the house. It had a dirt floor and a couple of cots. Oh, I forgot to tell you: Vic tried to escape, but one of the kidnappers brought him back. I think that took the wind out of both our sails."

Deputy Pendry, who'd been quietly taking notes, spoke up. "When did you find out they were going to bury you alive until the ransom was paid? That would've scared the shit out of me." He put his hand to his mouth as if realizing that it was the sheriff who should be asking the questions, then looked at his boss to assess if he was in trouble. There was no reaction from Sheriff Webster, other than apparent interest in Hugo's response.

"Well, Deputy, the one guy mentioned it on the boat. I thought he was pulling my leg at first. He said they were serious, that it would move things along. I had to break the news to Vic. He fell apart. God, it was painful watching him agonize about it. He begged me to pay them extra to let him go. I said I would, but it didn't do any good. Was I scared? You bet. But my philosophy is to steel myself to get through a situation and resolve whatever issues come out of it afterward.

"They took Vic first on the morning of the next day. I pleaded with the kidnapper to take me instead—told him that I would pay anything. It was the smaller man from the boat and some woman who came for Vic. We tried to fight back but were unsuccessful.

"It was about an hour later when the small man came for me. I was trying to stay calm. Just get through it, like I told you. The guy acted like someone down on his luck, so I took a chance. I told him that within a couple of hours, I could have five, ten million—whatever he wanted—wired to an offshore bank account with his name on it. He could let me go and no one would know. Right away, he said no, but I could tell he was thinking about it. I thought if I could get one of those guys on my side, maybe Vic and I had a chance.

"He didn't tie me up or anything. We left the house and started walking. I had my head down, following the footprints. The sand was broken around the edges, like Vic had dragged his feet. What I saw in those prints—desperation and fear—broke my heart. When we got to the burial spot, the sand was smooth, as if no one had been there. A metal cylinder was sticking out of the sand, and there was a device pumping air into the tube. It sounded like a ceiling fan on high.

"I yelled down the cylinder. 'I'm here for you, brother! We're going to get through this! I love you!' There was no answer. I'd heard one of them say they were going to give him a sedative, so I assumed he was asleep."

When Hugo paused to take a breath, Sheriff Webster took charge again. "Did the man bury ya then?" he asked.

"He showed me the box. It was about eight feet long with food, water, and the same cylinder, so I knew I would have air. 'Name your price,' I said. He just stood there staring at me. Finally, he said, 'Five million.' Of course, I said yes. I was free, dammit, free. And I would have given him twice that . . . three times . . . whatever he wanted. What a pathetic piker.

"My hope was that I could send you guys back for Vic. It wouldn't be that long. Not if I hustled. The guy gave me an account number. If the money wasn't there in forty-eight hours, he said he would dig up Vic and kill him, then come after me. I doubted he had it in him but played along."

"What happened after that?"

"I took off. It was getting dark, but I managed to find my way off the north end of the island, where I knew there was a sandbar that connected with Anibonie Island. I walked through the shallow water to the island and broke into someone's house. I was so exhausted I fell asleep on the couch. I was covered in mud, so I guess I owe those folks a housecleaning. The next day, your deputy showed up."

"Why didn't you try to contact us last night?" Sheriff Webster asked.

Hugo rubbed his eyes as if to indicate he was growing weary. "I didn't have a phone, and the house I broke into didn't have a working landline. I didn't see a light on in any other houses, and to be honest, I was so physically and emotionally wrung out I wasn't thinking straight. Have you found my brother? Is he safe?"

Sheriff Webster shrugged. "We found his burial site, like ya said, but he wasn't there. Are ya sure they didn't take him someplace else? Maybe they let him go."

A look of disbelief crossed Hugo's face. "He wasn't there? . . . I can't believe they'd let him go. I have no way of knowing, but they need at least one of us to ensure the ransom is paid. Poor Victor. Whatever they've done has to be terrible for him. And my wife . . . when can I see my dear Patricia?"

Sheriff Webster stood up and stretched. "Yer free to go whenever ya want. But we'll be calling ya later. Meanwhile, I would advise ya to hire a bodyguard or someone for protection. Those kidnappers are still on the loose. Do ya have someplace safe ya can stay?"

"You're saying I won't be safe at home?" Hugo asked, his eyes widening.

"Well, Mr. Clerk, there are only two of us, and we're still lookin' for yer brother," Sheriff Webster responded. He reached for the recorder and clicked the *Off* button. "I'm real sorry, but we aren't equipped for this. I can call some off-duty deputies I know from other counties for a protection detail."

Hugo asked if he could borrow Deputy Pendry's cell phone to call his attorney. When he turned his back as though he didn't want the others listening to his conversation, the deputy pulled the sheriff into the hallway outside the office door.

"I think we could use some of the firemen to help protect Mr. Clerk. Someone like Ray Santiago would be good, and he's off for a couple of days. Gene Miller, the iguana hunter, helped us find the burial sites. We could offer to pay them, although Gene would probably do it for free."

Sheriff Webster appeared to like the idea. "We've already broken all the rules. There's no guarantee I'm gonna be elected next year after people hear about how everything fell apart these last couple of days. Let's see what we can do to protect this man from further harm."

CHAPTER 30

When Wes strolled into the sheriff's office, he was shocked to see Hugo alive and seemingly well, despite his appearance. It looked as though he'd been underground without the benefit of a pine box. His face and clothes were caked with dirt, his hair tangled and matted. There were tiny sores and bug bites on his arms, neck, and face. Although there were no demons glaring over his shoulder, he seemed like a man who'd been to hell and back and was now enjoying the company of angels masquerading as law enforcement officials.

"Mr. Clerk! Thank heavens. You okay?" Wes asked, stifling the urge to give the billionaire a hug.

Hugo grinned. "I'm grateful to be here. Thanks for your part in the rescue effort. The deputy here's been telling me about you, Gene, and your lady friend, Leslie, searching the islands around here for me and Vic. It was kind of you."

Wes blushed, then recovered quickly. "I have so many questions."

"I have no answers," Hugo said, scratching his arms. "There are plenty of wealthy people on this island. Why did they go after us? And who are they?"

Wes took the last available seat in the office. Out of habit, he pulled out his reporter's notebook. "I'm wondering why anyone thought they could get away with kidnapping you in broad daylight." Out of the corner of his eye, he saw Sheriff Webster wince. "And what do we know about your brother's situation?"

"Sheriff Lake from the neighboring county loaned us deputies to check out the island where you found the boxes. We're waiting to hear back from them," Deputy Pendry chimed in. "Other than that, we got nothing."

Wes nodded, looking out the window and thinking about what he could post on the newspaper's website. He'd held back for fear of jeopardizing the search, but now that Hugo had turned up, Wes didn't feel as though he could remain silent. Maybe someone from the public would have information about Victor's whereabouts. As he watched the island residents go about their business, oblivious to the fact that two of their own had been wrenched from the safety of their homes, he wondered if Sara would oppose an article and website posting that alerted the public to the crime. It wasn't his objective to scare the few people who didn't go north for the summer, but he felt strongly that they needed to be informed.

His thoughts moved on to doing an interview with Hugo. He was considering how to approach the billionaire on the topic when he saw a familiar figure striding toward the sheriff's office, a man on a mission. He felt a surge of adrenaline. *That can't be Dan White.*

The ex-military man and presumed suspect was walking the street as big as you please. He didn't appear to have any weapons with him—no holstered knife. Just six feet four inches of rock-hard muscle, which, in Wes's estimation, was armament enough.

"Sheriff, my name's Dan White," Wes's nemesis said as he strutted through the door like a professional wrestler entering the arena for the big match. "I'd like to talk to you about a complaint I have."

No one said anything at first, including Hugo, who studied White briefly and then reached for his water, looking out into space as if he wasn't fully engaged in what was going on around him.

"Deputy, would ya get Mr. White a chair from the office next door?" Sheriff Webster asked. "Sorry, we're a little busy today, as ya can see. What can I do for ya?"

White eyeballed the others in the room, stopping at Wes, who was sitting off to one side, wondering what the hell was going on. "I saw you the other day. Are you, uh, Wes Avery, the reporter from Indianapolis?"

Wes nodded warily, remembering the scene at the four-way stop when White had flashed focal daggers his way. Now he was acting as if the two men were old college chums taking part in a surprise reunion. Wes wondered what kind of game White was playing.

"I thought it was you when I saw you in the village. I used to read your stories every day in the paper. What are you doing here in Florida? You retired?"

Wes shifted uncomfortably in his chair, his skepticism meter registering off the chart. "I moved down here several months ago. You've put on a few pounds of muscle since that day you threatened me with a knife. Was it six or seven years ago?"

White looked apologetic. "I am sorry about what happened. I'd just gotten out of prison, and things were rough. You showed up at my door unannounced, and I felt threatened. I intended to reach out to you later but got sidetracked. I hope there are no hard feelings."

"None," Wes said, thinking that he had crossed over into some alternate universe and none of this was really happening.

"That's good to know. I was worried that you were the one spreading rumors about me around town. That's why I'm here," he said, turning to Sheriff Webster. "The lady at the grocery store was acting weird to me and my girlfriend yesterday, and some guy who worked there told me that folks thought I had something to do with the bridge and cell tower. I want to make it clear that I'm not involved in any way with what happened. My friends and I are here on vacation. That's it." He slammed his hand on the desk for emphasis, startling the sheriff, who dropped the pen he was using to take notes.

Deputy Pendry set the borrowed chair next to Sheriff Webster's desk and moved to the other side of the room next to Wes, his face reflecting curiosity and awe regarding the office visitor.

"Well, Mr. White, there's been two kidnappings on the island. I'm guessing the word has gotten out among the locals, and they're a little jittery. But it looks to me like we can clear things up quickly with just a few questions," Sheriff Webster said.

Wes was at an angle where he could see Sheriff Webster unstrap the holster on his gun and click off the safety. He was sure White didn't notice the move.

"Mr. Clerk over there was one of the people taken," Sheriff Webster said, pointing in the direction of the disheveled victim. "I'm just gonna ask him straight out if he's ever seen ya before and if he thinks ya might be involved in the kidnappings."

Hugo looked surprised, then stood up and walked cautiously toward White as though he were examining a dog to determine if it was friendly or not. He peered at the man, scrutinizing his face and impressive build with what Wes thought was a look of admiration.

"Sheriff, I don't know this individual," Hugo said. "All of the kidnappers were big—muscular, like him—and wore masks. But if he was one of them, why would he be sitting in your office now? It doesn't add up."

White remained expressionless. Wes was shocked.

"Ya sure?" Sheriff Webster asked.

"Were you in the military?" Hugo asked, ignoring the question and pointing to White's tattoo. "Maybe Special Forces?"

White nodded.

"I imagine people often mistake you for a tough guy because of your build and the way you carry yourself . . . and perhaps the tattoo," Hugo said.

White smiled but said nothing.

"I'm looking for a bodyguard. The sheriff here suggested that a couple of people on the island could be helpful in that regard. But if you're interested and feel like you can handle it, I think you might be the better fit. I'll make it worth your while. You can protect me until my regular, Mick, returns. I'll try to contact him when I get home, but he's on a camping trip in South America and not scheduled to be back for another week."

White appeared to be assessing Hugo as he considered the proposal. "I've been a bodyguard and a bouncer, but I have a criminal history. I was found guilty of killing my commanding officer and served four years. I got out in 2014."

"Have you been a model citizen since?" Hugo asked.

"The sheriff here can check. I've had no arrests since my release."

Wes was feeling like any minute he might explode at the scenario unfolding before his eyes. He wanted to scream, *Are you fucking kidding me? You can't hire this man or anyone he's associated with. He's a killer and likely a kidnapper.* But even as he was sure White and his girlfriend were involved in what had gone down the last couple of days, he didn't have any real evidence. Hugo, who apparently hadn't seen White before, was seeking protection. And Wes had to admit that if you were in need of someone to watch over you, White had the appearance and bearing of a warrior.

"I'm headed home to get cleaned up so that I can go see my wife in the hospital and talk to my attorney about the ransom payment for my brother. Do you have a car, and can you give me a lift? I have a nice guest house. It's on the water," Hugo said, sounding as though the two men were already old friends.

White hesitated, then turned toward Sheriff Webster. "Are we okay? I want to make sure that I'm not going to be arrested for something I had nothing to do with. Mr. Clerk here says I'm not one of his kidnappers. I want that acknowledged here and now."

Sheriff Webster stood up. "We'll make sure the word gets out that yer not one of the bad guys."

"Appreciate that. And, uh, Mr. Avery, it was good to see you again," White said, flashing a grin in Wes's direction.

Wes cringed. *If this isn't a case of the fox guarding the henhouse, then I've lost my mind and all my instincts with it.*

eeƆCee

Wes arrived at the newspaper office and found Leslie waiting for him. She had seen Hugo at the sheriff's office and later in a golf cart, heading toward his home with a muscular man behind the wheel. She wanted to share this information with Wes and Randy.

"Did you know they found Hugo hiding in a house not far from the island where he was being held captive?" Wes asked before Leslie could say anything. She nodded. "Still no word about Victor's fate. I think Hugo is still planning on paying the ransom."

Leslie was joined by Randy, who emerged from his office and took a seat on the edge of Wes's desk.

"I saw him at the sheriff's office and then in a golf cart with someone I didn't know a few minutes ago," she said.

"That was Dan White, the former military guy I told you about. Hugo declared in the sheriff's office that he wasn't one of the kidnappers," Wes said, shaking his head. "That's a tough pill to swallow."

"That's bullshit," Leslie said. "Remember—we found the cigar band close to where the brothers were supposed to be buried. You said White was a cigar smoker. It's the only potential clue we have, but it feels valid. What reason would Hugo have for lying?"

Wes and Randy shook their heads. "Maybe he wasn't. It's possible Hugo never saw White," Wes said. "He told the sheriff that the kidnappers wore masks."

"How much danger is Hugo in?" Randy inquired.

"Maybe not as much as you might think," Leslie interjected before Wes could respond. "If Hugo plans on paying the ransom, White is now at his side, helping make sure that happens. Afterward, what reason does he have to harm Hugo, unless whoever masterminded these kidnappings wants Hugo dead?"

"Whoever that is," Randy added, thoughtfully stroking his beard, "we oughta try to figure that out."

CHAPTER 31

The lookalike goons were hanging out on the stern of the Sea Ray, casting lines, drinking beer, and occasionally breaking into raucous laughter as though one of them had shared an off-color joke with the others. Rick Howell, alias Mark Foxx, sat alone on the bow of the boat, thinking about what White had revealed to him forty-eight hours ago.

His freshly shaven face was two colors: dark on the forehead and white around his chin and lower cheeks. The scars caused by the barbed wire torture were at last exposed for the world to see. He fidgeted, checked his cell phone, all the while wishing he hadn't said yes to his friend's offer those many months ago. Even though the money he stood to make would set him and his dad up for life, he had come to regret his involvement with the kidnappings. Especially after White told him the identity of the mastermind shortly before Hugo was to be buried.

White's revelation and the subsequent events had motivated Rick to slip away earlier that morning for a meeting with a local attorney. Now he was back and waiting to hear from his friend. It was already 4:30 p.m., and no word. Rick wondered if there had been a last-minute change of plans. He worried that at any minute, the mercenaries would stop enjoying themselves and start asking questions he couldn't answer.

What Rick had shared with the five when they boarded shortly before noon was that their payments would be delivered in cash today—one hundred thousand dollars each. White would bring the second Sea Ray for them with their money on board. They would drive the boat to a popular waterfront restaurant in the nearby town of Venice. There, a car would be waiting to take them to a private plane at the local airport. It was the same small-town airport where the 9/11 terrorists had learned to fly, Rick remembered hearing, and in his mind, where the events that had led to his current situation began.

From Venice, they would travel to Atlanta and pick up an overseas flight to a destination unknown to Rick. He assumed they operated as a mercenary unit out of Europe, maybe Russia. He didn't know and didn't care. Good riddance to bad rubbish, as his dad liked to say.

Rick hated the goons and would be glad to see them go. They reminded him of the al-Qaeda terrorists. Their lineage and ultimate goals might differ, but the bent toward cruelty was there—held in check most of the time but ready to be unleashed at a moment's notice. He guessed they were capable of anything.

Lilith had a separate arrangement unknown to Rick. She was an attractive woman. *Strong and plenty smart,* he thought. He wasn't interested in women, but he wondered if she and White might hook up after this job was finished. They seemed well suited, but Rick knew his friend would never allow himself to become distracted during a mission, and Lilith hadn't expressed any interest in White that he was aware of beyond their professional relationship.

This would all be over soon. Out of respect for White, he just had to bide his time and fulfill his obligation. He got up, walked to the back of the boat, and grabbed a beer from the cooler. The others stopped talking. One stepped forward, blocking Rick's path back to the bow.

"Any word?" he asked. "We want our money."

"Nothing yet. Be patient," Rick said, making a gesture with his hand that he thought the man would understand to mean "chill out."

"It better be soon," the man said, grabbing Rick's arm and giving it a warning squeeze.

Rick wanted to tell them not to be mad at him. He had nothing to do with it. Instead, he jerked his arm away as if to tell the mercenary to fuck off without speaking the inflammatory words. Then he returned to his seat, twisted off the beer cap, and took a couple of sips.

It was about eight months ago that White had reached out to Rick and offered him the chance of a lifetime. For a couple of days' work, Rick could make one million dollars, tax-free. All he had to do was disable a swing bridge in southwest Florida and assist in the kidnappings of two brothers who lived on an island that was virtually abandoned in the summer months. No one would get hurt as long as the ransom was paid. Rick was working as a mechanic in a garage in Arizona and wanted a better life for himself and his father. He was forever linked with and grateful to White through their war experiences; there was no way he could refuse.

He had barely known White when the man risked his life and a promising military career to rescue Rick from the tortures being inflicted on him in a cave in Afghanistan. There were four men holding Rick, and White crept in under the blackness of night and took them out one by one as if reenacting a scene from an old Sylvester Stallone movie. Rick thought he was hallucinating as this mountain of a man appeared out of nowhere to inflict swift justice on his abductors, then carried him, battered and bleeding, to safety. Rick remembered little about the trip back to the platoon's campsite—only the sound of the three extra dog tags around White's neck clanking together as the soldier strode purposefully across the rough terrain, carrying a brother as if he was no burden at all.

Rick didn't hear what the commanding officer said to White when they returned, but others in the platoon told him. Not only had the CO refused White's request for men to help him on the mission to rescue Rick, but he was furious with White for disobeying orders and was advocating for the soldier to be court-martialed for desertion.

Two nights later, while Rick struggled to stay awake for fear of reliving the torture in his dreams, al-Qaeda struck the campsite. It was a small band seeking retribution for what White had done to their comrades. As the fight raged, Rick summoned whatever strength he had and slipped out of his bed and into the CO's tent, where he hid behind a pile of boxes. When the skirmish was over, the commander returned to his tent and lay down on his cot, fully dressed. As quiet settled over the area, Rick crept out from behind the boxes and crawled across the ground to the sleeping CO. He had to punish the man who didn't care about his life or White's future. He took the knife he had brought with him and ran it across the commanding officer's throat. The dying man had made no sound; only opened his eyes in surprise and stared at Rick as life ebbed from his body.

The next morning, the others told Rick about the CO's death. "How did the terrorists get into his tent?" he asked as though shocked by the turn of events. But the investigators knew it hadn't been the terrorists. They had failed to breach the perimeter. It had to be one of them, and the likely suspect was Dan White. Rick protested the accusation. When that failed, he went to the man to whom he owed his life to confess his crime.

"Don't say a word," White said, ordering Rick to keep quiet. "I didn't save you for the hangman's noose."

When White was found guilty and sentenced to life in prison, Rick went to him again. He said he was going to tell the authorities what really happened. White told him no for the second time.

"You suffered enough. You owe me the life outside that I will never have. Take care of yourself," White had said.

Six years ago, when White had been released from prison and justice had finally prevailed, even if unintentionally, Rick vowed that whatever this man he loved asked of him, he would never refuse.

ฒ⊃ℂ

Another hour had passed when Rick noticed a white boat with a green stripe coming their way. Even without binoculars, he recognized that it was the Fish and Wildlife rangers in their familiar state law enforcement water cruiser. He hoped they didn't recognize him as the former bridge tender and associate him with the bridge disablement.

"Hey there," the woman in the green shirt and matching pants said as they pulled alongside the Sea Ray. "Catching anything?"

"We, uh, don't know the limits, so we're just releasing anything that lands on our hooks," Rick said. "I got some guys that work construction for me. I'm treating them to a day off."

"Aren't you a good boss," the woman said. "Mind if I come on board?"

Rick nodded, even as he prayed the men didn't do something stupid, including making some smarmy remark about a woman in a uniform. Even in a foreign tongue, their body language would give them away. She headed for the stern, where the lookalikes were sitting around, trying to appear casual. One or two continued fishing.

"Little warm today," she said as she checked the cooler and found only water and beer in there. A couple of them nodded, fanning themselves with newspapers someone had brought on board.

Rick saw her walking toward the duffel bags, in which he assumed the mercenaries had stowed their passports, a few clothes and change of underwear, one or two weapons, and ammunition. He held his breath.

"Anything in here?" she asked, pointing to the identical bags that were neatly stacked in one corner.

"I'm guessing dirty underwear," Rick said. "You're welcome to check, but I gotta be honest, we've been out here a couple of days and no one had any toilet paper, so . . ."

"Tire tracks," she said and laughed. "I've got teenage boys. I know all about that. Give me a minute while I see if my partner has any questions. I left him running a check on your boat registration."

"You looking for something in particular or just fishing violations?" Rick asked, growing uneasy. He didn't know anything about the Sea Ray— in whose name it was registered or where White had gotten it. If there were questions, he would have to think quickly. Maybe claim it was rented by his boss, which technically was true.

"Coming on board," he heard a man's voice say. "Hot out here, isn't it?"

Rick wondered if temperature-related comments were the standard opening remark for law enforcement officers trying to assess whether they were walking into a hornet's nest, or in this case, a group of vipers. He noticed that the man had a piece of paper with him. He felt his stomach tighten when he realized it was the photo on his bridge tender's badge.

"Just wondering if you've seen this individual," he said.

Rick took the paper, examined it, and was happy to observe that the beard, which was almost black in the photograph, hid all signs of the now-prominent white marks on his chin and lower cheeks. He'd forgotten that was the case.

"Any of you guys recognize this man?" he said to the mercenaries, who filed up to him and murmured a chorus of *nos*.

"Sorry," Rick said, shrugging. "Anything else?"

The ranger squinted at the fishermen. "You guys brothers?" he asked.

"Cousins," Rick responded. "They're from someplace in Europe. I can't remember where. Their English isn't great, but they know how to wield a hammer. We've been making money hand over fist since the storm."

The rangers, both nodding, moved toward their boat. "We're gonna be back by here in about an hour," the woman said. "We're on our way to the causeway. I guess they've got a better photo of the man who sabotaged the bridge. You can see more of his face. Would you mind taking another look if you're still in the area?"

"No problem," Rick said, remembering Cap's birthday party a couple of weeks earlier when he drank too much and posed with his friend under a light that was sure to expose his facial scars. What had his friend unknowingly done to him?

After the rangers' boat pulled away, the mercenary who spoke the best English approached Rick and flashed a menacing look in his direction. "It's not good when the police are around. Why the delay?"

"Let me contact Dan," Rick said. He checked his watch, noted it was about 5:00 p.m. White had left him alone on this boat to manage a group of men who were, in his mind, uncontrollable. They'd grown weary of waiting for what was theirs and were spooked by the presence of the rangers.

"Pick up, pick up," he whispered as the phone continued ringing with no answer and finally switched to voice mail. "Uh, Dan, this is Rick. The boys are getting a little antsy about their payments. Give me a call."

When Rick clicked off his phone, he noticed that the goon who questioned him had been joined by the others. "Our money. Where is it?" a second man said, pointing his finger and then punctuating his remark with a poke to Rick's shoulder.

"Don't touch me," Rick said, straightening up and giving the man a shove. He knew he was taking a chance, but showing any sign of weakness was dangerous with this group. White didn't take any guff from them, and neither would he.

"Big man," he heard one of them say in a voice that sounded like the actor Arnold Schwarzenegger. "More like a little pussy." They all laughed and moved in closer.

"Back off!" Rick yelled. He felt himself being jostled by the men, who had been drinking all day in the hot sun. If their judgment wasn't good to begin with, it had definitely been affected by the alcohol and the heat.

"Knun ero za bort!" one of them yelled. There was a chorus of *das* as Rick felt himself being swept off his feet and thrown over the side of the boat and into the warm water.

He landed on his back and immediately flipped over. He was an excellent swimmer, and the water, though bathtub warm, was refreshing. He was confident he could make it to the shore without difficulty. *Bastards,* he thought. He was not looking forward to spending any more time with these men. White could handle them from now on.

After he'd swum a couple of hundred feet, he rolled over on his back again, paddling with his feet and trying to gauge the distance between him and the boat. The mercenaries were pointing at him, guffawing and slapping one another on the back. He raised his arm, extended his middle finger and shook it defiantly at them. They laughed even harder. Then he noticed one of them raise his arm and point it in his direction.

Is that a gun in his hand?

He flipped back over, gulped in air, and dove as deeply as he could, watching as the bullets sliced paths through the water on either side of him.

CHAPTER 32

Friday, July 16, 11:00 a.m.: Day Five

The messenger who brought the latest news from the kidnappers was not the young boy from before but a pair of fresh-faced young women in their twenties wearing bikinis under their see-through beach cover-ups. They had been eating breakfast and texting their friends when someone dropped an envelope on their table, along with two hundred-dollar bills. By the time they looked up, whoever it was had disappeared. The girls asked the waitress if she had seen anyone near their table, but she said she was busy with other customers and didn't notice anything. Written on the envelope were the words *Deliver to Sheriff.*

There they were, grinning at Deputy Pendry, asking if he would pose with them so they could post a photo on Instagram. He agreed, blushing, and held out the envelope so that it appeared prominently in the selfie. He hoped the sheriff wouldn't be upset with him for this breach of police protocol. It was, after all, harmless fun.

"Bye now, and thanks for bringing this to us," Deputy Pendry said as the young women departed, tittering and waving to him. "Hope I wasn't out of line," he said as he handed over the envelope and watched Sheriff Webster rip off the end, blow into it, and produce the letter without comment. He read it quickly and dropped it on his desk when he was finished.

"It says that Victor Clerk's alive. They're demanding the ransom be wired immediately. If it isn't, both Victor and Hugo will be dead within twenty-four hours," Sheriff Webster said. His voice was grim.

"How can that be? Did they include any proof?" Deputy Pendry asked, putting aside thoughts of young women and Instagram fame. "Hugo's got that White fellow protecting him, so I find it hard to believe they have any bargaining power. The state police and the FBI are still looking for Victor, but maybe we ought to ask Sheriff Lake if we could borrow more deputies to work out of this office." He didn't intend to overstep his bounds, but he thought he should emphasize their need for additional manpower in case the sheriff had the mistaken impression the two of them could handle the situation by themselves. "We talked about Gene and Ray. Mr. Clerk didn't seem enthusiastic about them, but in a situation like this, it feels like . . . uh . . ."

Sheriff Webster cleared his throat and held up his hand. "Not so fast, son. I think we should speak with Mr. Clerk before we pull together a posse of local citizenry. This isn't the Old West. We'll show him the letter and see what he wants to do. Maybe he'll be of a mind to get out of town. That's what I'd do in this situation with his resources—leave and let us worry about his brother."

Deputy Pendry nodded, turned off the TV and the coffeepot, then scribbled on the whiteboard by the door that they'd be back in an hour.

As they exited the sheriff's office, they could see a large crane lifting the remains of the cell tower off the flower shop and placing it in a dumpster. Deputy Pendry was glad they had brought their own crew to direct traffic, what there was of it.

When they arrived at Hugo's home unannounced, they were met by a bulky, rough-looking man standing by the opening in the wall that blocked Hugo's house from the street. His face was red, as though he'd spent a day on a boat, fishing perhaps. He was dressed in khaki pants and a tight, black T-shirt. He looked like he could stop an army.

Sheriff Webster pointed to his badge and then to the weapon holstered on the right side of the man's waist. "Ya got a permit for that?"

Without hesitating, the man produced a piece of paper from his shirt pocket and handed it to the sheriff, who checked and then returned it. "Ya work for Mr. White?"

The man nodded.

"I'm the sheriff, and I'm here to see Hugo Clerk. This is my deputy."

The man produced a walkie-talkie device from his left side, scrutinizing the two law enforcement officers as he announced their presence. "Send them in," came the reply.

Hugo, White, and a woman with short black hair were sitting in the area just off the kitchen. Hugo was reading the *Wall Street Journal*. White and the woman were scrolling through their cell phones.

"Sheriff," Hugo said, laying the *Journal*'s financial section on the coffee table nearby. "What brings you here? Any news of my brother?"

Out back, Deputy Pendry could see three others milling about as though on guard duty. He did a mental count. Hugo had six bodyguards, if you included the woman, who appeared strong enough to take down anyone who got in her way. He wondered if that would be enough protection against a band of determined criminals who had succeeded twice before.

"We got a letter delivered to us a few minutes ago. It claimed yer brother's alive and demanded ya pay the ransom in twenty-four hours—or else," Sheriff Webster said.

"They said Vic's alive? If there's proof or hope, I'll gladly pay the ransom. I don't know why, but I have the feeling he's dead. I'm reluctant to fork over two hundred million for nothing," Hugo said.

Deputy Pendry, sensing that Victor was about to be abandoned by his brother, decided it was time to speak up. "Excuse me, sir, but if there's any doubt, I think you should pay. And what about your wife? At some point, she could be a target if you don't cooperate."

He watched Hugo's face turn pink. He wondered if he should have kept his thoughts to himself, then saw the sheriff nodding.

"My deputy's correct. We could get help from the state experts, maybe the DEA guys, and bring the banks in to follow the money. These days, it's not so easy for criminals to move large sums around in secret. I think we wanna see proof yer brother's alive and arrange for his return before any transaction—"

"You think? *You* think?" Hugo blurted out, his face growing redder as he directed his ire at both the sheriff and his deputy. "You think I should put two hundred million dollars at risk on some piece of paper that claims my brother's alive after all this time? And some belief you have that my wife could be in more danger than she already is? Honestly, Sheriff, I haven't seen any evidence that your law enforcement skills merit any confidence on my part. You and your deputy have bungled this from the start. It was because of your incompetence that my brother and I were kidnapped and my wife nearly killed in the first place."

Hugo was now pacing. White and the woman exchanged looks that came close to surprise. Deputy Pendry wasn't sure how to react and looked to Sheriff Webster, who appeared unruffled by Hugo's criticism.

"I know you've been through a lot, but I can assure ya—"

"You can assure me of nothing," Hugo interrupted. The volume and tenor of his voice attracted the attention of one of the men standing guard at the back of the house. He glanced over his shoulder to see what was going on inside.

"Your job is to provide security for the residents of this island. For people like me, who bring money and prestige to this location and expect it to be a safe place for our families. You couldn't stop the bridge from being disabled or the cell tower from being blown up. You couldn't prevent my wife from being shot or my brother and me from being kidnapped in broad daylight. If you can't keep us safe, nothing else you do matters. Do you understand what I'm saying? You're worthless."

Hugo's face was fully red, the veins in his neck bulging. Deputy Pendry, taken aback, assumed that this display of temper was the result of the strain the man had been under. He saw Sheriff Webster straighten up and put his hand on his weapon. It seemed that he was also losing his cool.

"Under the circumstances, I think we've done as good a job as can be expected," Sheriff Webster said, obviously struggling to tamp down his anger. "No one can prepare for Armageddon. You wanted yer own security, and I agreed to that. If ya don't feel safe here, you can leave the island and return when ya feel comfortable again. No one's gonna stop ya. I suggest that's what ya do."

Deputy Pendry felt compassion for Sheriff Webster. He thought back to the tragedy of 9/11. If something like that couldn't be stopped, how did he and the sheriff have any hope of protecting people like the Clerks against a determined and apparently well-funded band of kidnappers who had used the element of surprise, just as the terrorists had done almost twenty years ago?

"That's exactly what I plan to do," Hugo said, folding his arms defiantly across his chest. "As soon as my wife returns from the hospital, we're flying out of here to Costa Rica. In the meantime, I'll decide what I want to do about the ransom payment. You can consider the kidnapping case closed. Finished. Goodbye."

Sheriff Webster narrowed his eyes. "You are not the law, Mr. Clerk. I'll decide when the case is settled. And as long as your brother is missing, the case is wide open," he said. He signaled to Deputy Pendry to follow him as he marched out the door.

"I'm calling the attorney general," Deputy Pendry could hear Sheriff Webster muttering as they strode down the street toward their vehicle. "Kidnapping's a felony whether Mr. Clerk wants to view it that way or not. His refusal to help us any further or follow our instructions could be an offense in itself." He glanced over at Deputy Pendry as they climbed into the car. "That asshole can't just dismiss us when a crime's been committed on our island, and possibly a murder. And who's going to pay for everything? The cell tower. The man hours. No, sir. We're not yokels."

CHAPTER 33

After downing breakfast at the restaurant across the street from the newspaper office, Wes was back on the blue bench next to the *Sun's* front door. He was scribbling on his notepad, trying to decide what to reveal to his readers through social media and what should run in next week's paper. It felt to him that a lot of news—most of it inaccurate—had already been spread through the local grapevine.

"When did you say the grocery's closing?" Wes asked when Randy came through the door and sat down beside him. He hadn't forgotten Randy's comment about needing cigarettes. The idea of having to drive off-island to pick them up at the nearest Publix was not something that appealed to him.

"Next week," Randy responded as he pulled his brown hair back into a ponytail and captured it with a rubber band. "I've been thinking about us getting Leslie and Gene together and continuing the search for Victor. I'm guessing the police are still looking, but a part of me feels like the authorities put him on the back burner once Hugo was discovered."

"Any thoughts about where you'd start?" Wes asked as he stuck his notebook in his shirt pocket and leaned back against the bench.

Randy shook his head and pursed his lips. "The sheriff called and told you that the kidnappers said Victor was still alive. They didn't say they had him. We know he's not underground, unless they buried him again, which is . . ."

"Highly unlikely," Wes said. "Especially with the alleged kidnappers babysitting Hugo."

"Yep, that's a real pisser, isn't it? Tough to figure that one out. Maybe White and that woman are just tourists like they claim to be." Randy fiddled with his beard for a few seconds, then waved away a mosquito buzzing around his head. "Changing the subject, we didn't have much in the paper about this today. What are your plans for next week?"

Wes shrugged and reached for a cigarette. "This whole thing's a shitstorm," he said, standing up and leaning against the railing to keep his smoke away from Randy. "I feel hinky about it. You know, suspicious. Dubious. This isn't your standard kidnapping—I'll give you that. But something else is wrong, and I can't put my finger on it."

"Did you tell Leslie about the latest ransom note and Hugo's reaction to it?"

"I did, and she's stumped like us. If the kidnappers are guarding Hugo, maybe it was sent to throw everyone off base. That was Leslie's theory. She's also still trying to figure out who owns Paraiso Island and if the LLC has any connection to the kidnappers."

"She'll come up with something soon. She always does," Randy said. "I think the best thing you can do is set up an interview with Hugo. Find out if he remembers something from his experience that might help his brother. I can use anything you discover to fill the hole I have on the front page. We still have to put out a newspaper every week."

Wes nodded. "I know, I know. I'll be surprised if Hugo wants to talk, but maybe he will. The answer's always no unless you ask." He gave Randy a pat on the back and strolled inside.

A female voice answered Hugo's cell phone. Wes was taken aback. "Patricia, uh, Mrs. Clerk?" he asked.

"This is Mary Smith." He thought the woman had a slight German accent but couldn't be sure. "How can I help you?"

"This is Wes Avery from the local newspaper, and I'd like to speak with Mr. Clerk. He knows who I am."

"He's very busy right now. I can take your number," the woman said.

"I need to speak with him. Now," Wes persisted. Whoever this woman was, he was not about to be stonewalled.

There was silence, and then Hugo's voice, sounding relaxed and friendly, came over the cell. Wes's immediate thought was that ignorance was bliss. The billionaire apparently was feeling comfortable among people that Wes was convinced didn't have his best interests at heart. It was scary, but at this point, there was nothing that could be done about it.

"Wes? Taking another trip? My plane will be available in a week or so."

"Thanks, Mr. Clerk. That's kind of you, but I'm not going anywhere for a while. Also, no word yet from *Architectural Digest*. Sometimes these things take time," Wes said, wanting to set a casual tone and then ease into the tough questions. Even with his brother missing and his wife in the hospital, Hugo sounded as though he was in a good mood.

"You wrote a beautiful article. Maybe they're waiting to do a beach-front edition."

"Could be," Wes said. "I know things are still up in the air, but I was wondering if you'd consider doing an interview about your harrowing experience. Word is out on the island, and people are interested in the security implications." He didn't want to say that people were interested because these days everyone was a voyeur wanting to get all the information they could about other people's lives. The more salacious the better. He remembered thinking that the newsfeed on his computer resembled the gossip rag *National Enquirer* in its heyday.

"I appreciate you asking. It's too early to do something on Victor and me. I told the sheriff when he dropped by that the kidnapping case was closed as far as I was concerned, but I haven't given up on finding my brother. I'm taking Patricia away as soon as she returns from the hospital. Same for Victor, if my men can find him. They're looking for him now, and I have a lot of confidence in them."

"Your men?" Wes asked, thinking that Hugo's response was very strange but not wanting to pressure him just yet. "I think the state and federal boys are also still searching."

"Uh, yes, but you know how that goes. I've hired a team of mercenaries recommended to me by Dan White. I feel they're more qualified than anyone around here. No offense meant to you and your friends."

Wes was too stunned to immediately comment. *The fox has expanded his territory,* he thought. He worried about the consequences for the Clerk family but knew he was helpless to do anything about it.

"Good luck to you," he said. "If they think they're getting close, I'd sure like to tag along and be there when the story breaks." When Hugo did not respond, he continued. "There's one more thing I want to share with you. It's about Victor's girlfriend."

"Ah yes, Billie. I hadn't given her a thought. She wasn't hurt when Vic was kidnapped, was she?"

Wes relayed the story of how Billie was discovered in Victor's safe room and her brief stay with Leslie. He mentioned that Billie had left the island for parts unknown, taking with her a substantial sum of money, a diamond ring, and some incriminating photos.

"What kind of incriminating photos?"

"The only reason I'm telling you this," Wes said, knowing he was now about to lie to Hugo and feeling no guilt about his reporter's bent toward manipulation, "is because I worry that before she left, Billie told a lot of other people what she shared with Leslie and me. You know how the word gets out on this island. I want you to be forewarned, especially since you weren't aware of what happened."

"Yes, yes, what is it?" Hugo asked, his voice reflecting his impatience.

"Well, she told us that your wife and Victor had a brief affair. That Victor was very sorry but kept photos of the two of them together. Nothing lewd. More like vacation snapshots of them holding hands."

Hugo was silent. Wes thought he was stunned and weighing his response. "Are we still connected?" he asked.

"Sorry. You reminded me of a sad period in my life. I was reflecting on what happened and thinking about how glad I was that it was resolved. Now you tell me that Billie has brought the whole thing up again. That's very sad for Patricia, Victor, and me. It was a mistake. When they admitted it to me shortly after it happened, I immediately forgave them. So you see, Billie was wrong. I knew."

"I'm glad I wasn't the bearer of bad news," Wes said, wondering about the conflicting stories.

"My wife is an extremely beautiful woman, and Victor was going through a tough time after his divorce from Sheila. I think Patricia felt compassion for him and his inner struggles, as I did. In a moment of weakness and pity, she let things go too far. They both realized immediately what they'd done, and it was over. Being family, we were able to put aside any hurt we might have had and reunite as though nothing happened."

It was Wes who was momentarily silent as he pondered how to respond. "You understand I won't print any of this. It's your private business and has nothing to do with the matter at hand," he said. "I can appreciate how hard it was for you. I remember when my wife left me for another man, I wanted to kill him. Then I realized that I was better off without her."

"My life would not be better without Patricia," Hugo said. "And I certainly had no intention of punishing my brother after it was over. I'm sorry you went through that. So, Billie left? Did she say where she was going?"

Wes was trying to figure out if he believed that Hugo had forgiven Victor and Patricia and moved on quickly from the affair when he responded. "Her note didn't have any details. Leslie might have a better handle on that. Billie stayed with her for a couple of nights."

Hugo laughed. "You know, if you're looking for the person who orchestrated the kidnappings—someone who had everything to gain and nothing to lose—you might think about the charming Miss Tsvetkov," he said. "Victor was planning on dumping Billie. She'd become tiresome and demanding. She always wanted more money. She grew up with nothing and was in pursuit of financial security. She told Vic that an old boyfriend of hers was, at one time, a mercenary in the Wagner Group. Maybe that's where the idea for this caper originated. Also, her native country is Bulgaria, which is one of the few remaining places into which you can transfer huge amounts of money, no questions asked."

Hugo paused. "Something for you to pursue with your good reporter's instincts. Sorry you didn't have this information earlier. Perhaps you could have stopped her before she left the island for parts unknown with my brother's money. And is now waiting for the ransom."

Shit, Wes thought. *Is Hugo on to something?* Who would suspect the scantily clad woman found dazed and confused in Victor's safe room? And why had she lied about Hugo's knowledge of the affair? If what Hugo was suggesting was true, cleaning out Victor's safe was a clever idea. It wasn't a stretch to believe that the beautiful young woman who already had a bagful of money would want even more. Wes couldn't wait to share the news with Leslie.

CHAPTER 34

Saturday, July 17, 9:20 a.m.: Day Six

Patricia was weary of her hospital bed, the questionable food, and the twenty-four-hour drip she had to drag with her to the bathroom several times a day. It had been five days since she had been shot, and Hugo had come to see her twice a day since he was discovered shaken but unharmed. He brought her flowers and professed gratitude that her life had been spared. A man he introduced as Dan White was always with him but said nothing.

"It's all my fault," he said on more than one occasion. "I shouldn't have sent everyone away. I thought you and I would be safe. There's no one on the island this time of year. How could I have known what those criminals had planned for us? I'm so sorry."

She asked about Victor only once. It was on the first day. Hugo told her he was still alive, but there was no further information, and he said that he didn't hold out much hope for his brother. When he gave her the news, it seemed to her that he was monitoring her reaction. For that reason and that reason alone, she held back the tears of worry she would normally have shed for a loved one in danger. Instead, she grasped and squeezed Hugo's hand as if her focus was on the pain he was enduring. Not her own or Victor's.

"I hope he'll be okay," she said. "No one should have to go through what the two of you have."

He seemed grateful for the answer and the lack of follow-up questions.

On the day Patricia and Victor had gone to him and told him about the affair, his initial reaction had been predictable: surprise, anger, hurt. But it was what had happened afterward that seemed odd to Patricia. Hugo never again mentioned their confession. His demeanor toward her remained just as it had been before her infidelity: solicitous and attentive. Some days, it felt like the silence and lack of comment about this indiscretion was worse than any punishment Hugo could have meted out to the two of them.

Then there were Victor's girlfriends. They came and went quickly, each a slap in the face. Each more of a punishment than the last. With Victor flaunting their vacuous beauty and, in Patricia's mind, diminishing what the two of them had confessed to each other—feelings they had shared for years and never acted on.

When Victor left and returned several months later with Billie, Hugo welcomed both of them into the family. Patricia also liked Billie's survivor mentality and spunkiness. She nicknamed her the Bulgarian Bitch, a moniker that Billie often used when referring to herself in Patricia's presence. In return, Billie called Patricia PP, for Patricia the Prude. It stemmed from an incident when the two women were shopping and Billie wanted to stop at a sex toy shop.

"I, uh, don't think I'm interested in anything like that," Patricia told her friend. "Hugo's fairly straitlaced. On and off. I'll leave the funky stuff to you and Victor and that mirror of his." She laughed when she said it, but the idea of Victor making love to someone else was painful. When Patricia saw signs that Billie and Victor's relationship was deteriorating, she was relieved and sad at the same time. Who would be next?

"Sweetie. How are you feeling?" Hugo's voice brought her back to the reality of her hospital bed. "I brought someone. He'll be accompanying you in the ambulance when you're released later today. His name is Leonid but you can call him Leo. He doesn't mind. Also, his English is acceptable unless you try to engage him in a lengthy conversation. He's armed for your protection. As long as those kidnappers are out there, we can't take any chances."

The man smiled and gave her a two-finger salute. Patricia nodded, sizing up her new bodyguard. He was significantly larger than Mick, who'd been with the Clerks long enough to be considered a member of the family but never invited to the dinner table. He was well over six feet, she guessed, and dressed in a white shirt and camouflage pants. His face was craggy—the lower half covered with bristle and the upper half dominated by bushy eyebrows. She wondered if Hugo would be able to track down Mick and ask him to return before his vacation ended or if she should try to get used to Leo's intimidating presence.

"The doctor told you I could go? I'm ready to get out of here." She laughed. "More than ready."

Hugo reached over and adjusted the pillow under his wife's head. "You're going to be recuperating in Costa Rica. I've already arranged for a nurse to meet us when we get off the plane this evening. If you have any medical issues, we can get you back here in a hurry."

Patricia felt a lump growing in her throat and struggled to keep the stinging in her eyes from manifesting into visible tears. *We're leaving the island without knowing what's happened to Victor? How can you do that to your own brother?*

"What about Victor and the ransom? Have you paid it?"

She couldn't read his face, although she was sure his expression changed ever so slightly from solicitous to . . . was it controlled anger? She had to ask about Victor. Not knowing was making her crazy. She'd been careful not to mention him since that first time, but any normal person would inquire about a missing family member. She wanted to scream at him, *For God's sake, don't abandon this man whom I love more than life itself.*

"Don't worry. We're still looking for him," Hugo said, the subtle annoyance in his expression disappearing into a sanguine smile. "By the way, I updated the boys on your condition today and convinced them to stay at camp for another month. They wanted to come home, but I arranged for them to work as counselors. I know you're missing them, but I think it's for the best for now."

Patricia tried to smile bravely, but it felt like everything in her life had spiraled out of her control, and she could only hang on and hope for the best.

CHAPTER 35

The Tarpon Bar was closing for a couple of months as it did every summer and offering a limited Saturday menu Leslie likened to a cleaning-out of the refrigerator before vacation. She ordered the creamy chowder with potatoes, corn, and a few bits of lobster. Her friend Deb Rankin, who managed the island's Gallery Centre where local artists displayed and sold their work, had the chicken pecan salad.

"You're telling me Wes thinks that Bulgarian woman had something to do with the kidnappings? Is he nuts?" Deb asked as she reached for the basket of rolls.

"As theories go, it has possibilities," Leslie said, crumbling a few oyster crackers into her soup.

Deb shrugged. "The woman volunteered to help out at the gallery. She was pretty, which was a plus for the older male artists and visitors. But when it came to being left on her own at an art show or reception, she was too easily distracted and didn't even do a good job of passing appetizers. She'd spot a good-looking guy and talk to him instead of working the crowd. I'm not criticizing her. Some people just don't have that talent, and Billie Tsvetkov did not. You told me she cleaned out Victor Clerk's safe. I can definitely see her doing that."

Leslie reflected on Deb's observation as she ate her soup, then moved on to what she really wanted to speak with her friend about. "I was at the county offices on Thursday, trying to find out who recently bought Paraiso Island. You heard anything about it?"

Deb shook her head, took a sip of iced tea and smiled at what Leslie thought must be fond memories. "Scooter and I like to fish there. Lots of sea bass, snook, and snapper in that area. We even had a sleepover one night when Scooter was feeling his oats and wanted something, um, different. We took our sleeping bags and hunkered down in that abandoned house. We lasted until 2:30 a.m., and then the bugs and the no-see-ums got to us. Too many broken windows. Shame, too, 'cause when they first built the house, it was nice out there. You find out who bought it?"

Leslie shook her head. "Not really. It's a limited liability corporation that's owned by another LLC. Super-secret stuff and no names of principals."

Deb laughed. "That's Florida for you. Full of intrigue, mystery, and the weirdest group of people you'll ever want to meet. I proudly include Scooter and myself in that category."

"Hardly," Leslie said, grinning. "You're interesting and fun, like so many of the people around here, and you know everybody. The names I'm looking for are Cain and Del. Any thoughts on who they might be?"

Deb motioned to the waitress that she wanted more iced tea, then tilted her head to one side as if considering Leslie's question. "There's Del, the artist from Mystic, Connecticut. Can't imagine him wanting to buy that old place, although it would make a great studio. Plus Michael Caine, the actor. I just saw an old movie of his on cable."

"Isn't his name spelled with an *e*?" Leslie asked, chuckling. "Imagine someone like him buying a scrubby island in Florida. Who in their right mind would want it? To do anything with it, you need plenty of gumption, a boat, an unlimited supply of money, and a reason."

Deb picked up her cell and punched in something Leslie couldn't see. "Here we go. Cain. First thing that comes up on the internet is Cain in the Bible," she said, turning the phone to show Leslie. "Cain was the oldest child of Adam and Eve. Says here Cain gave an offering to God, who wasn't pleased and preferred the present from his brother Abel instead. Cain was so jealous he murdered his brother. Your church doesn't preach the Old Testament, does it?"

Leslie put down her soup spoon. "I think it does. My mind strays now and then during the sermons, although that's a familiar story. Anyway, if Cain's dead brother was Abel, who was Del? That's one *l*, not two."

Deb scrolled on her phone. "An English baby name meaning 'valley'?"

"Look for Del in the Bible," Leslie said, grinning. "Let's stick with the Old Testament theme."

"How about Delilah? The woman who cut off Samson's hair and took all his strength. It popped up right away," Deb said triumphantly.

"I vaguely remember my mom taking me to see a movie about that when I was a kid."

"Don't you love the internet? Here's a nifty little story about the signs that someone in your life is a Delilah. She has the ability to pick up on your weaknesses and leverage them to get what she wants. She's not trustworthy and can twist every situation to make herself the victim. A Delilah nags a lot to get what she wants and uses your love for her against you. She tells you a secret and then torments you with the knowledge she's shared with you."

Leslie finished her soup, wiped her mouth with her napkin, and took a drink of water. "Not that I know her that well, but it does sound like Billie. Acting like she's a victim when she's actually the manipulator."

Deb scooped up the last bit of salad and excused herself to go to the restroom. "I think you might be barking up the wrong tree, but hold that thought."

Leslie paid for both lunches, all the while pondering what Deb had to say. Ruling Billie out completely because of incompetence seemed a risky thing to do. Hugo had told Wes that Billie had a Wagner mercenary for a former boyfriend. Maybe he was not only trained in combat but also in strategy. Then there was motive. Money was a factor, but Billie might also have wanted to get even with Victor for bringing her to America and then dumping her. Maybe she called the old boyfriend to set the wheels in motion. Then again, Hugo might have wanted revenge against Victor for having an affair with his wife. And was Patricia the devious Delilah? Wes had said Hugo sounded genuine about forgiving his brother and wife for the indiscretion, and the brothers continued to see each other socially after Victor and Patricia had confessed their sins to him. *I gotta get off this biblical kick,* she thought as she watched her friend strolling toward the table.

"Ready to go," Leslie said. "Let's take a little walk."

"In this heat? Are you crazy?"

"Don't be a wuss. I want to go by Hugo's place," Leslie said. "For inspiration."

"That's what I wanted to tell you," Deb said, grabbing her sunglasses out of her purse. "I wouldn't rule out Hugo. The desire for revenge is a powerful motivator."

"You think so?" Leslie said, nudging her friend. "While we're walking, I'll give you a bunch of reasons why I don't think Hugo masterminded these kidnappings. I'll start by asking why he would go to the trouble of going through a crazy kidnapping charade and extorting a hundred million dollars from himself? There must be an easier way to get even."

Because of the heat, Deb talked Leslie into using the gallery's red golf cart to drive by Hugo's mansion. The property was impressive, taking up the back corner of Laurel Street and spreading along the pristine beach for the length of at least two football fields, maybe more. Leslie had never been inside the restored home but had heard from Wes that it was beautiful.

"That's a creepy-looking guy standing by the entrance to the property," Deb said as she pulled up to the end of Laurel and parked by the guardrail that separated the road from a public beach. "You see how he glared at us?"

"Wes said Hugo hired some bodyguards. Don't worry. We're on public property."

Leslie stopped talking as she watched the man, who had a holstered gun around his waist, stride toward the two women. He wore a surly expression and a black T-shirt soaked through with sweat. His dark-green shorts stretched tight across his muscular legs. Leslie's first thought as he drew closer to the cart was that the man would benefit from a shower and, afterward, an attitude adjustment.

"What are you doing here?" he asked in a heavily accented voice, leaning in on the driver's side of the cart.

"Not that it's any of your business, but we're enjoying the view of the Gulf and having a friendly conversation," Deb said, scooting closer to Leslie.

Leslie cringed at her friend's cheekiness. This was not a man to be trifled with.

"Move on," he said, gesturing for her to turn the cart around and leave.

Deb reached for her cell phone and snapped several photos of the man, then began videoing him. "This is public property. Who are you to tell us we have to leave?"

Before Leslie could take any action to defuse the situation, the man had pulled Deb from the cart and was attempting to wrestle the phone from her hand. In response, Deb reared her foot back and gave him a kick in the shin. He grimaced, reaching for his leg, then smacked her across the face with the back of his hand, sending Deb and her phone to the sandy ground.

"No pictures," he growled as he moved menacingly toward the fallen woman.

Leslie hopped out of her side of the cart and snatched up a large, yellow flashlight Deb had attached to the back of the cart in case of an emergency. *This is definitely a disaster in the making,* she thought as she lunged toward the man and whacked him on the back of his head. He staggered, turned, and raised his arm toward her when Leslie heard a male voice yelling, "Stop! Back off!"

The man froze in place, rubbing the back of his head and making no attempt to hide his disgust at the order. Deb got to her feet with Leslie's help, dusted off the sand, then bent over to pick up her phone. The screen was cracked.

"You'll pay for this, jerkwater," she said, waving it in the armed man's face. She propped her leg on the cart and checked out her knee, reaching for a tissue in her pocket to dab at the blood.

Leslie turned to the muscular man with a large tattoo on his arm. Next to him was a woman with short dark hair.

"We were minding our own business, and this, this, uh, man attacked us," she said, trying to focus on the crisis at hand while realizing from Wes's descriptions that their rescuers were convicted killer Dan White and some unknown woman. Wes had said that Hugo had hired these people as bodyguards.

She watched White reach into his billfold and pull out at least twenty hundred-dollar bills and offer them to Deb, who was checking out her broken phone and muttering to herself.

"Sorry for any inconvenience. Our man here is trained to suspect everyone. He meant no harm. He just doesn't like having his picture taken," White said.

Deb started to say something, but Leslie interrupted. "This is a public roadway, and at sunset, it's going to be filled with people in golf carts, all with phones. He might want to stand behind the wall, not in front of it, during that time," she said. "The locals won't take kindly to some armed individual breathing down their necks as they watch the sun sink into the Gulf of Mexico. Not on this island."

White flashed what she read as a conciliatory smile in her direction. "The owners will be leaving soon for the season, so there won't be any more issues."

Deb, who had taken the money and stuck it in her purse, turned to Leslie as the two of them watched White and the woman disappear behind the wall that surrounded Hugo's home. The man with the gun resumed his post, all the while glaring at the two women.

"That was sure something," Deb said. "Attacked by a thug on a public street. I think he would have killed us if that other guy hadn't intervened. Luckily, I can still access my information."

Leslie was nodding but not really listening to her friend. *Leaving? Soon?*

"Could you drop me off at the newspaper office?" she asked Deb as they climbed back into the golf cart. "I need to run something by Wes."

"Sure thing. I'm off to the Verizon store. I've needed to upgrade my phone for a couple of years," she said. "I guess a scraped knee and a bruised cheek aren't too big a price to pay. But that guy's a menace to society."

Leslie sighed loudly. "Maybe next time you should ask before you start taking pictures of strangers. But since you have them, can you text them to me? I want to know why the guy felt so strongly about having his image captured. I'm guessing it wasn't because he didn't like the way his hair looked."

CHAPTER 36

Leslie bounded up the stairs and arrived at the newspaper office only slightly short of breath. Her morning walks had been slowed by the presence of Newton, whose stumpy legs could only carry him so far so fast—unless he spied a squirrel or an iguana. She wondered if her fitness level was deteriorating and hoped the same thing wasn't happening to her deductive instincts.

"Hi, everybody," she said, announcing her arrival to Helen, the receptionist, Sara, and Wes, who was leafing through the printed version of the *New York Times*. Randy appeared like magic from his work area, an expectant grin on his face.

"Wes, I need some sticky notes and your brain," she said. "Got a few ideas to toss around."

"You can use my back wall," Randy piped up, appearing eager to be included in any discussion that was about to take place.

"Great. I need you to print this photo for me," she said, sending Randy a text with a photo of Deb's attacker. Leslie marveled that it was crystal clear despite Deb being jostled about by her assailant. She'd moved quickly to capture his face. The video of him dragging her from the golf cart was too fuzzy to be useful.

"Who's this?" Randy asked, enlarging the picture with his fingers. "Reminds me of the tough guys we saw on the boat that day you got winged."

"He's one of the gatekeepers at Hugo's place. We had a little tussle with him, but Deb was able to grab this snapshot. Any chance you can send this to the sheriff to see if he's on a wanted poster somewhere?"

"Wanted poster?" Randy chuckled. "Do they still have those on post office walls?"

"Oh Randy, you know what I mean," Leslie said, blushing. "Guess who saved our butts, Wes? Dan White and some woman with dark hair, not a blonde. Curious."

Wes shook his head. "The sheriff was over there talking to Hugo, getting an earful about lax security, and saw the same woman. She said she was Mary Smith when I called to talk to Hugo."

A round of groans followed his statement. "So original," Randy said.

"Wig, Wes," Sara said. "It was probably the blonde you've been talking about in a wig."

Wes rolled his eyes and handed Leslie the sticky notes. She headed for Randy's area, followed by Sara and Helen.

"We have the victims—Hugo, Victor, and Patricia—on one side," Leslie said, writing their names and sticking them on the wall to the left. "Then we have a bunch of suspects, starting with Billie, Dan White, the lady with the braid, Rick, the two men Gene saw headed for Hugo's house, and the ones who kidnapped Victor."

"They could all be working together," Sara said. "I wonder who's in charge?"

"For fun, let's put Billie at the top of the suspects and say the others are working for her. Is Dan her former boyfriend?" Leslie said, moving Billie's name to the top of the group on the righthand side.

Wes shook his head. "I'm sorry. Billie's a gold digger, but I can't see her being the mastermind behind this. Besides, Hugo told me her former boyfriend was Russian, not ex-US military."

Leslie squinted at Wes, always ready to call him out for any signs of misogyny in his thoughts. "You're not saying she couldn't be in charge just because she's a woman, are you?"

"Never," he said a little too emphatically. "When it comes to evil, I'll concede that women are an equal-opportunity gender. But if she was about to get her hands on two hundred million, would she be worried about the chump change in Victor's safe?"

Leslie removed Billie's name and replaced it with White's.

"Definitely involved, along with his blonde friend," Wes responded. "He's smart enough to be the mastermind. But he's also military and good at following orders. I say he's in charge of the others in the gang but answers to someone higher up."

There was an affirmative murmur from the group. Leslie's eyes went from the suspect pile to the three victims. She reached out and put Patricia's name on top of the suspect group, moving White to one side.

"Whoa, that's a wild idea," Randy said. "Woman gets herself shot to look innocent while getting even with her ex-boyfriend and her husband for being rich assholes. You see that in movies a lot."

Sara, who had been quietly studying the list, spoke up. "I don't know, but I have the impression that Patricia could have died if Gene hadn't found her in time. I'd rule her out on that alone. There's a level of sophistication involved in that kind of planning that I don't think the average person has. She may not be average, but you know what I mean."

"I need some coffee," Wes said. "My brain has hit the afternoon lull, and you're making it work too hard."

Everyone laughed as Wes walked out of the room and returned a few minutes later with a large cup in his hand with printing that read *I'm sorry I offended you by using facts & logic.*

"What about Rick Howell? He's been at the bridge for several months now. He obviously worked out the plan to disable the structure. He wanted money for his father, and he knows Dan. The two of them could have figured this out together, with Rick being the brains and Dan being the brawn," Wes said.

Leslie moved the slips of paper around to comply with Wes's theory and then added a third category: *Motive*. She wrote down *money* and *revenge*, then stopped. She noted there was no support for the theory about Rick's level of involvement among the others, including herself. Her memory of seeing him at work was that he was the compliant type—not forceful enough for a leadership role.

"Moving on to Victor," Randy said. "He's still MIA, so it's difficult to figure out his story."

"Based on what you said, no one ended up getting buried alive, even though that was the big threat hanging over them, and the kidnappers made elaborate preparations for that to happen," Sara said. "You told me Hugo said he bought his way out of the ordeal. Victor's escape is a question mark. If he planned this, he wouldn't want to be buried. I say this is all his doing."

Helen nodded. "It sounds logical to me."

Leslie cleared her throat and moved Victor to the head of the suspects. "So, let me tell you about my lunch today." She shared her discussion with Deb about Cain, Abel, and Delilah. She was surprised that everyone in the office was familiar with the stories.

"Would someone be so arrogant as to name an LLC with such an obvious clue—one that involves brother against brother?" Wes asked. "That is, if he or she is involved in the kidnapping. Maybe there's no connection between the purchaser of Paraiso Island and the crime."

"Or maybe that was his or her little joke. Buy the land, knowing what the plan was, and play a game of cat and mouse. It's like when an author writes a book and sticks references in it that only she or he understands," Leslie said.

There was a collective shaking of heads.

"And Del could be Delilah, also a manipulative female from the Old Testament," Leslie added, reaching over and moving Billie's name back to the suspect pile, putting it next to Victor's name. She stood back as if seeking input from the others.

"Now I'm the one who needs coffee," Sara said, scratching her head. "With maybe a dash of whiskey in it."

Wes got up and added two sticky notes under the category that said *Motive*. One read *Hugo*, the other, *Victor*.

"You're right. Each had motive and the wherewithal to set this up," Leslie said. "Victor likely felt cheated out of the woman he loved and slighted by his father on the money end, if we can believe Billie. And Hugo could be consumed with the idea of revenge."

"Which one?" Wes asked.

"I'm still convinced it wasn't Hugo. But there's one person who could have the answer," Leslie said. "He just doesn't know it."

CHAPTER 37

Now that the search for Victor or his body was in the hands of the Fish and Wildlife rangers, the state police, and possibly the FBI, Gene Miller had returned to his job of reducing the island's iguana population. He had killed about nineteen reptiles on various properties and decided to head out to Victor's mansion to finish the job he had started before he was so rudely dismissed. Even if Victor never resurfaced, his island retreat was the perfect breeding ground for the pesky reptiles.

He followed the tire tracks that circumvented Victor's locked gate through small ornamental grasses and drove down the path to the waterfront mansion. He stopped now and then to pick off an easy target. *Blam!* One shot, one lizard. Before he reached the massive structure, he had nailed at least six of the critters. He could leave without any guilt and come back tomorrow. But he was there and still had plenty of ammo, and his motivation to do away with the pests was strong following the events of the last several days.

He parked his vehicle by the front entrance, then traipsed through the thick landscaping until he arrived at the pool. He immediately saw five iguanas sunning themselves on the deck like guests at a party. They were big ones and apparently didn't hear him coming. He could nab one easily. The others would scatter the minute he got off the first shot, but there was nothing he could do about that. He gauged his target, putting his sights on the daddy of the group. *Blam!* The creature squirmed for a few seconds, then stopped moving. His preference was to kill them immediately so that there was no suffering. He chided himself for not being a better marksman.

"Is that you? The iguana guy? Oh my God, it is." The voice came from the direction of the pool house, a smallish building with two glass doors and no windows.

Gene turned around and was so startled to see Victor Clerk running toward him that he nearly lost his balance and fell into the pool. "Jesus! You all right?" Gene gasped, catching himself at the last minute.

The man whom he'd last seen wrapped in a towel and arrogance was cowed. He bore bruises from what Gene assumed was a beating. He was unshaven and scruffy. His shoulders slumped. His gait was unsteady. Victor threw his arms around the iguana hunter and began crying unashamedly, his head against Gene's chest.

"It's okay. Pull yourself together," Gene said, unsure how to handle the embrace. He patted Victor on the back like a father comforting an upset child. "We've been looking for you—me and some others were part of a search party. I'm real happy to see you're alive."

The younger Clerk brother, who was two inches taller than his sibling, let loose of Gene. "I've been hiding here for the last two days, sneaking into the house for food at night, then sleeping in the pool house. I didn't want anyone to know I was here. What if the kidnappers discover I'm no longer buried and come back for me? I'm afraid to leave. Where can I go to get away from them? There's no safe haven for me."

As Victor fell silent, Gene did a quick check of the surroundings. The kidnapping victim was right. They were no longer in friendly territory. They needed to seek cover.

"Do you know anything about my brother and sister-in-law? Anything at all?" Victor asked.

"Why don't we go inside? We'll be safer there, and I'll tell you what I can," Gene said, trying to sound comforting, all the while wondering what the best course of action might be. Leaving Victor in the house with the kidnappers running loose was not an option. Should he encourage Victor to come with him to the sheriff's office? Or take him to his own home until things were resolved? He was stumped.

"Sit here," Gene said once they were inside and in a lower-level room that couldn't be seen from the outside. "You need something to drink? Water? A beer, if you've got any?"

"I'm fine. Help yourself. There's hard stuff in the bar. Tell me about Patricia and H. Are they still alive?"

"The missus is in the hospital but is gonna be okay. I found her. She was in pretty bad shape, but the clinic doctor saved her. Your brother escaped by buying off one of his kidnappers, the sheriff told me. He's back in his house."

"Alone? Is his bodyguard, Mick, back from vacation?"

Gene didn't dare tell Victor what Wes had said—that Hugo had hired the very people suspected of kidnapping him to be his protectors. "I can't say. Wes Avery, the reporter from the *Sun*, is my point of contact. He told me your brother contracted with someone to provide protection. You want me to call Wes and tell him I found you?"

Victor hesitated, then shook his head. "I'm scared to let anyone know, even Hugo. You said you discovered Patricia and then were part of a search party. After how I treated you that day when you came to get rid of the iguanas, why would you care what happened to me and my family? I was an asshole—and for no good reason."

"I was plenty pissed, I have to say," Gene said, chuckling. "But that doesn't mean I wanted something bad to happen to you. Underneath all that privilege baggage you carry around, I figure you're an okay person. Just trying to make it through this world the best way you can, like me."

"Oh God, you're so right," Victor said, dissolving into tears again.

As he waited for Victor to pull himself together for the second time, Gene checked his phone and noticed three missed calls from Wes. When he tried the service, he got no response. He wasn't about to leave Victor alone, but he also wanted to respect the man's wishes to keep his resurrection a secret for now.

"I gotta find a place where my cell phone works, if that's possible," Gene said. "Let's get you a cap and sunglasses—hide your face as best we can—and you can come with me. I'm happy to take you to my house. You can sleep in my son's bedroom. Or maybe you'd prefer a hotel?"

"I have no money," Victor said. "The woman who was living with me took everything from my safe and must have done something with my billfold, which has my credit cards. I'm not sure where it is or what happened to my dogs."

Gene chuckled at what he knew was going to be a moment of irony. "That's okay. I can loan you a couple of bucks. Your dogs are safe at the fire station."

"Thank you, thank you. I'll stay in your boy's room if that's okay."

Gene nodded, hoping Victor didn't start crying again.

Near the post office by the temporary cell tower, Gene got four bars. "Sorry, my phone wasn't working," he said before Wes could say hello. "Hold on.

"Can I tell him?" Gene mouthed to Victor, who shrugged as if to signal acceptance that his life was in the iguana hunter's hands. "You're not gonna believe who's sitting next to me: Victor Clerk."

There was a few seconds of silence on the other end. "I'm dumbfounded," Wes finally said.

"Yeah. It's a long story. He's okay but traumatized, obviously. I'm gonna take him home with me until we can figure out what else to do. He doesn't want the sheriff told just yet. He doesn't want anyone to know he's okay."

"With the kidnappers still out there, I get that. But I have a big favor to ask before you head off the island," Wes said. "You think you'd recognize the two men you saw coming onto the beach the day of the kidnapping? I thought we could check out the bodyguards at Hugo's."

Gene hesitated. "I guess so. I'm not a hundred percent sure. If you stuck them in a lineup, I might be able to tell them from the others. You're not expecting me to knock on the front door and ask to speak to them, are you?"

Wes laughed. "Hardly. This'll require reconnaissance. I'm texting you a photo of a bodyguard in case he was one of the two men you saw."

"I'm up for doing that. Maybe Leslie can watch over Victor. See you shortly," Gene said, agreeing to meet Wes in thirty minutes at the church near Hugo's home.

Gene contemplated several possible scenarios and decided that using his golf cart would give him more flexibility. He also wanted to pick up additional ammunition at the county office, where he kept his stash locked up, along with an extra rifle. He remembered Wes had turned down the use of a gun before, and he guessed Victor wasn't a big fan of them. But it made him feel better to have a backup weapon nearby. In the heat of a potential battle and when threatened, anyone could become a soldier.

When Wes's text came through, Gene nodded knowingly. He was sure this was one of the men he saw—or a close relative.

Victor rode silently with a blank expression on his face and no sign that he wanted to engage Gene in conversation. Gene wondered what was going through his mind. He had all the money anyone could possibly want, and still, his life had turned to crap. He'd been beaten and kidnapped, buried, managed to escape, and now felt like a hunted man. Gene had his family. Who did Victor Clerk have to make him feel loved?

When they switched to the golf cart, Victor yanked his cap down tightly, pulled his shirt collar up around his neck, and slumped down into the seat. A few minutes later, when they saw Wes and Leslie waiting by the church steps, he shocked Gene by announcing he was going with him to Hugo's home. "I haven't seen the faces of the kidnappers, but if they're holding my brother hostage, I'm not going to hang out with some female while you and the reporter do my dirty work," he said.

Gene's expression registered amazement mixed with admiration. "Your call," he said.

Leslie also protested being left behind until Gene came up with what she decided was a good idea. She and Wes could monitor the Clerk property from their vantage point at the church a block away and alert the deputy if there was any indication things weren't going well.

"This is a fact-finding mission, like I said, isn't it?" Wes asked, scanning the two rifles and boxes of ammunition in the back of Gene's golf cart. "Or are we preparing for all-out war?"

Gene grinned, then shot a glance at Victor. "Hard to say, but at this point, we're ready for both. I think."

Gene took off, turning the cart onto a property two houses down from the Clerks'. Victor was leaning forward and staring like a dog on the scent of a squirrel. Gene was feeling like he was back in Iraq on a mission against the enemy, although he didn't recall seeing golf carts in the Middle East.

They cut through the side yard, as Gene had done on previous occasions when he was in pursuit of reptiles on the property. He knew exactly where to park the cart so that it would be out of sight of the so-called bodyguards. There were several stands of ornamental grasses and flowering bushes the two men could use for cover. Beyond that, there were people on the beach resting under their umbrellas, providing a diversion. Someone had pitched a large cabana. Gene saw those people as helpful cover in his pursuit of his objective. He hoped that if things went south, they would have the good sense to get out of the way.

From their vantage point, Gene could see one of the bodyguards sitting under the pergola where he had discovered the bloody Patricia. His massive bulk covered most of the lounge chair. There was a glass on the table next to him and a bowl of something that Gene guessed were peanuts, which the man was downing as though he hadn't eaten for a while.

"You know this guy?" he asked, handing the binoculars to Victor.

"Fucking son of a bitch," Victor growled as he leaned into the shrubbery and adjusted the lenses to get a better look.

"That's a yes, right?" Gene asked. "Let me take a look . . . Yep, it sure looks like one of the guys I saw on the beach. Here comes someone else."

Victor snatched the binoculars from Gene. "Him, too. I know these assholes. Not so much by their faces but by their overall builds. It has to be them. How could my brother be so stupid? Dammit!"

Victor kept adjusting the binoculars and moving them about, totally absorbed in what was happening. It appeared to Gene that the more he saw, the more it felt like Victor was going to suddenly explode—like a cartoon character whose face turns bright red and smoke shoots out of his ears. Alarmed at what this could mean for their mission, Gene stood up and touched Victor's arm gently so as not to startle him.

"Easy does it. I know you hate these guys, but let's not do something foolish . . . and dangerous."

Victor turned to Gene; his face twisted in rage. "My brother's being 'guarded' by the same men who wanted to bury us alive. He has to know who they are. He must recognize them and feel powerless to do anything about it. We have to help him. Now! Give me your other gun! I'm going in shooting. I don't care what happens to me."

Gene remembered being in Iraq when the enemy had been nearby. Some of the young soldiers next to him had become crazed with an adrenaline-fueled lust for battle. You had to hold them back, urge them to follow orders, or things could quickly go wrong. He didn't know how many kidnappers were involved, where Hugo was, and whether he was in danger. He had to prevent Victor's anger from taking control and putting everyone at risk.

"Steady," Gene said, squeezing Victor's arm to signal that he was in charge. "Before we do anything, let's see what happens. Maybe others will join this little pool party. We want all of the bad guys out in the open." *Like maybe Dan White,* he thought as he watched the muscular ex-soldier emerge from behind the French doors, say something Gene couldn't hear, and then distribute cigars to the others.

"Oh God, it's her," he heard Victor say, then put the binoculars to his face again. Gene wished they'd brought a second pair as he watched Victor's face flush. Was he starting to cry again? The man's emotional range seemed limited—from sad to even sadder, mad to even madder. Maybe it was to be expected. It was obvious to Gene that Victor knew the woman with the long blonde braid who had now joined the others on the patio. Gene watched her strip off her clothes and dive into the pool, her every move scrutinized by the other three. *Damn, she's got a good body,* he thought.

He heard her yell, "Come on in—the water's nice, not too hot!"

One of the men pulled off his T-shirt, but White held up his hand as if to say no.

"Oh, come on," she taunted. "We're all friends here."

White shut it down again with a shake of his head.

"Fuck me," Victor said when a fifth person joined the crowd. He was wearing sunglasses, a man's straw fedora, white linen slacks, and a Miami-style, crème-colored shirt. He looked like he owned the world.

"Rico Suave," one of the men said loud enough for Gene to hear. "You got a hot date tonight?"

"Escorting my beautiful wife to Costa Rica," Hugo said, accepting the cigar White handed him, biting off the end, and pulling a gold Zippo lighter from his pants pocket. "Gather 'round, boys and girl."

The blonde emerged from the pool, wrapped herself in a towel, and joined the others in pulling up chairs to hear what Hugo had to say. Gene looked over at Victor, who was glued to the binoculars watching the group's every move, and wondered if he could read lips.

A sick, uneasy feeling had entered the pit of Gene's stomach when he saw Hugo emerge from the house. He couldn't shake it, and he knew the reason why. He didn't know how to break it to Victor. It was obvious from the manner in which he conducted himself that Hugo was not the helpless victim of a group of money-hungry mercenaries. No, from what Gene could see, there was no longer any question. Hugo Clerk was the man in charge. The mastermind.

Victor slowly handed the binoculars back to Gene. The knowing look he gave the iguana hunter said he had come to the same conclusion. "Let's go. We have to save Patricia from this evil fucking son of a bitch that is her husband and my brother."

CHAPTER 38

Leslie was sitting with Wes on the church steps, wondering how the so-called reconnaissance expedition was going when she caught sight of Gene and Victor speeding their way in the golf cart.

"Do we have any idea how Victor managed to escape his captives?" Leslie asked Wes, feeling pity for the pathetic figure who was now part of their team. "And why he doesn't want anyone to know he's been found?"

Wes shrugged. "All will be revealed in a few minutes," he said, pulling out a phone and snapping a picture as the two men approached. "I can already see the headline: *Iguana Hunter Saves Kidnap Victim.*"

"You can do better than that. Something catchier," Leslie said, chuckling, then wondered why it felt like she was making light of a bad situation.

When the two emerged from the cart, Leslie sensed something was very wrong. Maybe neither man could identify the kidnappers and they were now back to square one. The good news in that case would be that Hugo was safe and well protected.

"What is it?" she asked Gene.

He let out a heavy sigh. Victor whispered something that sounded like, "You tell them."

Gene said, "We saw at least four people and a woman that Victor was sure were the kidnappers and—"

Victor interrupted, "My fucking brother. He was talking to them like they were buddies, not acting like some helpless victim. Smoking a cigar and giving them instructions on what was going to happen next. We should have shot him, Gene. Killed the fucker on the spot. Oh yeah, he was going to save me by giving them another hundred million. He was willing to take my place and be buried alive first. That's what he said. He even cried for me. All laughable. And to think I bought into his bullshit."

Gene was nodding. "Like Victor said, it was pretty obvious who was in charge, and it wasn't the kidnappers-turned-bodyguards crew."

"Unbelievable! What a shocker!" Leslie said. "We have to go to the sheriff!"

"Not so fast," Wes said, running his fingers through his hair. "I heard Hugo deny ever having seen Dan White when I was in the sheriff's office. That's when he hired White to be his bodyguard. If Hugo's behind this, all he has to say is that Victor's wrong—confused or suffering from trauma. These guys resemble thousands of other tough guys, no one's been killed, and both brothers are safely home. The sheriff told me that Hugo already said he's not paying the ransom and, in his mind, the kidnapping case is closed."

"Was Rick Howell one of the men on the patio?" Leslie asked.

"Didn't see him," Gene said.

"How about a woman?" she added.

Gene nodded, but it was Victor who spoke up. "Lilith," he said. "She saved my life. She couldn't stand me being buried alive, even though she thought I'd survive. She got me out of the box; we covered it with sand so that no one would know. She said she would play dumb if they discovered I was gone. Then she told me to go to the north end of the island and stay put."

Leslie and Wes took seats again on the church steps and focused on Victor's story. Gene, standing by the back of the cart, opened the cooler and pulled out a beer.

Victor continued. "I found my way there and waited for her. I kept wondering if this was some additional torture my kidnappers had dreamed up: They would give me hope and then snatch it away from me, just like the night I tried to escape on my own. But shortly after dark, she showed up in one of those rubberized boats with a motor. In the moonlight, she was beautiful. I don't think I've ever wanted a woman more. She took me back to my place and told me to lay low for a couple of days. She said she heard that the boss was satisfied that the mission was accomplished. I never knew what she meant until today."

Wes started to say something, but Leslie interrupted. "She meant that Hugo thought you were history. Is that right?"

"Yes, I'm sure of it," Victor said. "Dead and buried was what he wanted. Maybe he was content to know that I was suffering, even if he wasn't sure I was dead yet."

"Jeez, and he's your brother," Gene said.

"This is probably going to shock you. Patricia and I had an affair after we realized we'd been in love for a long time. We couldn't stop ourselves after all the years of longing. I'm not proud of that, but I thought Hugo had forgiven us and we'd all moved on. What Hugo didn't know is that after our father died, I had the books examined, along with the will that our attorney, Farrell Rogers, drew up. It's taken the investigators a while, but they informed me recently that Hugo and Farrell colluded against my interests. My father wanted his money to be divided equally. Instead, Hugo got the lion's share, and the attorney got a big chunk, too. Farrell has no scruples; he'll do anything for money. It was hard for me to believe that Hugo would do something like that. It feels like I've never really known him."

Victor took a drink from the water bottle Leslie handed him. "No one needs as much money as we have. We can't even begin to spend it. That's one of the reasons I didn't go after more. Today, looking through those binoculars at that smug bastard ordering around men twice his size,

I realized Hugo won't be satisfied until he's taken everything from me, including my life."

Leslie felt goose bumps pop up on her arms. Victor's tale was a chilling one that matched its biblical precursor: the son who worked hard for his father's love and watched in pain while it was given to his brother. Then the loss of his wife's affection to this same rival. It had been more than Hugo could take. Leslie stood to put a comforting arm around this man she barely knew, realizing that she also had a nagging worry about what was going to happen next to someone else.

"If he feels that way about you," she said, "what are his plans for Patricia?"

Because they were trying to keep Victor under wraps while they executed their latest rescue plan, Leslie set him up in one of the church's Sunday school classrooms with Gene's extra county cell phone and a few instructions. His job was to call the hospital to try to find out when Patricia would be released and if she was coming by ambulance, then text that information to Wes. He was also to contact Cap Collier to see if the bridge tender was willing to help waylay an ambulance that could be arriving at any time. No one had Cap's number, but Leslie suggested leaving an urgent message at the office. Wes thought approaching Cap was a long shot but was persuaded to have Victor inquire. Finally, Victor was to get in touch with someone at the private airport nearby to confirm Hugo's scheduled departure time for Costa Rica. Victor often made his own travel arrangements on the family plane, he told Leslie, so he felt comfortable quizzing airport personnel, who likely didn't know that he had been kidnapped.

"Do the best you can, Victor," Leslie said. "We're counting on you." She thought he was okay with his assignments, but it was obvious Victor was still shaken by the revelation about his brother. There was no telling what was going through his mind.

Gene's task was to park his vehicle by the entrance to the airport and watch for the arrival of Hugo and his entourage. That was the stopgap measure in case Wes and Leslie were unable to intercept Patricia's ambulance.

Leslie wanted to include Sheriff Webster or at least Deputy Pendry in the plans, but neither answered their phones. She couldn't be sure if it was because of the spotty service or if both were busy. She and Wes decided they would check in later with law enforcement.

When they arrived at the bridge in Wes's SUV shortly after 3:00 p.m., Cap was sitting on the bench, waiting for them. He got up the minute they pulled into the parking lot and approached the car. Leslie was grateful that Victor had somehow gotten ahold of him. She lowered her window to say hello and could see that he was uneasy about this second encounter.

"I talked to the other guys about this. They don't feel comfortable trying to stop an ambulance. That violates all the rules," he said, fanning himself with a piece of paper.

"If it doesn't have the siren on, maybe you can direct it to one side. All we need is a few minutes to check on Mrs. Clerk's well-being. Maybe get her out of the back and into our vehicle. This is a matter of life and death," Leslie said, trying to calm the nervous man while downplaying his involvement.

"If you do something like that and I help, I could lose my job," he said, glancing nervously toward the office. "Does this have something to do with Mark Foxx?"

"Yes and no." Leslie hesitated. It was clear that Cap was a bundle of nerves, not really wanting to rock the boat or create problems for himself. She was sympathetic. He'd worked at the bridge for a long time but always faced the possibility that the wrong word or some idle gossip about him would get him fired. She had heard that it had happened before to a beloved tollbooth worker and never understood why.

"I can see you aren't comfortable, and that's all right. Wes will check with the people in the office. Thanks for waiting for us," she said. Even without asking, she knew the bridge office would be a dead end. Without some involvement from the sheriff or his deputy, the administrators would not support their plan to rescue Patricia and, if anything, would vehemently discourage any attempt to stop an ambulance.

"It looks like we're on our own," Wes said as they watched Cap limp over to his car and drive away.

"He's a nice man, but I think this has all been too much for him. I can't blame him for not wanting to get involved," Leslie said. She checked her phone to see if Victor had left them a message and found nothing.

They waited around for another half an hour and were getting ready to leave for the airport when they saw a white vehicle with the word *ambulance* written backward on the hood turn onto the road that led to the causeway. There was no sense of urgency on the part of the driver. His siren was silent, and his pace was slower than the speed limit. Leslie could see him talking on his cell phone and assumed he was alerting Hugo that they would be at the mansion shortly.

Leslie left the car, positioned herself by the side of the road, and at the opportune moment stepped out onto the street, frantically waving her arms. Wes moved quickly to the bench where Cap liked to sit and slumped down slightly as though not feeling well.

When the ambulance driver slowed at her insistence, then stopped, Leslie ran up to his window and did her best job of appearing alarmed. "Are you an EMT? My friend over there's having chest pains. Do you mind checking him out?"

The driver eyed her skeptically. "I'm on a run. I can call another ambulance."

"Please! My friend could be having a heart attack. Isn't it your responsibility to save lives if you can?"

He sighed, pulled the ambulance to the side of the road, grabbed the bag on the front seat, and exited the vehicle, heading for Wes, who was clutching his chest.

Leslie waited until the driver was engaged with the reporter, then slipped around to the back of the ambulance and yanked open the door. Looking out at her was Patricia, an attractive blonde in a wheelchair with a blanket over her lap. Sitting across from her on a stool, his back against the vehicle wall, was a man in his forties with a grizzled face. He was twice Leslie's size. Both of them seemed surprised to see her.

"Are we home?" Patricia asked warily.

"Uh, no. I'm with the bridge office. Um, we got a call about a suspicious ambulance headed this way and were asked by law enforcement to detain . . ." As Leslie stuttered and struggled to come up with a good excuse for intercepting the vehicle, she wondered why she and Wes hadn't considered the possibility that one of the kidnappers would be accompanying Patricia on the ride home. ". . . detain you until, uh, someone from the sheriff's office could be notified and, uh . . ."

The bodyguard got up quickly from the stool, hopped off the back of the ambulance, and faced Leslie, towering over her. "I don't think so," he said in a heavily accented voice. "Mrs. Clerk is coming from the hospital. We need to get her home now."

Leslie searched for a response that might intimidate the mountainous figure. "We can always call the sheriff," she announced, which seemed like the right thing to say. "He could be here in a few minutes. I'm sure you won't mind waiting. It's probably not a big deal."

"You call your sheriff. By the time he gets here, we'll be gone," the man said defiantly.

"It's okay, Miss," Patricia said, rearranging the blanket on her lap. She was wan. Without makeup, she appeared older than in the photos Billie had shown Leslie and Wes. "I'd really like to get home to my husband and my own bed. If the sheriff wants to stop by our place for any reason, he's welcome. I hope you understand—Leo and I aren't trying to be difficult."

Home is not where you want to go, Leslie thought, growing increasingly frustrated with her inability to halt the forward progress of Hugo's potentially murderous plot. Neither she nor Wes was armed or any match for the man in the back of the ambulance. There was no time to give Patricia a convincing argument about her precarious position. And even if the woman agreed to leave the ambulance and seek protective custody with Wes and Leslie, her bodyguard was not going to allow that to happen.

"What's going on here?" the ambulance driver asked as he approached the vehicle and saw Leslie speaking with his passengers. "I checked out your friend. His blood pressure's a little elevated, but he's okay. Probably a reaction to the heat. Sorry, but we gotta go. We're running late."

"Thanks for your kindness," Leslie said, relieved that he didn't question her further but also upset that she and Wes had failed in their attempt to rescue Patricia from possible harm.

"Well, that didn't work, did it?" Wes said when Leslie climbed into the front seat of his vehicle and slammed the door shut.

Leslie shook her head. "Dammit, one of the kidnappers was doing ride-along guard duty. There was no way he was going to let us take her, and in her state, she wouldn't have been inclined to go with us anyway. She doesn't know us from Adam, and it's doubtful that she would have bought our story. If I think really hard about it, it's even tough for me to believe."

"Why's that?" Wes asked, appearing surprised.

She paused for a minute as if collecting her thoughts. "Oh, I'm still not convinced Victor was telling us the truth. Both of these brothers are an enigma, not to be trusted. In my opinion, neither one is free from guilt in this odd situation. Luckily, no one has died. Yet."

CHAPTER 39

En route to the sheriff's office, they stopped by the church to pick up Victor and found he had disappeared without leaving a note or any indication as to where he'd gone. Leslie hoped he wouldn't try something foolish, like confronting his brother and attempting to save Patricia on his own. She assumed he had more sense than that but couldn't be sure.

A quick call to Gene confirmed that all was quiet at the airport. "Nothing happening yet, but there are a hell of a lot of iguanas on this property," he said, chuckling. "If only I had permission, I could clean this place up pretty quick."

Leslie laughed for the first time that day. "Hopefully you won't be shooting anything or anyone, but it's best that you stand by and save your ammunition. I'm guessing the Clerk plane will be taking off before dark. They've got about five hours of daylight left."

As Wes sped down the main road into the village for the sheriff's office, Leslie noticed there were at least two temporary cell towers on the island and pointed them out to him. She was glad to see the progress but worried that it could take months, maybe longer, before the primary tower was replaced, with no guarantee that service would improve.

"Where's the sheriff?" Wes asked as he and Leslie entered the office to find Deputy Pendry alone again, organizing a stack of papers in his inbox.

He shook his head. "He's at the dentist getting a root canal. What now?"

"The good news is that Victor Clerk's been found," Wes said. "The bad news is that we've lost him again. This time by his own choice, we think."

"I'd better alert Fish and Wildlife so that they can call off the search of the islands around here. Where was he?"

"Hiding in his house. Gene found him there. He seems to be okay, just frazzled from his experience, but who wouldn't be?" Wes said. "We're concerned about what he might do next, but it feels like we have a bigger problem on our hands than him."

He explained how Gene and Victor had gone to Hugo's house on a recon mission to check out the bodyguards and confirm that they were, in fact, the kidnappers.

"How can that be?" Deputy Pendry asked, his eyes growing wide. "Hugo said he'd never seen that White fellow before."

"We are ninety-nine percent positive he was lying," Leslie said. "And you're not going to believe this, Alex, but we think Hugo is the mastermind behind this whole scenario: the kidnapping of him and his brother and the hiring of the band of thugs to help him carry out his plan. What he didn't anticipate is that one of the kidnappers, the woman with the blonde braid, would take pity on Victor while he was entombed under the sand and release him."

"Wow. Why would he want to kidnap and torture his brother?" Deputy Pendry asked, looking like a ten-year-old eager to learn the facts of life.

"Seems like his brother had an affair with his wife, and Hugo was nursing bad feelings about it," Wes said, nodding as if to affirm that jealousy was an age-old reason for criminal activity.

"And I'm pretty sure that it was Hugo who purchased Paraiso Island so that he would have an out-of-the-way place to stage his revenge tableau. He must be Cain and Del LLC. I don't have any proof because the state of Florida protects the names of the people who own limited liability corporations, but it makes sense. We're also worried that he may now want to harm his wife."

Deputy Pendry shook his head. "Sorry, but I'm having a hard time buying that story. Mr. Clerk seems like a real nice fellow, and he's done a lot for this island. What evidence do you have?"

"None," Leslie said. "Except for Gene and Victor, who identified the people involved in the kidnapping—the ones who are now at Hugo's house. And by applying the duck test."

Deputy Pendry raised his eyebrows and mouthed, "Duck test?" Wes laughed.

"I'm sure Wes has used this before in his reporting: if it looks like a duck, swims like a duck, and quacks like a duck, then it probably is a duck," Leslie said. "There is overwhelming circumstantial evidence that Hugo planned all of this for revenge. Maybe it wouldn't hold up in court, but still."

The deputy hesitated, then nodded. "Okay. I'm convinced. We gotta do something. Call the sheriff. Go to the house and arrest Mr. Clerk. Something."

"Hugo's got a small army of mercenaries protecting him," Wes said, as the deputy reached for his cell phone. "We don't have the manpower to do anything on the island, but apparently, he's planning on flying out shortly on his private plane. I know he wants to take his wife, who's home from the hospital, but I'm not sure who else. Leslie and I think he's planning on doing away with Patricia in the tropics. If we can recruit our own militia to meet him at the airport, maybe we can stop him there."

Deputy Pendry was able to reach Sheriff Webster, who was still in the dental chair, and share this latest information with him. When he hung up, he explained that the sheriff would meet them at the airport and also contact Sheriff Lake in the adjoining county for additional help. Deputy Pendry was going to call Ray Santiago, the fireman, to see if he wanted to be part of the group. "It can't hurt to have as many bodies as possible," he said, "including the iguana hunter, if we know where he is."

"That's easy. He's already on the site," Wes said, "and has his guns and ammo with him."

CHAPTER 40

The off-island airport had two large hangars and an administration building that Wes remembered as luxurious for a small, local field. The one drawback was that there was no control tower, which meant that flying in and out after dark could be tricky. Wes remembered having dinner at Leslie's when the noise from a descending small jet was so close, they looked at each other as if questioning whether they should dive for cover.

The Clerks' jet was parked just off the runway, apparently ready for takeoff whenever the passengers arrived. One of the pilots was doing what looked to be a last-minute check of the outside of the aircraft. Wes remembered his recent excursion to Panama and how the young hostess, Sandy, had wined and dined him as he relaxed in a posh leather seat and enjoyed luxury he could never afford on a reporter's salary. *Those days are over,* he thought. He was sorry—not so much for missed extravagances but because his friend Hugo had turned out to be one of the bad guys. He still found it difficult to believe.

"What's the plan?" Gene asked when everyone had gathered near his truck, which was in the parking lot by the airport office.

Leslie had her arms crossed and was shifting from one foot to the other. "I'm willing to do whatever you want," she said, "but I think I might be better off manning my phone in some location where I can see what's going on. I can call 911 if we need more help."

Wes felt immediate relief and nodded vigorously. "In the office there," he said, pointing to the big building with the glass front.

"Gene, why don't you park your truck by the plane—just off the runway," Deputy Pendry instructed. "Ray and I will position ourselves close to that maintenance vehicle to provide cover for the sheriff when he gets here with Sheriff Lake's reinforcements. It should be anytime. Wes, you, uh . . ."

"How about I stick with Gene?" Wes asked and saw everyone, including Leslie, agreeing with him. It felt like they had a plan in place. Whether it would work remained to be seen.

"One problem," Deputy Pendry added. "The sheriff called me and said he can't legally detain Mr. Clerk because we have no proof that he was behind all this and has refused to prosecute—"

"What?" Leslie interjected. "We're supposed to stand by and watch him take his wife to certain death without doing anything to stop him?"

"If she objects to going with him, that's one thing. If she goes willingly, our hands are tied," Deputy Pendry said. "Not to mention that this airport is not in our jurisdiction."

"What's the sheriff going to do?" Leslie asked.

"Try to bluff his way through it. He said he has no intention of letting her get on the plane if there's any sign she's being coerced."

Wes flashed a grin Deputy Pendry's way. "At last, it feels like Bruce is getting the hang of his job."

CHAPTER 41

From the front seat of Gene's truck, with the air-conditioning on and the strains of "Rolling in the Deep" blasting forth from the radio, Wes watched a caravan of three Range Rovers progress down the access road toward the airstrip. He took a couple of deep breaths. This was not Mickey Mouse stuff they were dealing with. He knew it and sensed that Gene felt the same way. At least Leslie was out of harm's way if something bad should happen.

He watched the vehicles veer off the road and cross the grass, speeding toward the Clerks' plane. Behind them about a quarter of a mile and sending up a cloud of dust was Sheriff Webster. Catching up quickly with the sheriff were three other police cars; their sirens and lights off.

"The cavalry's coming," Wes said to Gene. "I wanna get closer. I'll take your extra rifle if that's okay."

"You sure?" Gene asked. "I thought you didn't like guns."

"I don't. But today, I'm a card-carrying member of the NRA," Wes responded. He felt as though his heart was in his throat as he departed Gene's vehicle, surveyed the area around them, and saw no place to seek cover. *What the hell?* he thought as he stepped boldly forth, moving toward the plane with Gene at his side.

Hugo and Patricia had departed their vehicle and were walking slowly toward the stairs that led to the open door of the plane when Hugo must have spotted Sheriff Webster and stopped. "What the fuck?" Wes saw the billionaire say. Patricia, apparently startled by her husband's comment, grabbed Hugo's arm, clinging to it like a little girl holding on to her father for security.

Within a few minutes, Farrell Rogers and the mercenaries had emerged from their SUVs. There were the five rough-looking goons, plus White and Lilith. *Definitely a mismatch,* Wes thought as he studied the size and heft of the opponents and compared them to himself and the others.

"What's going on here?" Hugo demanded as Sheriff Webster approached him.

"I've come to ask ya not to leave the country until some issues that could involve kidnapping and possibly murder have been resolved," Sheriff Webster said. Wes was proud of the body language the sheriff displayed as he uttered those words, probably rehearsed several times en route to the scene.

Hugo laughed and nodded toward Rogers. Patricia dropped her husband's arm and stepped back, a look of dismay on her face.

"Well, Sheriff, do you have any paperwork that would prevent the Clerks from departing the country?" Rogers asked. His voice was firm, but Wes noticed he was rubbing the scar on his face.

Sheriff Webster moved closer to Hugo and scowled at Rogers. "I have this badge and my authority as a law enforcement officer, and I'm telling ya that the Clerks are not going anywhere. Not today and probably not tomorrow. Maybe not for some time."

"Clearly, this is not *your* county," the attorney said. "Basically, you have no authority."

"These deputies here are working for me," Sheriff Webster said, gesturing toward the uniformed men standing off to one side. "I have authorization from Sheriff Lake to use them as I see fit. And what I intend to do is detain Hugo Clerk for fleeing a criminal investigation."

Wes heard a scream come from what sounded like the inside of the Clerk plane. He wondered if poor Sandy was in trouble for some reason.

When he and the others looked up, they could see Victor Clerk standing in the opening with a rifle in his hand. He fired off several shots in rapid succession, downing two of the mercenaries, then stepped back as a hail of bullets riddled the plane door in response.

It happened so fast Wes thought it amazing that more people weren't felled by Victor's bullets and the return fire. He and Gene ran for the iguana hunter's truck. The surprised deputies also dove for cover, as did the sheriff. The attorney sprinted for one of the Range Rovers and climbed inside. White leaped for the protection of his vehicle, with Lilith close behind. From his position at the rear of the SUV, he shouted orders to his men, who repositioned themselves on the airstrip in defense of what they anticipated Victor's next move might be. Hugo and Patricia were the only ones left in the open, frozen like two innocent civilians in the middle of a war zone.

A silence fell over the scene, along with a sense of impasse. As long as Victor was on the plane, Hugo couldn't use it to escape. As long as the mercenaries were there and probably upset about the wounding of two of their own, Victor couldn't leave the plane. Wes wondered if it was even possible for Sheriff Webster to get control of this nightmare.

Patricia, crying, began walking hesitantly toward the plane, stopping now and then to look over her shoulder. Wes wondered why no one, including Hugo, was taking any action to stop her and would have gladly done something if he could figure out what to do.

"Victor, darling, what's wrong with you? Please stop this," Patricia pleaded. "This isn't going to help anything. I love you. I don't want you hurt."

"I'm okay," Victor called out. "I don't want anything to happen to you. That's why I'm here."

Wes suddenly noticed Lilith striding fearlessly toward Patricia. She had no visible weapon. He remembered Victor saying that this woman had saved his life. Perhaps that was why she seemed unafraid, certain that Victor wouldn't take action against her and knowing she wouldn't be targeted by the kidnappers.

To Wes's surprise, Lilith put her arm around Patricia and began guiding her closer to the plane. "It's going to be all right," he thought he heard her say. Then she dropped her voice so that her words were only audible to Patricia.

Hugo's wife nodded as they walked, then stopped and looked at Lilith. "What?" Wes saw her mouth the word and then look back at her husband. She shook her head. "No. No!" Lilith pulled a tissue out of the side pocket of her white shorts, handed it to Patricia, then reached for her cell phone. Wes heard another phone ringing nearby and saw White answer. The two engaged in conversation for a few minutes, then Lilith started moving with Patricia toward the plane again.

"Victor, Patricia and I are coming inside. No need to be afraid. Neither of us is armed," Lilith called out.

Wes watched the two women climb slowly up the stairs to the plane. He recognized Sandy, the hostess, greeting them and closing the door behind them. He heard the sound of the engine roaring to life, saw the pilot—a woman—on the radio, and watched as she taxied the plane onto the runway.

Hugo, who had stepped behind his vehicle when Lilith joined Patricia, emerged from his place of safety and was running toward Sheriff Webster, screaming. His face was scarlet. His Panama hat had flown off his head and was tumbling in the breeze across the grass and toward the runway. "Stop them! You've got to stop them!"

"Can't help ya," Sheriff Webster said. He signaled to the deputies from the adjoining county that it was okay for them to leave. "I don't have jurisdiction in this county."

"What do you mean? They're stealing my plane!" Hugo said when he was in Sheriff Webster's face again with Rogers at his side.

"Yer plane? I bet if I checked the papers, I'd find out that it is also owned by yer brother, who happens to be on board."

"B-b-but what about these two wounded men here?" Hugo huffed. As he spoke, White and the other mercenaries were helping their fellow soldiers into the back of their vehicle.

Sheriff Webster paused for a minute and looked at Wes and Gene, who had joined the small gathering. Deputy Pendry and Ray were farther back but still within hearing distance. "If I'm not mistaken, these are the two men who allegedly kidnapped Victor Clerk from his house, beat him up, and attempted to kill him by burying him alive. This looks like a clear case of self-defense to me," he said. "For all Victor knew, these men were looking for him and planning to harm him again."

Wes saw White motioning to the remaining mercenaries to get in the Range Rover. "Mr. Clerk, our work here as bodyguards is done," he said as he joined the group but focused on Hugo. "You paid us this morning, and we'll be on our way. We've got to take these boys to the hospital."

"But your job was to get me safely to the plane and on my way to Costa Rica!" Hugo pleaded.

"And we've done that, sir. Gotten you to the airport. I don't think we're responsible for the plane departing without you," White said, glancing over at Wes and grinning ever so slightly.

Hugo glared at White, then turned and gestured to Rogers that they were leaving. White nodded to Wes and Gene and strode toward the vehicle where the mercenaries were waiting.

"That was something," Deputy Pendry said when Sheriff Webster had left, saying he was going home to nurse his sore mouth now that the immediate crisis had been averted. "Seems like someone needs to be arrested, but I'm not sure who and how. Bruce will decide that tomorrow."

"It was definitely a lot more exciting than fighting blazes that only happen once or twice a year on the island. And the sheriff was really cool under fire," Ray said. "I'm signing up for training. Uh, anyone know what happened to that woman in Victor's closet?"

Leslie, who had joined the group, chuckled. "She left, taking a chunk of Victor's money with her. I'm sure we can find someone more suitable for you, Ray."

Wes was gazing in the direction of the Clerks' plane, which was now no more than a speck in the sky. "What do you suppose will happen to Hugo now?"

Leslie put her arm through his. "I don't have the answer to that question yet, but I do know what's for dinner." She grinned and winked at Gene, who was waiting for Wes to join him in his truck. "It will be a first, and I've been assured you'll love it. It tastes just like chicken."

CHAPTER 42

Wes was still debating whether or not he enjoyed the iguana stew Leslie had served him. She had recited the recipe Gene gave her, but it seemed to Wes that you could mix anything with potatoes, onions, tomatoes, corn, and lima beans, as well as the right spices, and come up with a tasty dish. It was the idea of eating one of those spiny creatures that plagued the island that made him feel a little queasy.

The moon was barely a sliver in the night sky. An occasional wisp of breeze from the Gulf and the rotating fan Leslie had purchased a couple of months ago made sitting on the lanai pleasant. Wes sipped on a glass of white wine while Leslie dished up coconut ice cream with strawberries. Newton was dozing off to one side, having eaten the leftover stew and appearing to have relished every bite.

These moments of domesticity were satisfying to someone who had spent half of his life at a hectic pace. Mostly, it was about chasing the big story and the deadline that loomed, demanding to be met. But lately, with Leslie, there had been a lot more excitement than he had expected in this stage of his life.

"A penny for your thoughts," Leslie said as she handed Wes his dessert and settled into the chair next to his.

"I'm thinking about how fast my publisher is going to say yes when I remind her that before all this happened, you wanted me to do a feature on the island's emergency communications issues. And still do, I'm guessing," he said, scooping up a spoonful of ice cream.

Leslie looked unsure of her next comment. "Writing about it now feels like locking the barn after the horse has left. Still, it needs to be done and shouldn't be overshadowed by a story on Hugo and his criminal activities, which I assume you're planning on doing. It's still an issue waiting for a resolution. I can't figure out why he's walking around a free man after all that happened."

True, Wes thought. *And what else shouldn't take a back seat is what was going on the day I first saw Dan White and the blonde with the braid.* He reached for his wineglass and held it closer to Leslie.

"Are we toasting something?" she asked.

"Yes. For starters, you quitting that crazy, high-paying job of yours and coming to this island paradise with your mother."

"I'll drink to that. And let's toast the buyout you accepted at that awful afternoon newspaper, and to you coming to the same island I did," she said, clinking her glass against his.

"We're gonna need more wine," he said. "Because I'm not finished. I want to drink to someone who has brought a new kind of joy to my life, along with a certain unpredictability that I'm starting to enjoy." He paused. "To someone I have realized is the love of my life."

Leslie smiled warmly and touched her glass to Wes's. "So, the buck stops with me? That's a big responsibility."

"It is," Wes said, looking at her with anticipation. "I want you to marry me. You know that. I need to hear your answer."

Leslie stared at him for a few seconds as though trying to decide how to respond. "Marriage? I'm sort of in shock, which isn't good when my wineglass is empty. Hold on," she said. She got up and walked into the kitchen. Newton, who'd been ignoring the conversation between the two people who made up his world, got up and followed her, looking as though he expected something as a reward for being himself.

Wes heard her unscrew the lid on the dog's treat jar and say to Newton, "That's two—don't ask for any more until bedtime." He recognized the sound of the wine cooler opening and closing. There were a few other noises familiar to him: the uncorking of the bottle, the putting away of the corkscrew in the utility drawer, and her footsteps on the tile floor as she returned to the lanai. He wondered if she was doing this to torture him.

She sat down, poured more wine into his glass, then hers, and lifted it once more. An impish grin crossed her lips.

"Yes," she said. "For better or worse, my answer is yes."

CHAPTER 43

Wednesday, July 28, Twilight

From his father's backwater fishing boat, the ten-year-old boy and his dog, Buster, watched the furry creature slink across the shoreline toward the large mound on the beach. The boy could hear the piercing cries from others of his kind: *Ahoooooooo. Yip. Yip. Yip. Ahoooooooo.* But this one didn't respond. He was laser-focused on his objective.

"Dad! Look over there at that coyote by some big thing on the beach. What's he got?"

The boy lobbed an empty beer bottle toward the creature. When it hit a couple of feet away, the coyote jumped, then hustled toward a nearby clump of bushes.

"I'm gonna take the boat over there, son. Get closer," his father said. "If it's a fish, it's a big one. Could be a hammerhead. Maybe a manatee. Hard to see clearly in this light."

The man turned off the motor and let the boat drift closer to shore. He eased over the side into a foot of water, sloshing through the sandy muck until he reached the beach and the partly submerged mound. He nudged it gently with his foot. From behind the bushes, the coyote growled softly.

"Woohee, it stinks," the man said. He covered his nose and mouth and leaned closer to get a better look. "Shit, it's a body!" He jumped backward, lost his balance, and fell into the shallow water. The coyote retreated into the darkness again.

"We can't leave it here," the boy said when his father returned to the boat. "Should we call 911?"

"Not sure we'll reach anybody, but we can give it a try," the man said. He removed his jacket and wrung out the excess water. "I'm not bringing that thing on board. We'll never get rid of the smell. Go ahead. You make the call, son."

As the boy punched in the numbers and waited for an answer, the man wiped his face and hands with a red bandana, and the coyote emerged from his hiding place to once again examine the object on the beach.

"Dad, the coyote's back! You got something else we can use to scare him off? That beer bottle didn't work."

"Hold on," the man said as he reached into a box by the engine, pulled out a signal pistol, pointed it in the coyote's direction, and squeezed the trigger. A large, red flare struck the sand next to the animal, showering him with red sparks. He yelped and sprinted into the gathering darkness.

When the Fish and Wildlife rangers arrived by boat thirty minutes later, they tentatively identified the mound on the beach by the scars on the body's face and neck. It was Rick Howell, alias Mark Foxx, bridge tender, veteran, and kidnapper whose *shit life* had come to an end at age thirty-six in southwest Florida, just offshore of a tiny piece of land with a name that meant "paradise" in Spanish.

Cap Collier had worked as a bridge tender for fifteen years, and during that time, had never had one unauthorized visitor. Today, as he walked off his shift and saw a man in a suit waiting for him, sitting on his favorite bench, he could tell by the fellow's expression that he was about to have his third such caller. The other two, the reporter and his assistant, had created a stir by stopping an ambulance as it approached the causeway. He hoped this man was not a troublemaker.

"Mr. Collier? I'm Gary Clemons, attorney at law. The people in the office said I could deliver this to you in person."

Cap looked skeptically at the man, who was holding an envelope in one hand and tugging at the collar under his loosened tie with the other.

"What is it? I hope it's not a summons. I don't know anything about the Mark Foxx incident," Cap said, sighing.

He had heard from the others when he came to work that his friend had been found dead, washed ashore with a couple of bullets in him. Rumor was that he had also been involved in a plot to kidnap one of the local billionaires. Bill, a tollbooth worker, had told him that Mark's name was really Rick Howell and that he was former military who picked up a nasty case of PTSD in Afghanistan. Cap knew about the traumatic stress and the nightmares. He hadn't known Mark's real name was Rick.

"No, this isn't a summons. A couple of weeks ago, my client, a man named Rick Howell, gave this to me. He said that if anything happened to him—as in, he died—I was to give this letter to you."

"Why me?" Cap asked, looking surprised.

"I believe he considered you a friend and a man of integrity," Clemons said, handing Cap the letter and stepping back as if to say his work was done.

"Is that all?" Cap asked, limping slowly over to the bench and taking his usual seat in the shade.

Clemons shrugged. "There are instructions in the letter. They will be clear to you when you read what it says. When you need help, here's my card. My services are already paid for." Clemons grabbed Cap's hand as if to seal the deal, shook it, and left.

Cap studied the envelope, then did a survey of the three tollbooths and the office windows. One of the workers was gazing down at him. When she saw him looking her way, she waved. He nodded, wondering if she was being friendly or nosy, and returned to the envelope. He could open it and read its contents, or he could let the memories of his friend remain untouched. Whatever Mark—or Rick—had to say probably wouldn't change the way Cap felt about him. Despite their age difference, the younger bridge tender had been like a brother to Cap. He had listened to Cap's stories and didn't seem to care that he'd heard them before. On the weekends, they'd occasionally go out to dinner and talk about the state of the world. It was a bond that no one else shared with him. He sighed and opened the letter.

Dear Cap,

I hope the Cincinnati Reds win the World Series this year. I know that would mean a lot to you, and to me because you are my friend. If you get this letter, something has happened to me. I've been killed and probably not died an honorable death. I went for it, and things didn't work out. Maybe I'm better off.

I was employed by Mr. Hugo Clerk, who hired me and a bunch of mercenaries he found in some gun magazine. He wanted to stage a kidnapping because he was angry with his brother, Victor. His plan was for us to bury Victor alive so that he would suffer on account of he had an affair with Hugo's wife and was generally an asshole. Mr. Clerk thought he could pull off the whole thing because the local sheriff and his deputy were new and didn't know what they were doing.

I was paid $1 million for my part in the kidnapping. It was sent to an account in my name. Mr. Clemons, who delivered this to you, has all the papers you need to get to that account. I want you to have $250,000 for yourself to fix your bum knee and whatever else you need. The rest is to go to my dad. You have to watch over the money because he needs it for his *medical and living expenses and not for women and booze. I hope you will say yes to helping me.*

My attorney also has two other letters from me. The first he will deliver to Sheriff Webster. It tells him the same stuff I told you. What we did was not good, and I'm sorry I was involved. The second goes to the Department of the Army. It says that eleven years ago, during a raid in Afghanistan, I killed my commanding officer, Harold Kern, and allowed Daniel F. White to take the blame. Dan was released from prison after four years, but his record needs to be expunged. He was an innocent and brave man who suffered far too long because of my actions. A detailed account of the events is included in my letter to the army. I want to be remembered as a good person, if possible.

Your friend, Mark Foxx/Rick Howell

Cap let the letter drop onto his lap, reached into his back pocket, and pulled out his handkerchief. He wiped his eyes and blew his nose, shaking his head and letting a small sob emerge from his throat. He gazed out over the causeway and beyond into the blue-green water. In his mind, he could see the familiar figure walking toward him, waving and asking about the Cincinnati Reds one last time.

CHAPTER 44

Sometime Later, Date Unknown

When the Clerk plane returned to the local airstrip, still bearing the damage from the gunfire, Hugo Clerk had been full of questions for the two people who piloted Victor, Patricia, and Lilith to Costa Rica. The pilots had dropped off their passengers, filed a new flight plan, and headed back to their home base near Anibonie Island. One of the pilots had heard the trio talking about arranging another flight, but they didn't mention the destination. Hugo seethed about the outcome, angry that he had paid White and the others millions for a result that he considered less than satisfactory.

A short while later, Sheriff Webster dropped by to let Hugo know that the body of Rick Howell, alias Mark Foxx, the bridge tender who had been part of the kidnappings, had been found on the beach of Paraiso Island with two bullet holes in him. Hugo insisted he didn't know the man but, of course, was sorry that something like that had happened.

"I have no hard feelings, Sheriff, about the kidnapping and the lack of security here," he said. "I just hope that when I return—whenever that is—this situation will have been rectified."

Sheriff Webster told him to stick around for questioning at some future point. But later that day, Hugo made a few phone calls and flew to San Jose. There was a villa there he'd been thinking about buying for the last year or so. It was a private location with an expansive waterfront view and four bedrooms, not to mention access to the amenities at a nearby luxury hotel. Plenty of space for him and the boys when divorce and custody issues were worked out with Patricia.

As he sat by the pool waiting for his guest to arrive, he thought about his brother and wife and wondered where they were. And what about the blonde? Lilith Krueger was her name. She was damned attractive but had let him down just like the others. He had forced White to hire her. He was convinced that she was the one who released Victor from his coffin, but she had denied it, blaming it on Rick Howell, and Hugo had no proof to the contrary.

"Hello, darling."

He heard a voice dripping with honey calling to him. He turned to see the voluptuous Billie Tsvetkov, barefoot and clad in a red-and-orange bikini that enhanced her best assets. She was stepping gingerly on the rough tiles and carrying a bottle of champagne and two glasses.

He had been enchanted by Billie since the first time he saw her with Victor. When all his plans had gone south, Hugo called a private investigator and had her tracked down. She was hesitant at first about joining him in San Jose, saying she would think about it and get back to him. Two days later, she was on the phone, saying she could be at his villa in a couple of hours if he sent a plane for her. Later that afternoon, after three hours on the canopied bed in the main bedroom suite, Hugo wondered why it had taken him so long to start living the kind of life a man with his wealth deserved.

Their days together were blissful, but Hugo could understand why Victor hadn't wanted to make a lifelong commitment to this woman. Trust was the big issue. Could Billie be more than what she seemed—a woman solely out for herself and her own interests? The answer was no, which was why he convinced himself to think of her as nothing more than a pleasurable diversion for the next several weeks. He would eventually send her on her way. Well compensated, of course.

Billie set the champagne and glasses on a table between her and Hugo and spread the blue-and-white beach towel she was carrying on the lounge chair, bending over so that her delectable rear end flashed before him.

"Stop that," she said, giggling playfully as he reached out, pulled down her bikini bottom, and gave one cheek a squeeze. "We have more important business at hand."

"Oh," he said as he poured a glass of Cristal for her and held it until she settled into the chair and reached out to accept it. "What do you have in mind, you amazing creature?" he asked, pouring his own glass and raising it toward her.

She looked at him and then toward a clump of bushes off to one side of the pool. Suddenly, the glass shattered in his hand, and he felt something sharp hit his chest. He glanced down to see a white shaft with a red fibrous tailpiece hanging off it. He pulled it out, let it drop to the ground, and tried to get up. His legs were weak. He was feeling disoriented.

"That's what she has in mind," a familiar male voice said. The words were distorted. They didn't come from Billie but someone else.

Across the pool area, Hugo could see a woman emerge from behind a row of flowering shrubs. She was wearing white shorts and a tight-fitting top. A long blonde braid covered part of one breast.

"Lilith," he said, then looked to his left in the direction of the male voice. "White. What are you two doing here? I already paid you."

It was Billie who spoke first. "I called Victor to tell him about your phone call. He and Lilith reached out to Dan. I don't have anything against you, darling, but there are some people who have a big score to settle with you. I just happen to be their instrument." She poured herself another glass of champagne and took a drink. "Shame to let this go to waste."

White pulled up a chair next to Hugo and sat down. Lilith stood behind the ex-soldier, holding a tranquilizer gun.

"Yeah, old buddy, it's payback time. I'll make it very clear in the short time I have. Let's start with Patricia. Nice lady who finally remembered what you had in your hand before our guys showed up to pretend to kidnap you. It was a gun. You shot her, thinking her death would be blamed on us. I told you when I first took the job that I didn't want anyone dying. I was just helping you get even. Fortunately for her, you aren't an expert marksman."

White reached over and took a swig of the Cristal, then offered the bottle to Lilith, who said no. Hugo wanted to shake his head in denial but found it impossible to move that part of his body.

"Next was Victor," White continued. "We didn't find out until after the fact that you ripped him off—took the family money that rightfully belonged to him. Not that your theft mattered to any of us, but you were worried he would find out and take legal action. It turns out Victor wasn't exactly the evil character you portrayed him to be. At least not compared with you. And while we thought our job was just to scare him, it became obvious that it was your intention to put him under the sand and keep him buried there until he died a slow and terrifying death."

White stood up and checked his watch. "I got three minutes to finish this before you take a little trip to la-la land," he said, grimacing. "This was your worst crime: You hired a group of men who could follow orders but couldn't be trusted to act like human beings on their own. They killed my buddy, Rick. Shot him while he was trying to swim away from them. One of them told me about it. Otherwise, I wouldn't have known, and Rick would have disappeared forever without the proper send-off—a hero's burial in Arlington with his father and me there to say goodbye. Not that it means anything to you, but the letter he wrote saying it was him who killed our commanding officer, not me, is lost in military bureaucracy—thanks to the efforts of some friends of mine. You're a shit human being. All the money in the world can't change that."

White leaned closer and was now in Hugo's face, fading slowly in and out and getting more difficult to understand. "Try to remember what I said. You're going to have plenty of time to think about it."

Then everything went black.

Hugo had no idea what time it was when he began to wake, feeling groggy and out of sorts, as though he had lead weights attached to his limbs. He tried to move his leg but only managed to wiggle his toes.

That's good. If I work a little harder, I think I can. There.

His leg jerked and struck a solid object about twelve inches to the right. He opened his eyes but couldn't see anything except for a tiny speck of light above his head. Not enough to illuminate the area, but it felt like there was air coming through it. White hadn't killed him. That was a good thing. But where was he?

He raised his head and hit another barrier.

Ow! What the fuck?

Now he lifted his arms and began using his hands to examine his surroundings. First touching, then hitting, then pounding.

It was wood. All around him. Like a coffin.

"No, no, no, no, no!" he cried out.

Don't panic, he told himself. White had said he and Lilith weren't killers. Victor and Patricia wouldn't sanction murder. Billie was just along for the money.

He began exploring the area to see what he could find. Round? Yes, an apple. Water? Several bottles. Some other things he couldn't quite figure out. Finally, a flashlight and a piece of paper wrapped around it. He slipped off the paper and turned on the light.

You have been buried underground and have food and water to last for seventy-two hours. Your attorney has received a letter detailing your location. If he keeps this information to himself, one hundred million dollars will be wired into his account after four days. If he discloses your whereabouts to the authorities, he will be rewarded with the knowledge that he has saved your life and the possibility that you will be grateful enough to make it worth his while. We don't know what he will do. Do you?

Hugo folded the paper, turned off the flashlight, and closed his eyes. The only sound he could hear as he lay there—waiting and wondering—was the hiss of air coming through the small tube above his head.

What readers are saying about **UNDER THE SAND**

"*Under the Sand* is No. 4 in the Leslie Elliott series by Susan Hanafee and it maintains fully the excitement and captivating appeal of her first three offerings. In *Under the Sand*, readers become quickly enmeshed in a web of mystery and suspense. Our heroine, Leslie, and her journalist companion, Wes Avery, once again join forces with island law enforcement officers, as well as an array of colorful characters, to solve the kidnapping of two prominent local residents.

"The novel is much more than a fast-paced, whodunit; it is a penetrating portrait of human greed, lust, and jealousy. Yet, the darker side of human nature is not the full picture. Hanafee offers cause for hope and optimism, as honor and justice prevail at the end of this adventure. The Law of Karma is alive and well in *Under the Sand*."

> – Dr. Frank Johnson, Englewood, Florida

*

"Lies, betrayal, murder—paired with a major communication break-down—are among the plot twists that will keep you captivated by Susan Hanafee's latest thriller!"

> – Kris E., Kewadin, Michigan

*

"Susan Hanafee's latest mystery, *Under the Sand*, captures the reader along with kidnapped brothers and keeps you under her spell to the very last page.

> – Sue F., Florida

*

"I'm not a literary critic, but I am very critical. *Under the Sand* had me engrossed from page one."

> – Barbara W., Boca Grande, Florida

ACKNOWLEDGEMENTS

I wish to especially thank Bo Hamrick for sharing facts and providing inspirational ideas about the communication problems facing our little island setting after Hurricane Ian. My gratitude to Tom Hyman for starting me off on the right foot and providing invaluable editorial advice. Thanks also to the many people who read advance copies of the thriller and found it scarily plausible. As always, my deepest appreciation to the best possible partner a woman could have, Ian Rogerson.

ABOUT THE AUTHOR

Susan Hanafee is an award-winning for-mer reporter for *The Indianapolis Star.* She headed corporate communications for IPALCO Enterprises and Cummins Inc. before becoming a mystery writer. She resides in Sarasota, Florida.

Hanafee's blogs can be found on www.susanhanafee.com. Her previously published books include *Red, Black and Global: The Transformation of Cummins* (a corporate his-tory); *Rachael's Island Adventures* (a collection of children's stories); *Never Name an Iguana* and *Rutabagas for Ten* (essays and observations on life); *Leslie's Voice,* a novel, in which her heroine Leslie Elliott is introduced, and the mystery sequels, *Scavenger Tides, The End of His Journey, Deadly Winds,* and *Under the Sand.*

THE END